Vita Nova

MARINA HARLOW

HTTP://WWW.FACEBOOK.COM/VITANOVABOOK

Second Edition: September 2014

ISBN 978-0-615-96514-7

The characters and events portrayed in this book are fictitious. Any similarity to real persons, living or dead, is coincidental and not intended by the author.

Printed in the United States of America.

To my family. Thank you for your support and unconditional love. I couldn't have done it without you.

Masha

Prologue

I need to get away.

It's too dark to see where I'm going and the harsh gusts of wind are becoming much too fierce to withstand.

Something is very wrong.

It dawns on me that I'm alone and barefoot. Where did he go? Running as fast as my legs can carry me, I reach a small tower. It's pitch black outside and this is the only structure for miles. The weather is freezing.

"I'm glad you could make it, Emma."

I see waves of thick golden hair blowing in the wind as I enter. The girl's lilac eyes are almost too large for her face, reminding me of the dolls Jaq brings back with her from France. Though she is very beautiful, I can't help but feel some hostility behind her warm welcome.

There's a small silver amulet around her long neck. The cabochon in the pendant is made of lustrous tiger's eye and I'm transfixed by the swirls of honey and brown. I get this strange sense that I've seen the necklace before but I can't seem to remember much of anything right now.

Her sweet face radically contradicts the malevolent energy radiating from her core. I feel chills run up my body and I can't tell if they're from the breeze or the disturbing way she's suddenly looking me up and down, studying me. I do my best to disregard the fear coursing through me and try to find an opportune moment to run.

Before I can take a step toward one of eight visible gaps in the tower, she appears just inches from my face. I understand that there is nowhere for me to go. The girl is glaring at me with her remarkable set of eyes, which are now stained red.

I try to think positive thoughts, just in case there's no flashback at the end of this scene. My parents. Liam. Jaq. Unexpectedly, the faces of my loved ones disappear and I see him.

He holds out his hand to me and I stretch my arm as far as it will go. The boy's smile doesn't meet his eyes and I can feel his sadness growing as we both realize that he's simply too far away. I pull back.

This is the end.

No cherubs or pearly gates.

No white light at the end of an infinite tunnel.

This is it.

And then everything goes black.

One

"Wake up."

I heard the muffled sound before it left her lips. *Please, just a few more minutes.* The feel of my warm pillow and brand new goose down comforter was far too satisfying to part with. Reluctantly, I started to lift my head and heard more of that pestering noise.

"Wake up, wake up, wake u—"

"I'm up, I'm up," I managed to mutter to my overly enthusiastic best friend and new roommate.

It was the first day of the rest of our lives.

Jaq and I had known each other since our first year at The Astor School, New York's answer to prestigious academia. She had just moved to the States from Provence and was completely taken aback by the hustle and bustle atmosphere of a big city. From break-ups to prom nights to nights that were better left buried in the past, we were together for just about all of it. Newport University was a new chapter for us both.

I propped myself up onto my elbows, yawning drowsily and still half asleep. My new bedroom was less than a quarter of the size of my room back home and the twin-size bed would take some getting used to. From our small window, I looked out at the sunny day that awaited and leisurely placed my feet onto the cerulean rug that took up most of the floor.

Jaq's side of the room displayed photographs of her extended family with the French countryside in the background. An old teddy bear was lying peacefully atop a duvet adorned with a chic damask pattern. In the weekend we were given to settle in, we bought matching table lamps for the two wooden nightstands and a couple of black leather ergonomic desk chairs. The ones provided by the university were so worn and uncomfortable that we were forced to take action.

I brought a few paintings from home and nailed them to my side of the room. It was a series I did toward the end of my last year at Astor, just after my dramatic breakup with Aiden.

Three square pieces, each a portrait of the same flaxen-haired young woman. Her expression in the images changed from innocent to stern to menacing. Painting had been my escape since I was a little girl. I would sit in my bedroom overlooking the Hudson River and cover blank canvases with bits and pieces of my vivid imagination. I would sit in my room for hours illustrating the woman who relentlessly haunted my dreams.

After more than enough procrastinating, I finally rose from my bed and began getting ready for the day ahead. In the meantime, Jaq brewed two large cups of coffee and sat at her desk, undoubtedly daydreaming about what college would actually be like. Classes. Boys. Parties. I had spent all summer wondering the same thing.

We were both majoring in European History and our schedules were pretty much identical, apart from one elective. Jaq chose a French to ensure an easy A, while I opted for International Business. After countless arguments with my father about what I should study, I compromised on a business class to soothe his nerves. He felt that I would never have a steady financial future with the major I had chosen. According to my sweet mogul father, there was no money to be made in the field of history and he believed it was merely on a childish whim that I picked it. Even still, he allowed me to make my own *mistakes* as he saw it, and I couldn't be more pleased to take the opportunity.

As we made our way out of the dorm, it became evident that we had quickly gathered a group of admirers. I decided to wear a pale lavender top, black leggings and boots. Jaq could have stepped right out of *French Vogue* with her tight black miniskirt, white blouse accented with her customary golden Fleur-de-Lis necklace and bright red pumps. She always walked a fine line between runway model and harlot and I loved her all the more for it. I had always preferred to be elegantly understated. Risqué never did suit me, no matter how much Jaq relished in dressing me up in her barely-there ensembles.

As we passed other students on our way to class, it looked as if everyone had decided to put on their Newport apparel like there was some dress code we were mercifully unaware of. Newport U t-shirts, sweatpants and jerseys enveloped the immense campus, reminding everyone where they were. Just in case someone forgot.

Now fully awake, I was able to take in the beauty of my new home, which looked like something out of a bed and breakfast brochure.

Red maple trees lined cobblestone streets leading us to a cluster of historic buildings. I thought about how much the setting resembled all of those landscape wallpapers that came standard on computers.

Red and white banners stood on either side of us. One after the other, they followed the path as far as the eye could see. The red ones displayed the letters *NU* in bolded white while the white ones all had a giant red mustang in the center, up on its hind legs and ready to attack. For a fleeting moment, I felt like I was in a sea of peppermints.

Giant signs were everywhere we turned, welcoming freshmen to the next four years of our lives. Little kiosks were set up in the massive Ellis Student Center for the various groups and organizations we could join. Jaq spotted a sorority booth and smirked widely at me. We had made a pact that any kind of organized extracurricular activities would be out of the question if one of us had no interest. And she knew the only way to get me into a sorority would be via blackmail.

The campus was huge and the number of unfamiliar faces seemed endless. I was in a sort of harmonious chaos, reminding me so much of New York. I thought about how surreal it was that I wouldn't be back home again for a few months. This

"Let the games begin," Jaq roared as she pulled me toward orientation.

The auditorium was noisy and packed with students, leaving us with minimal seating options. I looked around and felt a stab of excitement as we made our way to two empty spots toward the back. Within a few minutes, a thin man in his fifties stepped up to the podium and began to address the audience. Dean Nathaniel Turner spoke with a sly undertone and I immediately got one of my bad vibes. I had always been good at reading people. Okay, I was great at it. I could always tell if someone had bad intentions. It was like a heightened instinct I was born with. The man's hair was more salt-and-pepper than black and he was clearly overdressed in a sharp navy suit and red silk tie. *Well, he obviously didn't get the memo.* I let my mind wander and started to remember my old auditorium at Astor, paling in comparison to Newport's opera house of a lecture hall. I was impressed at how vast the campus was as a whole and how much old-world charm it possessed. The latter was why I decided to place Newport on my top list of colleges. When I visited last fall, it was merely to check out a place I never thought I'd ever really end up. When I thought of Rhode Island, all I saw were lighthouses and seafood. A three and a half hour drive from Manhattan was more like a flight into another universe. Jaq loved the school just as much as I did and we were thrilled when our acceptance letters came in the mail.

Before long, everyone started shuffling out the door. I realized I had zoned out through the entire speech and hoped this wasn't a sign of things to come. Due to an unwavering curiosity of all things, I considered myself to be a pretty good student, especially in the subjects I liked. College was my opportunity to dig deeper and truly understand the romance in Europe's turbulent history. The closer we got to the exit, the more eager I grew for my first class.

"Welcome to *Age of the Vikings*," greeted a young professor as everyone took their seats. She had wavy auburn hair and couldn't have been older than thirty. Her black-rimmed glasses rested gently on her smiling face as she examined the room. "My name is Professor Quinn and I'll be your tour guide into the realm of the Vikings this semester."

The class was pretty large, over forty students in total. Once everyone found a spot in the smaller auditorium, the professor instructed each of us to stand up and introduce ourselves. *I hate this part.* It felt like an excuse for everyone to quietly scrutinize one another without having to feel awkward about it. I had assumed these uncomfortable preambles ended in high school but I was sadly mistaken. I lightly tapped my left heel against the deep burgundy nylon carpet and braced myself for the moment I had to stand up and deliberately make small talk with everyone and no one all at the same time. I deemed it unbelievably invasive and unnecessary.

"My name is Emma Dresden. I'm from New York and—"

"Speak up, honey!"

At that moment I knew Quinn was going to pose a great threat to my serene learning experience. It was like a seed had just been planted. I could feel the anxiety building up as I mustered the strength to politely repeat myself without throwing my notebook at her in the process.

"My name is Emma Dresden. I'm from New York and I'm majoring in European History."

I guess this is what an AA meeting must feel like. I sat back down relieved that my introduction was finally over. Suddenly, I heard the most charming sound coming from behind my chair.

"Andre Talon," the boy began confidently. "Born in Russia, raised all over the place and majoring in International Business."

The darkest eyes I had ever seen peered into me as he gracefully returned to his seat. They were so dark brown they could've been black and I couldn't help but look away timidly as the next student introduced herself. It took all of my willpower not to turn around and stare at his exquisite features. Forget *French Vogue,* Andre Talon looked as though he could have graced the cover of *GQ* wearing nothing but a burlap sack. He was tall and masculine with dark hair that subtly brushed over those piercing eyes that were like portals into another dimension. There was a tiny beauty mark under the corner of his right eye that complemented the flawlessness of his pale skin brilliantly.

"This place isn't going to be so bad after all," I covertly text messaged to Jaq.

"This course will give you a glimpse into the world of the Vikings," Quinn continued once our introductions were finished. "We'll go over everything from their origins in the late eighth century to their rise and fall. Feel free to ask any questions you may have throughout the semester. I expect full participation from each of you and I want us all to be familiar with one another."

The woman had read my mind. I was more than ready to get familiar with one student in particular. As I turned around to pass Andre the syllabus, chills traveled up my arm as I returned his smile and shifted back to face Quinn. His fingers were inexplicably cool as if he were out playing hockey or something before getting to class. I could feel his presence behind me like there was some kind of cliché magnetic pull between us.

He was wearing a fitted black t-shirt that wrapped itself snugly around his toned arms. Lean and muscular, he had a boyish face and this archetypal beauty that I couldn't seem to get enough of. Michelangelo could've sculpted that jawline and I still didn't think it would have looked as good. A few moments into my daydream, I felt my phone start buzzing. As I bent down to grab my bag, I noticed someone was talking to me.

"Hey, I'm Chris," the boy on my right whispered.

"Hi. Emma."

Okay, he was pretty cute. He had baby blue eyes and gave off a bit of a bad boy feel, which was definitely my style. Dressed in jeans and a red Newport University t-shirt, he ran his fingers through his brown hair and actually looked a little nervous.

"There's a party tonight at the Sigma Phi frat house. You should come if you're not doing anything."

I was always curious to see if real frat parties were as entertaining as the ones I saw in movies. I convinced myself it was time to get the ball rolling on this whole college experience thing and politely acquiesced.

"That sounds like fun. I'll talk to my friend and see if she's up for it."

"Cool," he said with a smile that revealed more satisfaction than I'm sure he meant to let on.

I finally got a chance to check my phone and it was a text; a winking smiley face from my ever so eloquent best friend.

Most of class went by quickly, especially since there wasn't much to do on the first day. Quinn went over the syllabus and told everyone to read the first two chapters of an obscenely large textbook, blandly titled, *A History of the Vikings*. Once we were dismissed, I turned to formally introduce myself to the beautiful distraction sitting behind me. When I saw that he had already gone out the back door, my promising college experience started to look slightly less impressive.

"Maybe he had somewhere he needed to be," Jaq said, attempting to lighten the mood. I just stared at her blankly. "Maybe this is his way of playing hard-to-get," she tried again to no avail.

"Maybe he has a girlfriend," I considered. *Or a boyfriend.* "Or maybe he's eternally damaged and saving me from himself."

"Come on, Em! You can't expect two of Newport's most eligible bachelorettes to miss out on the first party of the year!"

My lovable best friend spent over an hour trying on every dress in each of our closets in turn. She was the sister I never had. When Jaq first moved to the States, it was clear she went through a major culture shock. City life was quite different from the promenades and picturesque buildings of her native Provence. The Astor School was considered the best private high school in all of New York and both of our families insisted on the finest education money could buy. We quickly learned that our fathers were in the same field, handling mergers and acquisitions at rival firms, and we hit it off instantly. Jaq and I met in our freshman history class and we'd been best friends ever since. She was the exotic, raven-haired femme fatale and I was her wholesome blonde counterpart.

We took about a year off after high school to travel Europe. After a month or so of coaxing, our parents finally agreed to let us go so long as we only stayed at the accommodations of their choosing and we called them twice a day. It was by far the most incredible experience of my life. We had the privilege of admiring fine art at the

Louvre and walking along the Thames in the moonlight. By living in six different cities for a month or two at a time, we were able to immerse ourselves in the various cultures. Each place was a small yet meaningful chapter in the chronicle of our lives.

I was still upset over what happened with Andre and decided to curl up in bed listening to my iPod without any intention of getting dressed. I shut my eyes for all of one minute before Jaq threw a violet dress over my face. I had worn this dress once before to some debutante's birthday party. It sat tight at the waist and the full skirt reached just below my butt—not the most demure ensemble and quite fittingly, it belonged to Jaq.

"As your best friend," she started with an air of authority. "It is my responsibility to make sure you have some fun around here. Besides, maybe the sexy Russian will be there."

"Something tells me frat parties aren't really his scene."

"Maybe not, but that other guy from Quinn's class was cute too and he seemed interested. If you don't want to go for yourself, go for me. After all, I have yet to meet my American Sweetheart."

She whipped out her only viable weapon and once I caught a glimpse of that innocent frown, I was helpless.

"I'm not sure frat boy and American Sweetheart really belong in the same category. But for you, I'll go."

An hour and twenty minutes later, we locked the door behind us and made our way to the Sigma Phi frat house, all dolled up and ready to embark on our first ever college adventure.

I couldn't even count how many kegs of beer I saw while walking from the front door of the frat house to the backyard. Students were playing various drinking games, all with the same goal in mind: to get as wasted as humanly possible. We were both wide-eyed with excitement as this was our first college party. Everyone seemed like they were having a great time. The older frat boys were hitting on freshman girls who loved every bit of the attention. Pledges walked around like servers, making sure everyone's cup was filled to the brim.

"This is *amazing*," Jaq whispered as we found a private corner next to an untouched keg.

"May I offer you ladies some jungle juice?" asked one of the pledges with a large pitcher in hand. He was wearing a loose red tie over his Newport t-shirt and looked completely ridiculous. "You won't even taste the alcohol."

"I'm fine, thank you," I replied politely, but then immediately saw the scolding look coming from my friend. She seductively pulled the boy's tie toward me and insisted he fill my cup anyway.

"We're here to have a good time, remember? Let's forget about You-Know-Who for just one little night and enjoy this!"

Halfheartedly, I feigned an amiable smile and raised my especially classy red plastic cup to hers. "Cheers."

Frat Boy was right; whatever they put in that jungle juice tasted like nothing but sweet punch. Jaq and I spotted a couple of girls that lived down the hall from us and walked over to say hello. Olivia Adams and Isabel Fiore were both Art History majors and speaking with them put me right in my element. There was something about Isabel that seemed off but I swept those thoughts away instantly. *This is my first frat party and I'm going to enjoy myself, damn it.*

"Have you been to the Rhode Island Museum of Art?" Olivia asked us eagerly. "There's a Dalí exhibit that opens early next year."

"I love Dalí!" I cried out, surprising myself at how uncharacteristically loud I'd gotten. Perhaps the jungle juice was working better than I initially thought.

Dalí was one of my favorite artists of all time and I was elated to have the chance to see his collection up close again. Jaq and I went to an exhibit of his in London and the security guards were forced to usher us out of there because we had no intention of leaving. Well, at least *I* had no intention of leaving; she didn't really care either way as long as we made sure to stop by Harrods afterwards. I looked at my dear friend with my own exploitable weapon, a set of well-trained puppy dog eyes, and silently informed her we were going; whether she liked it or not.

Before long, our favorite pledge came back around and refilled our empty cups. He wasn't a bad looking guy. In fact, I was pleasantly surprised at how many handsome boys decided to come together in the Ocean State. He was tanned with dirty blonde hair and hazel eyes, but seemed like he'd be better suited as a friend than anything more. I pictured us hitting the beach in his imaginary Jeep with a couple of surfboards tightly secured to the roof.

"I'm Logan," the boy said coyly, interrupting my visions of sunshine and waves. "A woman as beautiful as you has got to have a boyfriend around here somewhere keeping an eye on you."

How very caveman of you, Frat Boy.

"Actually, Emma is *very* single," Jaq immediately disclosed, much to my dismay. I had really hoped for a carefree night and I knew it was about time to remedy the situation.

"I'd like to apologize for my friend. It looks as if she's trying to sell me off to the highest bidder." I narrowed my eyes at my foreign instigator playfully.

"Where do I put in my bid?" Logan asked.

"Listen, you seem like a really sweet guy, but—"

"No, I get it. I didn't think you'd actually go for me but it was worth a shot, right?" He forced a delicate smile and glumly walked over to one of the beer-pong tables, leaving me feeling like a total jackass.

"Poor kid," Jaq muttered. I shot her an accusatory glance. It wasn't even Logan's fault since my mind was clouded with all things Andre. I was just about to head home when Chris came by with some more jungle juice.

"Hey, Emma." The grin on his face was palpable.

"Hey, Chris. This is my friend, Jaq. Thanks," I said as he handed us new plastic cups.

"Hey, Jaq. It's nice to meet you."

"Likewise. If you two will excuse me, I'm going to see who's winning over there." She gave me one of her conspiratorial glances and walked off to let me flirt in peace. Intentionally dodging Logan, she strolled over to some action at the other side of the party, leaving me to entertain Chris. I instantly spotted her target as a tall blonde guy dominating the beer-pong table. He already had a few girls fawning over him and that was just the reassurance Jaq needed to go in for the kill.

It took about twenty minutes of talking to Chris before I started to look for my escape. As nice as he was, it was clear that I wasn't the best company at the moment. I knew nothing about Andre but he made his way into my head and I couldn't for the life of me get him out. His dark, knowing eyes were permanently etched into my mind. I apologized to Chris and told him I had a raging headache, searching for the nearest exit.

"It's that jungle juice. You never really know if it's a good batch until it's too late. Want me to walk you home?"

No, I'd prefer to teleport myself into Andre Talon's bedroom. But thanks anyway.

"I have to find Jaq. It was good to see you, Chris, and thank you for inviting me. I had fun." I gave him a friendly hug and walked toward the beer-pong table where I last saw Jaq. She was nowhere to be found so I messaged her that I was leaving. Less than a minute later, my phone buzzed with a response.

Jaq [12:18am]: I've officially found my American Sweetheart, ma chérie! Don't wait up! :)

I couldn't help but smile. Jaq was such a free spirit. Every twist and turn, every new acquaintance; it was all an adventure to be had and I admired her natural verve. She explored her environment with arms wide open and it was marvelous to watch.

I eventually made my way through the crowd and found the front door. The frat house was only a few blocks from my dorm and the night was exquisite. The first touches of autumn were felt in the brisk September air. This was my favorite time of year. The leaves were beginning to take on a vibrant pattern of reds, oranges, browns and greens. As much as I hated the winter, autumn was a season I was truly unable to part with. I always thought all Caribbean islands ultimately looked the same. Palm trees were meant for weeklong vacations but there was nothing like fall with its multitude of colors and cool breezes.

On my way back home, I realized I kind of liked suburbia, dull as it appeared to me at first. The picturesque state of Rhode Island didn't possess my own little island's incomparable exuberance by any means, but it had its own distinct charm. I liked how serene this place was overall. Earsplitting horns and sirens were permanent background music in Manhattan, so during my first night in Newport, I could barely fall asleep. The silence I was so unaccustomed to became deafening and I simply lay in bed for hours listening to the aberrant nothingness. I recently got used to Newport's constant stillness and grown to appreciate it more and more as the days went by. A block from the finish line, my peaceful walk was rudely interrupted by the pestering sounds of four drunken men incessantly arguing over something or other. They were coming straight toward me slurring some incomprehensible expletives. *Of all nights, I have to be wearing this tight-ass dress and heels. Classic.*

"Hey, baby!" the portly boy yelled at me.

The one that looked like a linebacker stumbled in my direction until he came so close that I could smell the rum off his breath. I thought about how much time it would take for me to remove my shoe and jam the four-inch heel into his foot. *Catch me if you can.*

I was about to bend down for Operation: Stiletto Smackdown when out of nowhere, a tall man put his arm around my shoulders. I couldn't really make out his face but the smile he wore was menacing.

"I see you've all become acquainted. Now back the fuck off before you get hurt. The alcohol will only mask the pain until morning."

It was strange, I felt all sorts of negative energy coming from the other guys, but his was calm and bright. It was as though he were enjoying this.

The linebacker started to laugh as the short one raised his fists, ready to fight. That mere invitation was all it took for the fearless stranger to accept the challenge. Once Napoleon attempted a punch, the guy seized his hand instantly and I saw a look of sheer pain in the boy's face. He fell to his knees and the remaining three took their positions around him.

"You think you're tough, bro?"

The overweight one surprised us all when he leaped at the man at full speed. It didn't even seem fair when all he did was casually step to his right before we all watched

Chubby land face first onto the sidewalk. Two down, two to go.

The linebacker and the lanky one decided to team up and come at their opponent together. They charged at him like raging bulls but the guy didn't even flinch. He merely stared at them in amusement. I had to admit it was sort of fun to watch. Lanky tried to punch him from his right side while Linebacker attempted a kick at his left. Both boys were instantly pinned to ground with the stranger looming over them threateningly.

"Apologize to the lady," he ordered the terrified jocks. He spoke so coldly that a chill crept up my spine.

"We're sorry," they whimpered in unison.

He looked into each of their eyes and told them they never saw us. They were to run home and fall asleep because they had a long day tomorrow. Their eyelids were heavy and bed never sounded so inviting. I'd never seen anyone attempt to literally plant thoughts into people's heads before. *Did he really think it would work?*

"Off you go," he commanded as if to a group of unruly toddlers. He then turned to me and I saw for the second time a flash of those black penetrating eyes that met mine just this morning. I even made out the faint little beauty mark below his right eye and took a deep breath.

"Are you hurt?"

I froze, unable to speak, and simply looked up at him like a deer in headlights. Andre, the guy whose face was perpetually etched into my mind was standing right in front of me. He had just beaten up four people without breaking a sweat and looked me up and down, seemingly pleased. This had to be a dream. After what seemed like ages, the silence finally broke as I found my voice.

"I'm all right. Thank you for saving me."

"It was my pleasure," he said smiling. It finally hit me that he'd been speaking in an English accent this whole time and I couldn't quite understand why. He was about as American as I was when he first introduced himself earlier in class. His teeth were perfectly white and my body tensed at the aching sensation I felt while studying the luscious set of lips that framed them. I'd bet just about anything that they felt just as soft and masterful as they looked. "You shouldn't be out this late by yourself. It isn't safe for a girl like you."

That one statement had managed to snuff out whatever lust I was feeling right then and there. *A girl like me? What the hell is that supposed to mean?* Granted, I was in a skimpy dress and high heels, but in my defense, the dress wasn't even mine! The angry New Yorker in me came out to play and I must have turned about three shades pinker. My original gratitude and desire instantly faded into a lethal dose of irritation.

"Well, I'll try to take your unsolicited advice into consideration," I said, a bit more sardonically than initially intended. "Girls like *me* need to be getting home so thanks again for the rescue. I appreciate it."

He pursed his lips, face downcast, and took a step toward me. Gently, he placed his hand on my shoulder, carefully avoiding any sudden movements. When he gazed down at me, I noticed the whites of his eyes took on a scarlet hue. His face looked unnaturally serene as he began to speak.

"All you will remember of this night is that you came straight home, uninterrupted, and fell asleep. There was no fight. I was never here. You saw no one on your way back to your room. Do you understand?"

Seriously? I didn't know whether to laugh at him or just go with it. I could easily have turned around and started walking back to my dorm obediently. No such luck.

"Whatever you say. I'll just go ahead and forget that you kicked some major ass less than five minutes ago. Won't tell a soul. Wouldn't want anyone to think a girl *like me* needed saving anyway." With that, I turned on my heel and headed directly to bed.

It took all of twenty minutes before I was showered, dressed in an oversized t-shirt and safely tucked away under the covers. Jaq wasn't back yet so it occurred to me to check my phone for messages. I forced myself out of bed and walked over to the chair where my purse was sitting. I grabbed my cell and threw my head back into the comfort of my soft pillow. When I clicked it on, I saw two new messages, both from Jaq. I took in a deep breath and prayed she was all right. My paranoia was not unwarranted given the night I just had.

Jaq [12:57am]: I love college!!

The next one was from fifteen minutes ago.

Jaq [1:42am]: I'll be home soon. Bonne nuit!

I let out a sigh of relief that my friend was safe and plugged my phone into the charger by my nightstand. I had just attended my first college party, drank something called jungle juice, witnessed a brawl in my honor and been spoken to like a child by my rather eccentric yet gorgeous crush. All in all, my night could've been worse.

Two

"Réveillez-vous!"

There was a large cup of scalding black coffee only a few inches from my face. The smell was strong enough to wake me and I slowly lifted my head, reaching for the mug. *"Emma and Chris, sitting in a tree,"* Jaq crooned, fully energized as usual.

I sat up, trying to mimic her enthusiasm and set the mug on my nightstand for it to cool down. *Ah yes, last night.* I made a conscious attempt to change the subject to something Jaq wanted to discuss and avoid a topic I didn't. "Before we get to that, I vaguely recall reading a text about you and your American Sweetheart. Do tell."

Her face lit up like a thousand Christmas lights as she hopped onto the bed beside me. She was in a red silk robe that reached just above her knees and her make-up from the night before hadn't been rinsed off. Jaq washed her face before bed religiously so it must have been quite an evening.

"Oh, Em. He's perfect," she breathed. She glanced at me with a dazed look in those pale blue eyes and I sensed the intense energy radiating from her skin. She was all passion and excitement when talking about this guy.

"Oh, he's such a gentleman and he's confident and so incredibly sweet. We spent an hour just talking about everything. And like a half hour getting to know each other better, give or take."

She gasped playfully and raised her hand to her mouth in mock disbelief. I couldn't help but smile. It was our golden rule that giving up the goods on the first night was never a good idea.

"And?"

"And … he's an amazing kisser, definitely good with his hands – should anything in the room break, of course." She paused and took the opportunity to wink at me. "So far, I can't find anything wrong with him. Is it fucked up that that's what freaks me out the most?" Her mood went from elated to nervous in the blink of an eye. "I'm so used to settling for decent that it's hard to picture myself getting someone I really want. Anyway, we have plans to have dinner this weekend."

"No, I get it." And I did. I knew just what she meant about settling.

I thought about Aiden for the first time in months last night. Not that I would ever date him again, but I just remembered certain things about our relationship that I could never tolerate now. As much as he continuously hurt me, Aiden helped me figure out what I was now looking for in a relationship long-term. And more importantly, what I wasn't.

"But," I went on. "It's always a learning experience. You just have to take those past relationships at face value and leave them be. If this guy, whose name you haven't even told me by the way, is as amazing as you say he is, then just be yourself because that's who he'll fall for the hardest."

"Tristen," she sighed. "His name is Tristen. Hey, what time is it?"

I didn't care. I took a sip of my coffee and leisurely grabbed my phone off the charger.

"8:07."

Uh oh. Wait for it ... Wait for it.

"We're late! Oh, no! Come on, we have to leave in less than an hour!"

Jaq hated being rushed and consequently rushed everyone around her to take the edge off of her building anxiety. I packed up the rest of my books into the black Longchamp shoulder bag Jaq's parents got me for my birthday and checked to make sure I looked presentable enough to face the aftermath of last night. *Bag, check. Phone, check. Coffee, check.* In a record forty-five minutes, we were out the door.

Everyone seemed to be sitting in the same seats as yesterday so I found my spot and secretly hoped that I might be sitting in front of Andre all semester. Though I preferred he would find his way into the seat directly to my left. All of a sudden, I felt a tight squeeze on my right arm and saw Jaq beaming. A tall blonde guy in a grey t-shirt and basketball shorts walked over and sat next to us. He gave Jaq a sweet kiss on the cheek, making her surprisingly giddy. That side of her rarely came out in public.

"Emma, meet Tristen. Chérie, this is my best friend in the whole world, Emma."

His blue eyes were sincere and by his calming energy alone I could see why Jaq liked him so much. He wasn't like any of the pretentious guys she dated back home. He also looked like he could kick just as much ass as Andre had last night. *Definite alpha male.* I liked him already.

"It's nice to meet you, Emma."

"Likewise, Tristen. You weren't in class yesterday,"

I noted. *Let the interrogations begin.*

"Yeah, my parents had something they needed me to do, so today's officially my first day."

I felt another squeeze coming from my left arm. I turned around hoping to see Andre but sadly, it was just Chris.

"Good morning. I'm glad you made it home all right."

"Thanks." I made it home more than all right but that wasn't something I needed to concern him with. "And thanks for inviting me. It was fun."

I turned my attention to the front of the room, thinking about my chauvinistic savior and where he'd been lurking. Quinn hadn't arrived yet so I guessed there was still time for a fashionably late arrival.

"Good morning, everybody! It seems we have a new addition this morning," she informed us as she marched into the room rather too enthusiastically. *I'll take one of whatever she's having.* "Tristen, why don't you stand up and introduce yourself to the class."

Jaq's American Sweetheart rose from his seat and assertively walked up to the front of the class. He stood at 6'4" at least, about an inch or two taller than Andre. His dark blonde hair casually swept his forehead as he spoke.

"Hey. I'm Tristen Valgard. Business major. Born and raised here in Newport. Apparently, I come from a long line of Vikings so that's pretty much why I decided to take this class."

So Tristen was a Viking. Well, that explained a lot. I looked over at him once he was back in his seat and he began to morph into the images I always had of what the hot sort of Vikings would have looked like. Not the burly ones who drank too much beer and raided villages, but the tall, sexy warriors people would make epic movies about. From his size alone, he could easily take on most of the guys in our class, with the exception of the gladiator who was burning my skull with his gaze. Andre's energy was like nothing I'd ever sensed before. It was bizarre but even though I hadn't seen him come in, I felt his presence behind me.

After assigning another few chapters of reading and a small paper, Quinn dismissed our class and everyone started to shuffle out of the auditorium. Chris looked like he was about to tell me something when one of his friends pulled him off to the side to discuss some Sigma Phi-related matter. I was somewhat relieved that I'd been able to dodge him without seeming unfriendly. I instinctively turned to look for Andre, half expecting him to have darted out the back exit again. Instead, he was observing me with those piercing eyes I'd grown so fond of. In a split second, he took my palm into his own and lightly kissed it, making me feel as if my knees would give out at any moment. I was yet again at a loss for words.

"I wanted to apologize for last night. I'm sorry I spoke so peculiarly to you. I guess it was all that adrenaline from the scuffle. I'd like for us to start again. I'm Andre."

It was taking all of my strength to keep calm. My heart felt like it was beating out of my chest and it was the only sound I could focus on at that moment.

"And you're Emma," he stated. I noticed his words were spoken without a hint of last night's English drawl. Okay, enough was enough. I cleared my throat.

"Sorry. Hi. Yes, I'm Emma. Are you okay? Don't get me wrong, you put up a hell of a fight, but you must be sore after all that."

Andre's lips slightly twitched displaying a trace of amusement. He looked down at me earnestly and assured me it'd take more than a few college kids to rough him up. I always believed confidence and even a bit of cockiness was acceptable in a man if he could back it up with actions. And judging from the incident last night, Andre certainly proved himself worthy of such talk and then some.

I looked around us and noticed we were the only two people left in the room. We stopped outside the back entrance and studied each other for a few spectacular moments. The way he looked at me made me feel like I was naked. Not so much in a carnal way but more as if I were being examined. I felt completely exposed as he somehow breached the walls I had instinctively put up for so long.

He was in designer jeans and a black blazer that was definitely custom-tailored. Jaq would've been especially pleased with his posh garbs. I had to admit the boy was fully aware of how good-looking he was and he wore exactly what he knew complemented him. I mustered the courage to look him in the eyes and briefly lost myself in their darkness. Unwilling to succumb to his charm just yet, I snapped myself out of whatever love spell I was under and smiled. He returned the gesture and I noticed that his high cheekbones rivaled my own. His skin was so smooth that from the looks of it, it could have been softer than mine. He was far too beautiful and just as lethal. For the first time in my life, I felt unquestioningly out of my league. Distracted by my own thoughts, I almost jumped back when I felt the touch of Andre's hand against my arm.

"May I walk with you to the dining hall?" he asked me with a note of hesitation in his voice. "I overheard your friend Jacqueline saying she'd meet you there after class."

"Sure, why not?"

Play it cool, Em. Play it cool.

On our walk to Chapel Hill, Andre told me about growing up abroad. His childhood was spent in Russia and then he and his family moved to London in his teens. I had never been to Russia but imagined it to be a stark and dreary environment for a young boy to live.

"One thing I never would've expected was ending up in Rhode Island," he declared. "Of all places, I honestly didn't see that one coming. Why did you leave New York? There are far superior universities over there."

It was getting slightly cold and a sudden gust of wind sent a chill all throughout my tense body. Andre immediately removed his jacket and placed it over my shoulders. I supposed chivalry wasn't entirely dead after all.

"Don't get me wrong," I explained. "I love New York. I grew up there and it'll always be home, but I needed a change. I wanted to go somewhere completely out of my comfort zone and … well, this was it."

"And Jacqueline? She's your best friend?"

"Yes. We've been friends for a long time. She's become like a sister to me. We decided college wouldn't be the same if we were forced to spend it apart. So, once I decided Newport was where I was headed, Jaq sort of just followed suit like it didn't matter any which way. I guess she just trusted me enough to decide for us both."

Our conversation was cut short as we approached the entrance. Chapel Hill was Newport University's colossal dining hall. It had all the usual regurgitated cafeteria food one would find in any American school but there was also a salad bar, fast food place, and a sandwich shop. Jaq and I both needed at least a couple hours after waking before food sounded remotely appetizing. There was a small break in between classes so we took that opportunity to have our breakfast. She was sitting at a secluded table in a corner eating a bowl of oatmeal and a fruit salad as Andre pulled out my chair and introduced himself to my awestruck friend.

"It's a pleasure to meet you, Jacqueline. My name is Andre. You ladies enjoy your breakfast. Emma, I hope to see you soon."

It seemed I wasn't the only one who felt the paralyzing effects of his company because Jaq just stared up at him mesmerized. When we saw that he was finally out of earshot, she widened her large blue eyes and shot me a look of pure envy.

"Em, he is *so* hot! I mean you have to be seeing what I'm seeing, right? *Ridiculously* handsome."

Oh, I'm seeing it. I haven't missed a beat.

"He's not bad," I shrugged, trying to mask the stink of infatuation I was sure floated in the air around us. It was almost annoying just how well we knew each other.

"Say what you want, Em. I can see it in your eyes. You just watch, chérie. He'll be yours in no time."

I wondered if she was right. Could I have finally met someone new? After Aiden, I kind of shut myself off to the possibility of any sort of romantic involvements. Sure, it had been over two years since we broke up, but Aiden and I ended on pretty awful terms and the thought of venturing into another relationship seemed unrealistic.

The night before our three-year anniversary, it was brought to my attention that the person I had been in a serious relationship with slept with at least four different classmates while we were together. To top that off, when I went to his apartment to confront him, he unwaveringly denied it. It was only when he got to the part where he saw us getting married that I heard a rustle coming from inside his closet. Low and behold, awkwardly sitting in his massive walk-in was none other than Astor's biggest skank, Amy Price. Oh, she had a price all right. The dirty broad was on clearance.

"I don't think I'm ready to date just yet. I mean we just got here. I should probably settle in first, right?"

I didn't have to hear Jaq reply to know what she'd say next. The look on her face spoke volumes.

"It's already been two fucking years since you left that lying, two-timing dickhead. Not all guys are like He-Who-Must-Not-Be-Named. He's his own special breed of asshole and he'll find his other half soon enough. It's about time you found yours."

"My own special breed of asshole?"

"You know what I mean!"

I let out a long sigh. Jaq was right; I needed to start letting my guard down more. Two years was sufficient time for me to get my shit together and move on with my life. I stood up with a newfound sense of optimism and went to grab a Greek yogurt and some fruit. As I passed the other students, I smiled to myself, considering the countless possibilities life had in store.

It's dawn and there are hedges six feet high all around me. I'm in the middle of a life-size maze. Running to one end, turning right, then left, it's apparent that there is no escape in sight. Finally, I reach the center of a clearing where Andre stands waiting. In his hand he holds the same amulet as that lady always wears in my dreams. The tiger's eye gemstone glimmers in the sunlight as he takes a step toward me.

"This is for you," he offers with one of his heartfelt smiles.

I run to him and hold on as tightly as I can. He returns my affections by pulling me closer. I am safe now. Nothing can harm me when I am with him.

"I'm so happy you're here," I whisper softly into his chest.

I raise my chin to kiss him and as I look at his face, I realize that the arms that cradle me are no longer Andre's. I am staring into the ominous eyes of a woman. Suddenly, the sky turns black and as I loosen my grip, I trip over my dress and fall backward.

The stranger takes a step closer and smiles at me, revealing a pair of sharp fangs. She bends down and takes a lock of my hair into her hand. I keep telling myself this can't be real; this has to be a dream. The woman lets go of my hair and her lilac eyes meet mine.

"Who are you?" I breathe, the sound of my climbing heartbeat growing louder under my skin.

"Camilla," she whispers, just before going for my throat.

The weekend came and went as quickly as it always had. If only America had a four day workweek. I'd even settle for siestas. Jaq and I grabbed our newly purchased insolated travel mugs and headed back to reality. Well, if reality happened to be the ninth century.

Quinn was rambling on about some raid when, out of nowhere, Chris took the rug right out from under me and leaned in close to my ear. I could feel his warm breath against my skin.

"Let me take you out this weekend."

I froze, eyes forward. Not to toot my own horn, but I'd turned down so many guys in my life that this should've been easy. But it never was. I hated telling people I wasn't interested in them. More than that, I hated knowing the reason I wouldn't give them a chance had nothing to do with them in the first place. I was emotionally damaged and had yet to meet my match.

"I think it could be fun," he went on as my mind clouded with reticent thoughts. "We can go wherever you want. Your choice."

I started to feel antsy while my brain took an early lunch. I didn't like being caught off guard and incapable of getting out of a particular situation. Chris basically had me cornered in the middle of class and I was forced to answer him on the spot.

We had spent a while talking at the Sigma Phi party and from what I gathered, he seemed like a pretty decent guy. He had a rough upbringing and overcame some seriously heartbreaking obstacles to get accepted here. He lost his entire immediate family in a tragic car accident and lived nearby with his violent alcoholic uncle. I knew I enjoyed his company and maybe if it were based on that alone, I'd have given him a fair chance. Unfortunately for us both, there was something missing. There had always been something missing these past couple years. *Well, it's now or never.*

Before I was given a chance to politely decline, Andre rested one hand on my shoulder, giving me a neatly folded piece of paper. Chris was clearly taken aback by this and I could see him stirring in his seat out of the corner of my eye. I glanced at each of them for a split second and noticed the glacial stare in each set of eyes. They looked like two wolves competing for a piece of meat and the idea of them entering into some old-fashioned duel over me brought an amused smile to my face as I unfolded the note.

I'm quite certain I'd be much better company. How about Friday night at 8? My choice. Andre.

I was unable to see Andre but I knew he was staring directly at me. His eyes burned a hole through the back of my head and his energy from behind my seat was off the charts. Right on cue, Quinn dimmed the lights to show us some slides and everyone fell silent. I sneakily ripped off a small piece of paper from my notebook and jotted down a quick response. Chris must have known what I was plotting because his glum sidelong glance said it all.

I folded my little note with tender loving care and casually placed my hand behind my head as if fixing my hair. Immediately, I felt Andre's hand deliberately sweep across my palm as he took the letter from me. Just then, I felt a rather large ball in the pit of my stomach as I looked down at Quinn, feigning interest in all things Viking. I realized I wore a giant smile from ear to ear and thanked all things holy that Andre was behind me and didn't have the pleasure of seeing the ridiculous look on my face. Chris definitely thought I was a lunatic or at least had some serious issues. To his credit, he did attempt to look away and focus on Quinn for a while.

It was the first time in years that I had felt that euphoric sensation, a blend of excitement and anxiety, deep in my belly. It was such a bizarre feeling that I began wondering why I always tried so hard to avoid dating. But it occurred to me that moments like these came few and far between. To be honest, the butterflies that everyone always spoke of never actually came for me. I didn't date because that energy that made the entire room reverberate in bursts of warmth hadn't appeared until now. In that one glorious moment, everything had finally come together.

I woke up early and decided to make a large pot of coffee before getting ready for class. As I waited for it to brew, it dawned on me that it was already Friday, my first date with Andre. A quick peak inside my closet revealed nothing remotely eye-catching. I hadn't been on a real date in so long that I felt completely out of my element. I gave him the note on Monday and he hadn't brought anything up all week, so maybe he'd forgotten we made plans. There was no sense in stressing what could have been a total nonissue, but what if he actually showed up?

I couldn't risk being in pajamas if he did in fact decide he wanted to see me and Jaq and I were scheduled to be in *Portraits of Roman Society* in less than two hours. There was no possible way we could squeeze in a shopping trip before class so I sat back down on my bed miserably.

Jaq's alarm suddenly went off like a cannon, startling me to the point that I almost dropped my cup. I immediately felt an instinctual urge to throw something at her phone but held back, knowing no good would come of it. She set her ringtone to the loudest setting available and if I weren't usually such a late riser, it would probably annoy the hell out of me. I poured some coffee into her mug and added a splash of milk, just as she liked. Her arms started to reach for it as I walked toward her. After a few sips, she was sitting up and looking at me suspiciously.

"Why are you awake before me?"

Jaq would just end up finding out about my date when I started getting dressed tonight regardless, so there was really no sense in hiding it. It wasn't like I kept things from her anyway.

"It appears I have a date this evening," I revealed with an innocent smile.

She immediately put her coffee on the nightstand and leaned forward. I was surprised nothing had spilled to the floor in the process. The energy around her was like sunlight. Her lips twitched until there was a childlike grin stapled to her astonished face.

"You have a date! With Andre? Tonight? Why am I only hearing about this now?"

"Honestly, I forgot. It didn't really hit me that it was really happening until this morning. And I have nothing to wear."

She took another sip from her mug and a deliberate smile appeared on her doll-like face. With nothing short of determination, she got out of bed and started getting dressed.

"What are you doing?" I asked. We still had a bit of time before we needed to be in class.

"You and I are going shopping, chérie. Tonight is a rebirth."

I raised an eyebrow at my now wide-awake best friend. She had already managed to slip into a casual knee-length dress and put her hair in a loose bun.

"You're going out with someone new, Emma," she continued matter-of-factly.

"Your sunglasses are in your bag."

"*Merci.*"

She was basically ready, toothbrush in hand while I was still lounging on her bed. I miraculously found my motivation and put on a pair of jeans with a simple white tank top.

"You haven't had a first date in what, five years?" Jaq went on. "This is your opportunity to see that not all guys are Aiden Cunningham. You're finally giving someone a chance, chérie."

Was I really that bad? Did I deliberately choose to be single because I assumed I would just get hurt again? Mercifully, Andre reminded me nothing of the pompous douchebag who broke my heart. So I convinced myself I was going to have fun and whatever happened, happened.

"We won't have enough time to shop and go to class," I considered out loud. "Have any suggestions?"

"I suggest we go get a professionally made cup of coffee, no offense, and then head to Orchard Street and hit up the boutiques. We'll have a day of it."

"What about class?" It was only the second week and cutting class was already a feasible option. *Not good,* I thought to myself.

"We went to the first one of this Roman crap. It's just going to be a bunch of slides and a reading assignment, which we can get later. Let's get Cinderella looking fly for the ball."

"I can't believe we're already cutting class," I muttered to myself as we walked into *Flora,* Newport's only halfway decent dress shop.

"Em, this is college! No one will even notice we're gone. Besides, I'm not sure if you got the memo but shopping trumps lectures."

That was very true; shopping did trump lectures any day of the week. Nevertheless I still felt guilty for using a date as an excuse to miss class. I really wanted to start the school year off right. But we would have already been late after our particularly unhurried chat over espresso. I just needed to put my game face on and focus on the task at hand.

"I don't even know what to look for since Andre hasn't told me where we're going. He made it very clear that the location will be his choice."

I started to feel some seriously ethereal energy close by, but saw no one other than a severely orange high school girl at the register. Working at the nearby tanning salon would have been a much more appropriate job for her. She offered her expertise but we politely declined. Tangerine couldn't help me if I didn't know what I was looking for in the first place.

"Oh, Em, this dress would be *perfect* on you!" I heard Jaq squeal from somewhere in the back of the store. When I walked up to her, she was eyeing a pale mint sundress with a low V-neck that traveled down further than I would've liked.

"You don't think it's a tad bit … revealing?" I muttered, wondering if she were serious.

"Revealing? Please! The moment Andre sees you he'll have a heart attack."

I wasn't sure heart attack was the look I was going for. *Oh, what the hell?* Why couldn't I indulge my best friend? After all, I didn't have to buy the first dress we saw.

"Okay, I'll try it on," I agreed hesitantly.

It looked stunning. The light green hue went so well with my eyes and that intense vibe I felt when we first entered the store got stronger. Even Tangerine looked flustered.

"I think we've got ourselves a winner," Jaq purred with a look of sheer satisfaction written all over her face.

As we walked back to our room, I couldn't believe they convinced me to buy that dress. Maybe I could spill something on it at the last minute and be forced to change. It fit so well though, seeing as how there was so little fabric. Jaq was right about one thing; Andre was going to have a heart attack when he saw me. Sadly, I wasn't quite sure it would be for the same reason we were hoping for. He didn't seem like the type of guy who wanted his girl in micro-minis or anything of the sort. *Oh, well.* We dropped off our shopping bags and headed over to the history wing where *Early Modern Europe* awaited our arrival.

Class flew by and I still hadn't thought of a topic for the Vikings essay I'd been assigned. It was due in a few days and all my thoughts were devoted to Andre. Quinn seemed pretty lenient about what we could write about as long as she got a feel for each student's individual interests.

After doing a bit of research, I came across the legend of the sólarsteinn, a sunstone that helped the Vikings in their navigation from Norway to America, centuries before Christopher Columbus set sail. When held up to the sky, it was thought to reveal the position of the sun. People believed it kept the sun on course and protected the earth from evil. I could only find one existing image of the stone. It had golden bands encircling strips of espresso and caramel, eerily resembling the necklace I always saw in my dreams.

Six pages and two cups of coffee later, the paper was finished and I could finally start getting ready for my date. I decided to take a hot shower and couldn't help but think of home. There wasn't that sense of privacy I was used to here. Bringing a basket full of shampoo and shower gel back and forth from the communal bathrooms was quite a step back from my spacious en suite in New York.

Fond memories of my parents, so unbelievably compassionate and loyal, filled my head as the warm water splashed onto my skin. There was always a home cooked meal prepared at my house and the teakettle was somehow always hot. My mother was the polar opposite of Jaq's. While Mrs. Avignon never once missed a Fashion Week in the years I'd known her, my mom never failed to see me in some stupid class play or painstakingly watch over me to make sure my fevers didn't climb too high when I got sick.

My father was my go-to whenever I needed grown-up advice. He was a businessman through and through but he always made time to take his children to ballgames and even taught me how to ride a bike when I was a little girl. I thought about how much I missed my older brother. Liam always pushed me to be better. He'd had me up on a pedestal for as long as I could remember. But they were far away. And this was another chapter.

I'm late!

Two hours of prepping for my date with Andre and I still wasn't ready. Pacing the room in my latest barely-there green dress and nude pumps, I looked to make sure I had everything. *Wallet, check. Lip-gloss, check. ID, check.*

"Stop it! You're making *me* nervous," Jaq groaned. "It's going to be fine. So get that worried look off your face and go have fun before I go for you. And judging by how sexy this guy looks in a pair of jeans, you know I wouldn't complain."

The playful grin she sported managed to lighten my mood. Just then, I heard a knock come from the opposite side of our door. *I guess he remembered after all.* Jaq gave me a quick hug, careful not to smudge my make-up, and handed me my purse.

"*Merde,*" she whispered in my ear, wishing me luck in her native tongue.

Before my hand touched the doorknob, I turned back to face my encouraging friend and silently pleaded with her to let me play sick and stay home without a struggle. The look in her eyes told me wimping out was a completely viable option … over her dead body.

Andre was a sight to be recAndreed with. Dressed in a pair of dark wash jeans and a black button-up, he wore a sweet, genuine smile as I greeted him at the door. He looked me up and down thoroughly, as if carefully surveying every inch of my body. He extended his hand to me and I instinctively took it, following him out to his car. *His car!*

"Wow," I breathed.

He walked over to the passenger's side as I stood there like a statue, gawking at the piccc of history in front of me. *Built in the early sixties at the latest,* I thought. For all I knew, it could've been even older than that.

"1955 Porsche 550 Spyder," he announced as we both paused to admire the manmade work of art. *Boys and their toys.*

I nodded in genuine awe of how beautiful it was. The car looked like it had rarely been driven. Each curve was vigilantly sculpted and there wasn't a single scratch or dent. Damn, it looked *really* expensive. And fast.

We drove to a secluded hilltop about an hour from campus with the most incredible views of Narragansett Bay. Down below, I saw an incalculable amount of diamonds shining in the water. Andre popped open the trunk and took out a few bags and a wine bottle. He put them on the ground and grabbed a large blanket. I walked up next to him and reached my arms out. Understanding, he handed me one half of the blanket and we laid it out in a spot overlooking the bay. He started to go through each bag when I finally broke the silence.

"Whatchya got there?"

"Food. You are hungry, aren't you?" he asked me thoughtfully.

"I could eat." And that was the truth. I hadn't eaten anything since the croissant Jaq and I split this morning. "What kind of food?" It smelled like it could be Italian. I may have been the only person on the planet who wasn't crazy about Italian food.

"Italian. I didn't know what you liked so I went ahead and just got chicken, some shrimp and steak. Well, and pasta, of course. Little bit of everything. I hear everyone loves Italian so I thought it would be the safest choice."

Part of me didn't have the heart to tell him his plan backfired. The other, much larger part of me was on a mission to prevent future *safe* choices.

"Actually, I'm not really that big on Italian food." The poor guy looked like he just missed the first shot in the championship game. I took a quick peak at the bags and noticed the words *Vicente* written across them. That was one of the most high-end restaurants in the state. "Not that I *hate* it," I quickly added, feeling like a total ass. "There are a few things I actually really like. I just don't ever crave it much. Thought I'd tell you in case we have another one of these scenic dinner dates."

Andre looked more relaxed, seeming somewhat pleased that I revealed that minor detail about myself. He started piling a bit of everything onto my plate until there wasn't any space left to fill. I looked down at the mountain of food and determinedly accepted the challenge.

Once I couldn't physically consume another bite of pasta, I put my plate aside and shifted closer to Andre. He turned his body to face me and just gazed into my eyes for a while saying nothing. I wondered what he was thinking. Maybe I had some oregano in my teeth and he couldn't bear telling me but couldn't look away either. And that was precisely one reason why me being in the mood for Italian was a rarity. *Case in point.* My face could have looked like three-car pileup and he was simply rubbernecking. *Not cool.*

"You know the view's over there," I said, pointing toward the Narragansett. Distraction was the only logical tactic in this type of situation. There was a trace of a smile forming on his face.

"See that's purely subjective."

That bizarre feeling in the pit of my stomach returned in force. I hadn't finished everything on my plate, but whatever I did eat couldn't seem to keep still. From the intense energy that pulsated around us, I felt myself shudder. Andre rose and hastily walked over to his car. I could have sworn it took him like half a second to get back with a jacket in hand. He put his mysteriously warm pea coat over my shoulders and I suddenly felt much better.

"Hey, I've been thinking. The night we met you had an English accent. Why is that?" I asked.

Andre looked as if he'd been caught off guard and tensely cleared his throat. "I spent many years in London so it's sometimes easier for me to revert to British, particularly when I'm angered," he smirked uneasily.

We spent most of the evening discussing our travels and what our respective plans were for the future. Basic date talk, I thought. We spoke of our favorite pubs in London and a mutually loved café that overlooks the River Thames. It was surprisingly fun having someone other than Jaq to talk to about that part of my life. London had such a unique ambiance and I had the privilege of experiencing both the regal and the grungy.

Andre's parents passed away when he was just a boy and he'd been trying to figure his life out ever since. I couldn't imagine losing one loved one, let alone two. That was something that could potentially break me.

"It happened so long ago that I rarely think of it. Nature's way of keeping the balance is all," he said matter-of-factly.

Nature's way of keeping the balance? Really?

I didn't understand how he could be so nonchalant about the death of his parents. Maybe they'd had some seriously deep-rooted issues. Even still, I felt a red flag rise up in my mind.

As Andre brushed his fingers through his lustrous brown hair, I noticed something glistening on his hand. He wore a silver ring on his middle finger and it looked kind of like there was a tiny engraving.

"It belonged to a friend of mine a very long time ago," he said, following my gaze. "I never take it off. Kind of like a good luck charm."

"It's beautiful," I whispered. It really was. When he stretched out his hand for me to take a closer look, I spotted a barely noticeable tiger's eye gemstone set opposite the text, which I still couldn't decipher.

"Vita nova," he answered my thought. "It means *new life* in Latin."

"And your friend? Are you still close?" What I really wanted to know was whether or not the ring I'd been admiring had come from an ex-girlfriend.

"Camilla." *Shoot me now.* "Quite fittingly, she gave me a new life," he said looking down at the silver on his finger.

I was going to be sick. How did I always manage to fall for the wrong guy? *I mean throw me a bone here.*

"Where is she now?" was all I could ask, not quite sure I really wanted to know.

"Oh, probably out plotting world domination somewhere," he grinned. He was probably reminiscing, the bastard.

Great. Well, this lovely evening just took a turn for the worse. I felt my territorial nature rearing its ugly head as I shifted uncomfortably beside him. I was taken by surprise when, all of a sudden, he wrapped his arm around me and lowered his lips to my ear.

"She is simply an old friend, sweet girl. You're the one I want. Just you."

I turned my head until we were less than an inch apart. He didn't give me a chance to think. All I felt was the softness of his lips against mine. Andre pressed his firm body into me with one hand resting on my back and the other on the nape of my neck. He lowered me to the ground and I barely even noticed the little rocks underneath the blanket digging into my thighs. I felt his hands investigating every inch of me. He was studying the curves of my body as I blissfully melted underneath him.

"I think we should head back soon," I mumbled halfheartedly, forcing the words out of my mouth one by one. I convinced myself that if we didn't stop ourselves now, it would have been impossible to do so later. And I wasn't that kind of girl.

When I lay in bed later that night, I thought about the words etched into Andre's ring. *Vita nova.* I imagined the glint of the delicate stone in the moonlight as I shut my eyes.

This is exactly what this is.

Three

The last few weeks had gone by without a hitch. Andre and I saw each other as often as classes and studying would allow and I was all caught up in my coursework. Quinn even started to grow on me, so that was definitely a good sign. Jaq and Tristen were also getting more serious and he had recently invited her to meet the family. It was a big step in her opinion and one she wasn't taking lightly.

"You think it's too soon, don't you?" she asked anxiously as we perused the racks at *Flora*.

Jaq had had a total of two, for all intents and purposes, serious relationships in her life. Serious merely implied that they hit the year mark since she hadn't even met the first one's parents.

"I think it's as good a time as any. Meeting his mom and dad isn't a marriage proposal, Jaq. He just wants to show you off to the people he loves."

"It's true," Isabel chimed in. "He's just taking things to the next level. I *wish* Taylor brought me around his family more."

"You're both right. I'm just so nervous about the whole thing. The last time I met the parents I accidentally spilled cranberry juice all over my ex's poor mother. I could tell through her pearly veneers that she wanted to slap the shit out of me."

I couldn't help but laugh. I remembered that night as if it were yesterday. Jaq took a cab straight to my place, burying her puffy, teary-eyed face in my pillows for hours. She was so embarrassed that she avoided Chase for over a week. Eventually she ended up leaving him for some up-and-coming actor but that's neither here nor there.

"You think that's bad?" Olivia asked, trying to lighten the mood. "I once showed up in a miniskirt and stilettos to meet *my* ex's holier-than-thou Catholic family. In my defense, they were Louboutin's."

Jaq decided on a modest knee-length dress with flutter sleeves that left just about everything to the imagination and we all hoped for the best. I don't think I'd ever seen her in anything so demure and proper. She transformed from sex kitten to Stepford wife before our very eyes. As much as I was impressed by this *all work and no play* version of my best friend, it sort of seemed like we were in a parallel universe. The entire dress was solid beige without a hint of ... well, anything really. We spent another few minutes making sure we hadn't missed anything and then walked across the street for a light lunch.

"Well?" I mumbled, still half-asleep. "How was it?"

Jaq had met Tristen's parents last night and I knew she'd been really anxious about the whole thing. We toned her make-up down to a 4 out of 10 and completed her outfit with the same nude pumps I wore on my first date with Andre. Anyone who didn't know her would've assumed she was some high-powered attorney or executive. I wasn't sure Tristen was really prepared for her extreme make-under.

She rolled over onto her side and started to shake her head. I was about to get out of bed to console her when a slight smile formed on her face. Then she started to laugh uncontrollably.

"You know, I was so worried," she said in between giggles. "I thought they were going to hate me, *ma chérie*. But they were the sweetest family. His mom was so nice and his dad kept offering me more food. Definitely made up for what happened at Chase's house."

I was relieved; thinking the last thing she needed was to feel any less incredible than she really was. This was a good time in both our lives and I intended to keep it that way.

"I'm so glad. You have no idea how worried I was about you last night. It took every ounce of my willpower not to text you and check on Mrs. Valgard's ensemble."

"Funny," she said narrowing her bright blue eyes at me teasingly. "Her ensemble is just as bright and colorful as when I first saw it, I assure you."

"Bright and colorful?"

"Bright and colorful," she repeated. "Apparently, Mrs. Valgard just *loves* to stand out in a crowd."

"Welcome to the family," were the only words I could muster before giggling uncontrollably myself.

Once our fit of laughter subsided, Jaq and I changed into our workout gear and headed to the university gym for our usual fitness routine. About a month ago, we had accidentally stumbled upon the massive building as we were exploring the eastern part of campus. The moment we went inside, I noticed a bright pink class list posted up on the wall in front of us. What we saw written on that piece of paper now managed to influence both of our schedules. Spinning classes, yoga, Pilates. You name it; this place had it. Jaq and I signed ourselves up that same day and we'd been regulars ever since.

A bit of cardio and a good stretch a few times a week did wonders for the soul. Even my nightmares were becoming less frequent. If getting sweaty was the price I had to pay for a good night's sleep, so be it. My slimmer waist was just an added bonus.

I put my gym bag away and locked it shut when Primrose Pierce greeted us with her usual innocent smile. We met her last week at yoga and she seemed so sweet and timid that she made me feel like a rebellious strumpet in comparison. She was only seventeen and apparently some sort of whiz kid. Her flaxen hair was so lustrous and unbelievably sleek, even up in a ponytail. My hair was just as long and blonde as hers but it didn't have the volume Prim's had. When she first introduced herself, all I could do was scrutinize every strand enviously.

"Hello ladies," Prim softly purred as she stuffed a green Puma bag into the locker next to mine. "How did meeting the parents go?"

"Much better than initially anticipated," I answered in Jaq's stead. She was fumbling with one of her shoelaces and seemed too distracted to find her manners.

"Have you met your boyfriends parents yet?" she asked me with inquiring eyes. The girl was so unsullied it seemed as though she were living vicariously through our respective romances. But as harmless as Prim appeared, I had only just met her and didn't feel it was appropriate to divulge Andre's personal baggage.

"No, I haven't. Maybe one day," I told her with a look that kept her from pressing the issue. I hadn't lied. Maybe one day I really would meet them. And I prayed that day would be a very, very long time from now.

"I'm sure you'll meet them soon," she whispered thoughtfully.

I felt a tiny hint of negative energy suspended in the air but it left as quickly as it came. My paranoia was clearly getting the best of me. I draped a cute little Newport University gym towel around my neck and picked up the purple yoga mat at my feet.

The instructor devoted the last five minutes of class to meditation. We all sat cross-legged with our eyes closed and I tried unsuccessfully to clear my head. The thought that I'd never get a chance to meet Andre's parents, at least in this lifetime, loomed in my mind. I wondered how he spent the holidays since he'd basically been on his own since they passed. I envisaged him discussing business tactics with my father while my mom and I helped Rosa, our housekeeper for all intents and purposes, put the finishing touches on the Christmas roast. Images of my own family quickly assuaged the melancholy sentiments I felt about his tragic past. I would just have to invite him to spend the holidays with us. It was that simple.

Quinn was going on about some tower the Vikings had built right here in Newport just over a thousand years ago. She said it was called the Old Stone Mill, a cylindrical structure made of lime-mortared fieldstone. Four of its eight pillars faced the main cardinal points of a compass and legend had it, the townspeople would gather around it on the eve of the autumnal equinox offering animal sacrifices to the evil spirits that haunted them. To say they were superstitious was an understatement. *Maybe they didn't have any sage to burn.*

Class dragged on until I could barely keep my eyes open. When we were finally dismissed, I looped my arm through Andre's and we walked over to Chapel Hill. Jaq and Tristen were off doing their own thing so we decided to quiet my rumbling stomach and get some breakfast. I went for my usual Greek yogurt and fruit while Andre decided on plain black tea with a slice of toast.

"You know, you really should eat more, honey," he chastised, taking a sip from the steaming paper cup in his hand.

"Says the guy who barely ever eats."

"You're a woman, Emma. You need to keep your strength up, especially since you've been working out so much lately."

"And you're a man, Andre. You need to keep *your* strength up in case you have to defend my honor again."

"Defending your honor is something I take very seriously. You can rest assured that I'm getting all my nutrients and then some," he grinned.

"And so am I. Yogurt is very high in protein if my sources are correct."

"Indeed they are, but you could stand to gain a few pounds, if I may be so bold. You know how beautiful I think you are, but I want to make sure you're healthy as well."

"Why, Mr. Talon, are you saying you want to keep me around for a while?"

"For a long while," he said taking my hand in his. "And I'd prefer it if you remained as vigorous on the outside as you are on the inside."

"I'll see what I can do," I sighed.

"That's all I ask."

The following night, I did as I was told and left my plate spotless. The look on Andre's face was one of utter disbelief. I didn't even mean to eat that much but after my earlier kickboxing class, I was famished.

"Dessert?" he asked with a far too satisfied grin on his face, shamelessly taking advantage of the situation.

"Chocolate lava cake, please."

I hadn't had lava cake since I got to Rhode Island and if the boy wanted me to eat more, I wasn't about to protest. *Go hard or go home.* He gestured to an attractive brunette who immediately rushed to his side. The waitress didn't even look in my direction. I could have been buck-naked and I doubt she would have noticed me sitting there. Her concentration was hopelessly devoted to my charming boyfriend and I was merely occupying an otherwise vacant chair.

"How can I help you?" the girl asked him beaming. She flashed a brazen smile, which I noticed was way too big for her heart-shaped face. Okay, maybe I was just feeling a bit territorial tonight. Andre hadn't taken his eyes off of me since she got there and I could see that he was downright tickled pink by my discernible possessiveness.

"The beautiful lady will have one order of chocolate lava cake," he said indifferently. "That is all."

Well *that* certainly got her attention. For the first time all evening, the waitress turned to look at me. I could feel her large honey brown eyes scrutinizing me from my head to my waist as that behemoth of a smile suddenly left her pretty face, her mouth tightening into a thin line.

He's all mine, bitch.

"Of course," she muttered and left us with a set of downcast eyes.

"You didn't have to do that."

"Whatever do you mean?" he asked with an air of mock surprise.

"You know what I mean. You didn't even look at her when you ordered."

"Well, it's only fair she get the same treatment as she's given my girlfriend. Don't you agree?"

Girlfriend. I loved it when he called me that. It had been so long since I had been called someone's girlfriend. I had to admit it gave me a warm, fuzzy feeling inside.

"Besides," he continued. "I still plan on leaving her a generous tip as the service was otherwise excellent. So all in all, no harm done."

When we got into the car, Billie Holiday's "I'm a Fool To Want You" started to play softly. Andre had such an eclectic taste in music. From Beethoven's symphonies to the latest hits, he tried to appreciate every genre for what it offered. He had once explained to me that even a mediocre song was still worth listening to because it was ultimately a story someone needed to convey to the world.

"To share a kiss the devil has known," I crooned along lacking both rhythm and grace. I'd always been the first to admit that singing was certainly not my strong suit. But with a very select few people, and usually in cars for some odd reason, I would permit myself to shamelessly jam out.

Andre smiled down at me as he took note of my musical handicap. He gently swept his cool fingers along my cheek and I felt myself shiver at his touch. He had a hunger in his eyes and parted his lips slightly, leaning toward me. We were undoubtedly holding up the valet, but nothing really mattered to us just then. He tilted my chin up to reach his mouth and kissed me sweetly. His lips were a blend of fire and ice. Whenever he kissed me, it was as though I were being catapulted into some euphoric dream world where everything was in its right place.

We passed Main Street and turned onto a secluded road that was a shortcut leading back to the campus. Before I could muster up a scream, someone jumped out in front of us and it felt like Andre had somehow managed to swerve out of the way before I ever saw the man coming. The car came to an abrupt halt and he instructed me to wait inside. He was gone before I could get a word out. I took off my seatbelt and turned around to try and see what happened. No one was out there and my head was suddenly pounding. I must have hit it against the passenger's side window when Andre slammed on the breaks.

As I touched my aching forehead, I realized it was wet and when I looked down, saw a streak of blood on my fingertips. "Great," I muttered to the empty driver's seat. *This is just perfect.* I had blood on my face, not to mention the sizable bump that would almost certainly need tending to once I got home. It took every bit of my feminine dignity to keep the tears from overflowing out onto my cheeks.

"Well we didn't hit anyone and as far as I can tell, he's long gone by now," Andre assured me as he got back in the car. "You're wounded!"

His reaction was better suited for someone who'd been trampled on by an elephant.

"A little banged up but I'll be fine. Not exactly the look I was going for. Don't worry. I'll take care of it when I get home."

"Emma, I'm so sorry."

The whites around his deep brown eyes suddenly turned scarlet and he sped off without saying another word. The silence was deafening as I looked out the window, trying my best to think about anything else. He wouldn't look at me the entire ride back and I wondered if that whole "beautiful lady" spiel was all talk. I knew I looked like a not-so-hot mess but this was taking it to an extreme. *It's only a little blood.*

When we finally pulled up to my dorm, Andre apologized yet again but continued to keep his eyes facing front. He didn't even kiss me goodnight and as I walked out of his car, I felt more pained by his reaction than by any bump or scrape I'd gotten from the stupid accident.

Coffee. I could smell the sweet aroma all around me and when I opened my eyes, I saw Jaq sitting right beside me. She was already dressed in her workout gear and held my favorite Picasso mug in her hands. I purchased it at the MoMA a few years ago and it had one of the most thought-provoking quotes I'd ever read written upon it. *Everything you can imagine is real.* I sometimes found myself staring at the words and conjuring up some profoundly peculiar conceptions. What if there was so much more to the world than met the eye? This couldn't have been all there was. I believed it with every fiber of my being. Or at least I wanted to.

"Good morning," I mumbled and thanked her for my liquid breakfast.

"My pleasure, *ma chérie.* I heard you crying last night. What happened?"

Privacy was pretty much nonexistent in a college dorm room. I told Jaq all about the car wreck and Andre's subsequent emotional detachment. She just sat by me, hanging on every word without interruption.

"I wouldn't overthink his brooding silence, Em. He was probably just really upset with himself for swerving the car and getting you hurt, *non?*"

"You're probably right." I let out a breath I didn't realize I was holding in. "It's just so crazy how one moment, we're kissing and everything is so perfect and then I get a little head wound and it's like I cease to exist."

"I'm sure he was just concerned. Andre doesn't seem like the fickle type."

"I know. I'm overthinking things as usual. I'm sure everything's fine."

She placed her hand on my shoulder and squeezed it a bit too firmly for my liking. I was still feeling pretty sore. "Everything *is* fine. I can hardly even see the mark from the accident. If you hadn't told me, it probably would have taken me a good ten minutes to notice."

Mark? I slowly got out of bed and walked over to the full-length mirror attached to our door. There was a small red spot with a few cuts that were already starting to heal. It honestly wasn't as bad as I thought it would be.

A knock from the other side of the looking glass startled us both. I opened the door and saw a young delivery boy in a navy blue polo shirt holding an especially large bouquet of purple peonies and white ranunculi. The arrangement was absolutely breathtaking and it took me a second before I went to my purse and handed him a tip for his troubles. I assumed Tristen decided to be romantic so I handed them straight to Jaq.

"As much as I adore my darling Tristen, I'd bet my life those aren't for me," she chuckled with a slight echo of melancholy in her voice. There was a small fragment of despairing energy floating in the room but I attributed it to my own fit of melancholy.

The sweet fragrance traveled all throughout our tiny room and attached to the luxurious ivory wrapping paper was a small note card with a neatly penned inscription.

To my beloved Emma,

Words cannot express how deeply sorry I am for hurting you last night. I haven't been able to think of much else since and it pains me to know that I behaved so inappropriately. Please let me know you are well and allow me to make it up to you somehow.

Yours, Andre

I set the card down and crawled back into bed. In one swift motion, Jaq pulled the covers from over my head and studied me for a moment. I took another sip of my coffee and then took my phone off the charger.

"Are you going to thank him?"

"To be honest, I'm not really sure what I'm about to do. For one thing, I don't think he's ever spelled out his first name before. If that's not a sign of remorse, I don't know what is."

I managed a small half-smile as I pictured Andre inspecting each petal until he was completely satisfied with the arrangement. I typed and deleted and retyped a jumble of thoughts until there was one cohesive message.

Emma Dresden | 10:15am: Thank you for the flowers. They're lovely. I'm okay, just sore. I don't think I could stay mad at you if I tried. & as for making it up to me? You better.

Jaq gave me her seal of approval and I hit the send button. Almost immediately, my phone buzzed with a reply.

Andre Talon | 10:16am: I'm relieved to know that you're all right. Please allow me to atone for my shoddy behavior. I have a surprise planned for you tomorrow night. Say you'll come.

After such a grand gesture, it was nearly impossible to have refused him.

Our yoga instructor was a slender redhead in her mid-forties. She wore her cherry-colored hair up in a messy bun and used the word *Namaste* more times than I felt were necessary. It took all of my self-control not to laugh when Jaq toppled over, trying to master her eagle pose. She looked like a little totem pole pretzel, standing with her arms and legs crossed in front of her. Well, that was until she hit the floor with a loud thud.

"Balance, ladies. We must learn to balance our bodies in order to balance our minds," the unusually nimble woman professed. "Jacqueline, you're doing very well. The eagle pose is a difficult one to master, even for some intermediate yogis. It requires strength, endurance and unwavering concentration."

Jaq looked like she wanted to shoot somebody and Ruby was as good a target as any.

"Now, I'd like for everyone to lie on your bellies with your legs raised behind you. This is what we call the locust pose, done to strengthen arms, legs and the muscles in your lower back. Jacqueline?"

Apparently, Jaq had had enough yoga for one day and nearly ran out of class. I quickly grabbed our mats and followed her into the locker room, awkwardly dragging the two vinyl sheets behind me.

"Why'd you run out? We've seen Penelope fall at least ten times and let's not forget about Wobbly Wendy."

"Oh, *chérie,* it's not that. That was just the icing on the cake. Prim told me earlier that she saw Tristen with another girl a couple days ago. I guess that's why I lost my balance. I just kept thinking about him with someone else. The idea of it sickens me."

"What? What do you mean with another girl? What was he doing?" I asked perplexed.

Her expression was heart wrenching and as I saw the tears welling up in her eyes, I could feel mine start to water. She buried her face in her hands and wept quietly when Primrose walked into the room.

"He was having lunch with some blonde tramp. No offense, Emma."

"Seeing as how we're both blonde, none taken," I muttered irritably.

"I just … can't … believe it!" Jaq whimpered. "He's everything I've ever wanted. How could I have been so stupid?"

"Guys are pigs, Jacqueline. I'm just glad you know now before things got serious," Prim said matter-of-factly.

As far as Jaq was concerned, things already were serious. I for one didn't see it coming. The way Tristen looked at her, it was like nothing else in the world mattered. They were like two peas in a pod and I was sure that there had to have been some sort of logical explanation for his apparent indiscretion.

"Listen, we can't jump to conclusions without knowing the facts. Prim, where did you see him?"

"He was having lunch with the harlot at Chez L'Ami. I saw them sitting outside the restaurant engaged in what appeared to be a *very* entertaining conversation."

"How do we know it wasn't his cousin or his sister?"

"Jessica's hair's as black as mine," Jaq sobbed. "She was adopted."

"Well I have a brother and I don't hold his hand when we're at a restaurant. Or any time for that matter," Prim said adding fuel to an already blazing fire.

"You're not helping here, Prim. I think you should confront him and see what he has to say, Jaq. There's no sense in getting all worked up about what could be one big misunderstanding."

My words of wisdom seemed to have flown right by her as she collected her things and started for the exit. With sheer determination written all over her blotchy red face, she stormed out of the locker room leaving me alone with the little flaxen-haired instigator.

"Well, if it were me, I'd certainly want to know," she muttered.

"Agreed. But I think you could've handled it a bit better, Prim."

"It's a good thing Andre doesn't keep any secrets from you. Right, Emma?"

There was almost a hint of cynicism in her voice as she asked me that. Her large, doll-like eyes were studying me expectantly as if she'd purposely planted a seed of doubt that had no place being there in the first place. Andre was a great guy and this naïve little girl who hadn't had any real dating experience had no right messing with my picture-perfect vision of my man. I refused to play her passive aggressive game and promptly sauntered off to find Jaq.

Maybe in her twisted mind, Prim did do the right thing by telling Jaq what she saw. But seeing my best friend so sad and helpless made me think otherwise. There had to have been some reason Tristen was having lunch with another woman, and so help me, I was going to figure out what it was.

I noticed my coffee tasted way off as I sat across the street from Placebo Music. I skimmed the pages of the

Picture of Dorian Grey novel in my hands, eyes glancing toward the record store in front of me every now and again.

Tristen had been in there for half an hour already. I thought I might have missed him leave and started to put my book away when I finally saw him exiting the store. He was heading back in the direction of campus, holding a bag with what looked like a few vinyl records. I got up and followed, leaving an overly generous tip given what I'd just forced myself to ingest. Whoever said all black coffee tastes the same clearly hadn't had the pleasure of sampling Planet Java's extra special blend.

We walked about two blocks down when Tristen slowed at a small bookshop and stepped through its large rustic maple double doors. Through the window, I spotted him meeting with some blonde woman. I could only see the back of her golden head. Tristen didn't look like he was too excited to see her so that was a good sign, at least for Jaq's sake. From my vantage point, I saw she wore tan linen pants that flared out just a little and an oversized white button-up tucked inside; the short, slender girl had style, I gave her that.

She led Tristen to a small wooden table and motioned for him to sit. There were a few leather-bound books set in front of them as the girl flipped through each one in turn. I hoped that maybe they were study partners, that Prim had made an innocent mistake. I lurked outside for another few minutes, trying to get as much Intel as possible. Once I determined that nothing seemed out of the ordinary and Tristen hadn't been sporting any bedroom eyes for his companion, I thought it was all right to leave them be. After all, I couldn't exactly storm in on the two of them with nothing to go by except a harmless rendezvous at Circe's Book Shoppe.

"What are you doing?" I heard a familiar voice ask from behind me. When I turned around, Andre was peering down at me suspiciously. *Busted.*

"Oh … hi," I murmured, trying to mask the shock in my voice. I had just been caught spying on my best friend's boyfriend and wasn't prepared with a suitable response. He repeated the question.

"Let's walk," I said, quickly grabbing Andre's hand and pulling him after me.

I explained the purpose of my reconnaissance mission as Andre listened attentively. He didn't seem to think I was being creepy, which was an added bonus. Instead, possibly in an effort to compensate for his recent thoughtlessness, he offered to help.

"I don't want you following him anymore, Emma. Whatever your gym buddy saw is hearsay. Let me get to the bottom of this, okay? Boys talk."

Why hadn't I thought of that? I should have just gone to him straightaway. Boys did talk and Andre would have probably gotten more out of Tristen by simply asking than I could have with my amateur espionage tactics.

"Okay," I agreed.

"Promise me," he said more seriously this time. *Geez, okay.* I wondered what crawled up his perfectly sculpted butt all of a sudden.

"I promise."

Four

We pulled over by the Goat Island Lighthouse later that night and I was immediately taken aback by its splendor. The small granite structure took on a life of its own, shining a vibrant red light overhead. Andre sat in one of the Adirondack chairs overlooking the Narragansett Bay and gestured for me to sit on his lap. He apologized yet again for the other night and I'd had enough. I turned around, wrapping my arms around his neck, and gave him a small peck on the corner of his mouth.

"There's no need. I must have looked awful after hitting my head. It's no wonder you wouldn't look at me."

I could see my answer had upset him. *Did I say something wrong?* He shifted in his seat but held my arms in place when I tried to loosen my grip. Andre gazed at me for a moment before speaking.

"Emma, you're so beautiful. There are things you don't know about me quite yet. And I promise you, if I ever have the opportunity to explain myself, it will all make sense."

I honestly didn't care anymore. For all I knew, he was in bad car accident as a child and the experience haunted him. But he looked so ethereally striking that all I could think about were his lips on mine. I didn't need any more apologies. Andre's dark features contrasted so brilliantly with his luminous pale skin that even the sight of the Claiborne Pell Bridge in the background couldn't hold a candle to his image. I took his face in my hands and kissed him mercifully. His smell consumed me with its light traces of lavender and musk. He placed one hand on the small of my back and the other clutched onto my hair as he kissed me back eagerly. He took all his grief from our last date and turned it into a yearning passion. I could taste his longing for me as his tongue brushed against mine in earnest. We'd acquired a rhythm that only paused briefly when coming up for air.

"Andre."

I heard an unnervingly familiar voice in the distance interrupting our heated moment. Instinctively, Andre stood up with me still holding on to him and set me down on the ground gracefully. He shielded himself directly in front of me as if safeguarding me from our uninvited guest.

"I send you to complete one final task before I grant you your freedom and *this* is how you choose to repay me?

By making out like a reckless schoolboy when you should be hard at work?"

For a split second he looked livid, but then quickly regained his composure and wrapped one arm around my waist possessively.

"I'm handling it," Andre said impassively.

"You better be," she shot him a sinister smile. "You are my progeny, Andre; I love you. But don't you dare confuse that with leniency. You and I both know that's a trait I haven't possessed for centuries."

When I finally made out her face in the dim moonlight, I could hardly believe my eyes. *What the hell is* she *doing here?*

"Prim?" I asked bewildered.

Her expression was oddly dark and menacing. She suddenly looked quite different from the bashful gym rat I had been doing downward facing dog poses with. Prim glared at me curiously until I started to feel like I was some sort of science project on display.

"Hello, Emma. How are your stretches coming along?" she asked nonchalantly but with a bit more intensity than I was used to coming from her. Andre's initial ferocity receded for a moment as he looked from me to her, visibly perplexed. Prim didn't wait for my response and turned her attention back to the man beside me.

"I've been keeping an eye on things since your arrival in this revolting town. I expected more from you, Andre."

"We've already been through this, Camilla." He looked exasperated, speaking so low that I was surprised she heard him at all at the distance she kept between us. "I will ring you as soon as I've procured the grimoire. Until then, what I do and whom I do it with is none of your concern."

"Until I release you, child, everything you do is my concern. That is something you will come to understand if and when you ever decide to become a maker. Drain half the city dry for all I care, but do not embarrass our line by consorting with a petty *human.*" The last word rolled off her tongue with palpable disgust.

"If I ever choose to become a maker, I will give my progeny the freedom to consort with whomever he or she pleases, so long as that relationship does no harm."

"But it does," she quickly cut in. Her expression was much like a mother scolding her adolescent son. It was so bizarre to watch since Prim, or Camilla, looked like a child next to him. "It does do harm. What you've failed to learn in all your years is that love between our two species is unquestionably reprehensible. One simply *cannot* devote himself to the source of his sustenance. You must forget about your pet at once and finish what you set out to do for me. My patience is wearing thin."

"I've been shadowing the boy for months now and I have a clear idea of its location. A few of my contacts in London and Berlin are working on a way to infiltrate the barrier Nathaniel placed around the perimeter." He glanced at me for a split second before continuing. "My relationship with Emma has in no way affected my work, Camilla. You have my word. So if it pleases you, I'd like to salvage whatever is left of my evening."

As quickly as she had appeared, Camilla vanished into thin air and I was left standing there, stunned and speechless, with a million different thoughts racing through my mind. Andre took me by the hand and silently led me back to the bulky wooden chair we had just occupied. I sat on his lap, curling myself into a ball, and rested my head against his chest. He ran his hand delicately through my hair and coiled a lock around his fingers. Even though I couldn't see his face, I knew him well enough to be certain he was deep in thought.

"How do you know Camilla?" he finally asked me, burying his face in the now undoubtedly tangled bird's nest that was my hair.

"Jaq and I met her at the gym, but she introduced herself as Primrose Pierce for some reason. I think the more important question here is how *you* know her."

Andre's brooding silence was maddening and I raised my head to face him. His guard was definitely still up, but the longer I peered into his eyes, charcoal in the darkness, the less tense he appeared. After what seemed like an eternity, he startled me by lifting me into his arms without warning. He put me down by the scattered rocks at the edge of the grassy precipice and we just stood there, watching the water ripple in the bay. I'd had enough of his melancholy nostalgia for one night and brushed my hand along his cheek, attempting to bring him back into the present. He gazed down at me with the gloomiest face I'd ever seen.

"When I was just a boy," he began, choosing his words carefully. "My father threw a party at our estate. Every year, our friends from all over the neighboring towns came to celebrate the Feast of Avalon with my family."

I had never heard of such a holiday and found myself relieved that he was finally opening up to me about his childhood. All I really knew of Andre's parents was that they died a very long time ago. Hearing about his past meant we were making some serious headway where our relationship was concerned.

"Once the party was well under way," he continued. "I decided to take a walk in the gardens. My mother had designed an actual maze in our backyard made of tall evergreen hedges. I would play in it as a child, hiding from my parents and au pairs. That night, I ventured deep into the labyrinth as I did every so often and came across a beautiful girl. She was the epitome of everything I'd ever hoped for in a bride and I remember thinking she looked like an angel." He paused for a moment and held my hand to his heart.

"At first, I assumed she'd been one of our guests. She was dressed impeccably and it seemed like she belonged there, simply choosing to escape the crowd as I had. I asked the girl if she was lost and she just smiled up at me." I leaned against him, hanging on to every word as he reminisced about his probable ex-girlfriend. "Back then, it was customary to take a lady on a stroll as a means of courting. It was the only way young men and women were able to speak privately. With the advent of my mother's maze garden, however, we had all the privacy in the world that night.

"The girl told me she was there for the party; that her parents were inside and she needed some fresh air. We spoke about everything from music to religion to politics. It was the first time I was able to truly debate without someone watching over my every word. You mustn't forget, Emma, my life wasn't like it is now."

From the way he was talking, it sounded like he was some sheltered aristocrat; that or he grew up in the Dark Ages. *Russia can't possibly be* that *repressed,* I thought to myself.

"Anyway, once we reached the center, we stopped walking and just looked at each other for a while. The very sight of her captivated me and it honestly felt like we were the only two people left in the world." I felt my territorial alter ego come out of hibernation as he went on.

"She asked me if I wanted to protect her, to keep her safe. In exchange, she would grant me eternity. Had I known then what the consequences would be, I'm not sure I would have made the same choice."

Andre was visibly exhausted. His eyes were half shut with his mind seeming as though it were battling a thousand painful memories all at once. I placed my hand on his cheek and encouraged him to continue.

"I was foolish and she was predatory. I was only twenty; my whole life was ahead of me. But I eagerly accepted my role as her guardian. I thought of it as a badge of honor, something to be proud of. I was at an age where I should have been married and I thought I'd finally found the one. That night, Camilla took me to an abandoned farmhouse nearby and—" He looked down at his ring. "And gave me this ... *vita nova.*"

I was beyond confused at this point. Firstly, he made it seem like this all happened ages ago and now I'd come to learn he was twenty when he met her. Secondly, I failed to understand what exactly she needed protection from. "So you became her bodyguard, basically?"

"Basically, at first," he nodded. "That night in the farmhouse, the night of the party, I died. The girl I met had been something I never would have considered possible. She led me to an open space where the entire sky was illuminated with stars. I saw her as my salvation from the life that awaited me back at the estate. Camilla offered a new beginning and I took it without a moment's thought. We were standing there, gazing up at the sky, and she kissed me.

"Before I could understand what was happening, I felt her teeth pierce my neck and I became paralyzed for a short while. I remember the initial sharp pain of the bite like it was yesterday, and how quickly it turned euphoric. I remember her holding me in her arms as she used her fingernail to make a slit in her wrist. Like an infant at his mother's mercy, she fed me her blood. I obediently drank from the bitch as she damned me for all eternity."

For the first time since we'd met, I genuinely thought my boyfriend had lost his marbles. At some point during his spiel, he had mentioned he'd died. Then there was all that talk about him drinking Camilla's blood. Every instinct told me to turn on my heel and run, but I just stood there captivated with his story.

"I awoke the following night in a large attic with an insatiable thirst rising inside me. My throat felt like sandpaper and I couldn't swallow. I was suddenly conscious of absolutely everything all at once. I smelled the mold growing beneath the floorboards and stew simmering in the kitchen. I could hear mice running behind the walls and people talking below. It was as if every sense was heightened and every emotion magnified. Camilla took me downstairs, pointed to a family at the dinner table and told me to pick my first course." His eyes looked pained as if he were replaying each moment.

I couldn't believe what I was hearing. My sweet, uncomplicated college romance had just taken a turn for the extreme. Surely Jaq hadn't had to listen to such nonsensical drivel from her boyfriend. The last thing I wanted to do was upset a man who was obviously in need of some serious mental help so I did the only thing I could have done. I played along.

"So do you even value human life? Or are we just something on the menu?"

I regretted my words as soon as they came off my tongue. Playing along was one thing, but I knew what I had said was downright cruel, even given the circumstances.

"Emma, do you really believe I look at you like you're something on the menu?"

Andre was so hurt by my reaction that he let go of my hand and started walking toward his car miserably. I followed him, mirroring his sadness and trying to make sense of it all.

"So you kill people to survive?" I asked meekly.

"No, I don't. Most vampires have evolved, Emma. We own blood banks all around the world so we don't need to kill. Some still do of course, but so do humans. I didn't want you to find out like this," he muttered. "I would have kept it from you for as long as possible, but given what happened tonight, I owed it to *us* to tell you about my past."

Vampires. I imagined Dracula and Nosferatu and Lestat; all literary characters that were too farfetched to be real. Andre walked in the sun and had enrolled himself in college, for goodness' sake! I didn't want to believe I was living in some B-rated horror flick. But after seeing his distraught face, I needed to know more; even if did sound completely ridiculous.

"And you can force humans to do what you want?"

Was that what he did to the assholes that tried to hurt me the night we met? Was that why they listened to him so submissively and left us alone? I started to wonder how many times I had been coerced. How many of my memories had been erased? Did he force me to do things I wouldn't have otherwise done? I couldn't believe it. Was everything up to this point just one big lie?

"It's called compulsion," he murmured. "And yes, I can compel humans to do as I command, all of them but you. I still haven't figured out why, not that I would ever compel you even if I could."

"How would you know you couldn't compel me if you hadn't already tried?" This was all too much to bear.

"The night we formally met, when I scared off those kids. I wanted you to forget it ever happened. I didn't want you to remember how frightened you were. I thought it'd have been easier that way for both of us. I never planned on falling for you, Emma. I was here to do a job and leave as soon as possible. But when I attempted to compel you that night, you just looked at me as if I were crazy.

"And that's when I knew. There's something very different about you. It's your blood; it's unlike any human being's I've ever encountered. When I smelled it in the car after the accident, I couldn't get enough. It's why I couldn't look at you. My eyes would have given me away and I wasn't ready to tell you everything then. But I am now."

"I don't know what to say," I whispered, unable to look him in the eyes. "Thank you for being honest with me, I guess."

I still didn't believe a word he'd said, but the despondency in the air around us was too intense to ignore. Could he have been telling me the truth? It wasn't possible.

"If you're really a vampire, may I see your fangs?"

The words left my mouth before I realized what I'd just asked him. Did I actually expect two pointy canines to appear from out of nowhere? He stood beside me at the hood of his Porsche and thought hard about my request. I sensed Andre was still upset, but he finally looked down at me with eyes tinged with crimson. When he opened his mouth, I gasped as I caught a glimpse of two sharp fangs flashing in the moonlight.

Five

The Annex was the only place in Newport that understood the science behind a good espresso. It seemed like the perfect place at which to continue our surreal conversation from the night before. Andre and I had left off with a plan to meet for coffee the next morning. After spending the night replaying Andre's confession in my head, I decided that it was in no way going to be a deal breaker for our relationship. I shared so many wonderful moments with this man. Who was I to judge a part of him he can't control? It took a little while but I'd mostly come to terms with the fact that he'd been around since before my great-great-grandfather, eerie as it was. Considering he still looked like a fucking supermodel, it really wasn't all that difficult. He had wisdom only years of experience could bring paired with the body of a young athlete. All in all, I had no right to complain about his diet.

We ordered our drinks and sat down at an old wrought iron garden table. The chairs were cushioned with plush forest green pillows and there were giant Art Nouveau posters along the walls inside. My favorite thing about the place was its large outdoor seating area in the back, which had the most spectacular views of Wickford Cove. Olivia recently told me that the owners locked up that part of the café for the winter, so we only had a few more weeks to enjoy it.

"So, you're supposed to get her a book of spells," I whispered as inconspicuously as possible over my iced Americano.

"Yes," Andre said in his regular tone of voice. "We can speak freely here," he informed me with a slight grin. "It's an ancient grimoire that Camilla has been trying to get her hands on for the better part of a thousand years. It originally belonged to Alexander Valgard, a very powerful mage … err, witch or sorcerer, whatever you want to call it. He and his family lived in this area back when Camilla was still human.

"Alexander murdered Camilla's first love, Theron," Andre continued. "Legend has it that a spell capable of bringing Theron's soul back to her is in this grimoire. She would ultimately need to find another vampire's body to use as a vessel, but should she succeed, Theron's spirit and all of his memories along with it will have returned. He'd have the strength of his thousand plus years and the mind of the sixteen-year-old vampire he once was."

I took another rather large swig of my drink, trying to mask my disbelief. The girl I'd been laying on floor mats with was actually some immortal creature on a mission to resurrect her former lover, a teenager with more power than he could possibly handle if ever brought back. *Who said Rhode Island was going to be boring?*

"Many centuries ago, when the Vikings inhabited what is now known as Newport, a small community of mages settled here. Edgar, Theron's father, had come to this town once he realized what his son had become. It was the only way he knew to protect him. The mages were able to do their spells and Theron could hunt animals freely. But very soon after they arrived, the young vampire started to become indifferent to humanity. People were disappearing left and right and the town grew fearful.

"Alexander watched this go on for months before he called a meeting with Edgar. Too many people were afraid and asking questions and Alexander couldn't afford to risk exposing either of their kind. He made it clear that Theron was solely to feed on animals if their family wanted to be welcome there. Edgar naturally complied and told his son to do the same."

"I can feel a *but* coming on."

"But," Andre said with a playful smile. "Theron was young and irrational. He considered it offensive that these *humans* were telling him what to do. Alexander needed to pay for insulting him. So Theron decided that it was wise to kill Alexander's wife. It was his way of settling a score. When the man finally found her body completely drained of blood ... Emma, are you sure you want me to go on?"

I was imagining the story play out in my head, wondering what Newport would have looked like all those years ago. I took another sip of my drink and nodded.

"When the man saw his dead wife, he went mad. It's been said that Alexander's rage was felt for miles. He conjured up a spell that was able to entrap Theron's soul inside Camilla's amulet."

"Tiger's eye," I muttered, surprising us both. It was as though I'd heard this story once before.

"Yes. Alexander did some magic compelling Theron to enter what we now know as the Old Stone Mill. You see, mages don't believe in disrupting the balance of nature by taking the lives of others, innocent or otherwise. So, he stripped Theron of his protective talisman and made him stand there as he chanted a spell separating his soul from his physical body. But here's the kicker: Camilla meant everything to Theron. She was the only person he truly cared for other than his father. As a token of appreciation for what happened to his wife, Alexander made Camilla watch as Theron's soul was locked away inside the little gemstone on her silver pendant. Once the spell was complete, he gave her the necklace back, fostering this crazy sense of wasted hope that she's carried with her for centuries."

"So why didn't she just go and get the grimoire once he let her go and undo the spell herself?" I asked feeling like my logic should have been blatantly obvious.

"Mages aren't your typical humans, Emma. They're extremely intelligent and quite powerful. Whatever that grimoire's locked away in, it's going to be harder to crack open than a vault in a Vegas casino. They've probably chosen a state-of-the-art safe, updated annually of course. And that's not to mention the confining spell, which has to be broken once the safe is cracked."

"How is it that you and Camilla can walk in the daylight?" I thought out loud, going completely off topic.

Andre raised an eyebrow. "One foot after the other," he said flippantly. "Quite simple, really."

My glare let him know that I wasn't in the mood. I had learned way too much creepy stuff in the last twenty-four hours to be patronized by Count Chocula. Andre cleared his throat giving him enough time to decide whether to continue pushing my buttons or play nice. For his own sake, he chose the latter.

"Myth. Sunlight does nothing to us. For so long, though, we've lived on a nocturnal schedule out of convenience that I actually prefer it to, say, morning rush hour. But now that so many of us exist, we've learned to adapt to the human timetable."

"What else?" I asked him wholly engrossed in Vampire 101. I had literally embarked upon the history of an unknown species, hidden to the outside world. It was like studying European History on acid.

"Garlic. I can eat it without fear of imminent death. Wooden stake through the heart won't work on me, but will work on most others. Let's see. I don't sleep in a coffin. I don't have to sleep at all, really. I do it to relax more than anything. I can eat food but I don't really enjoy it as it gives me no sustenance. I can taste and smell it all much more sharply than when I was human, but I don't like it the same way anymore. I love the taste of a good whiskey, though. And hot green tea. Don't know why."

"Hmm."

"Now, sweetheart, I think we've gone slightly off topic."

"Camilla and the pendant," I said.

"Yes. When a vampire is turned, his or her maker is responsible for them until their release. In return, the progeny must abide by any rules the maker sets. Some makers are stricter than others, kind of like parents with their children. The only way for me to truly be free of her is to challenge Camilla to a duel and win or convince her to release me by fulfilling this last assignment. And we've known each other for far too long for me to kill her if I don't have to."

I shuddered at the thought of Andre being at this woman's beck and call for so many years. I could totally understand why he would want his freedom. I'd been trying to get away from my brilliantly dysfunctional family since I was thirteen.

"Camilla's always given me carte blanche to travel, work and do whatever else that pleases me. But there's an incessant sense of responsibility that comes with being a progeny. She didn't turn me for love. If she had, our relationship would be much different. If I were to turn someone I love vampyr, it would be for an eternal partnership; I wouldn't expect anything in return. But for

Camilla, my immortality was more of a mutually beneficial arrangement in her eyes; one that I'd very much care to end."

"I can't imagine what it's been like for you all these years, being indebted to the woman that killed you."

"It's taken me a very long time to forgive her for that. Nevertheless, I *have* forgiven her and I've come to terms with what I am. No sense in drowning in something I can't change. But it's such a gnawing feeling that, be it tomorrow or a year from now, I'll have to pack up and do more of her dirty work. That's what bothers me the most. She made me a promise that I'll have earned my release with the procurement of the grimoire and Camilla's never gone back on her word in all the centuries I've known her. Once that book is in her hands, I will officially be liberated of my duties. And it's about time. I've paid my fucking dues."

"Why do you both wear tiger's eye gemstones? Is it a vampire thing?"

"Sort of," Andre smirked, looking down at the silver band around his finger. "A few years before her mother was killed, Alexander's daughter, Ariana, created a couple of special talismans for a boy she'd fancied."

"Theron."

"Yes. Ariana was deeply in love with Theron. She enchanted a ring and a pendant as a token of her affection and loyalty to him. Tiger's eye has been coveted since antiquity and Ariana blended its properties with silver to shield its wearer from the laws that bind my kind to the earth. A wooden stake through the heart would kill any vampire. With this ring, decapitation is the only way to truly kill me. And ripping out my heart. I don't normally divulge that little tidbit, but now you know. Try not to use it against me if I'm ever late picking you up."

"I could think of other, much more brutal ways to express my anger," I teased.

"I supposed as much," he grinned. "Anyway, I've always believed Ariana expected Theron to turn her so that they'd walk through eternity together. Unfortunately for her, Theron had already been courting Camilla. When he turned her, he gave Camilla the pendant for protection."

"How did Theron's ring end up on your finger?"

"That night in the attic, when my human life ended, Camilla told me I'd been reborn. We aren't natural beings, Emma. We don't procreate or pass on to maintain the balance. That's why there are things that affect vampires more so than humans. I think of it as nature's way of finding equilibrium within the species. This ring keeps me at an advantage. Ariana was powerful for her age. Without her talisman and Camilla's generosity, I'd be much more vulnerable."

I stood up and positioned myself firmly on Andre's lap, wrapping my arms tightly around his shoulders. He instinctively buried his head in my hair and we just sat there in silence for a while. I needed a moment to take in all that I'd heard.

"There's something I haven't yet told you, Emma," he muttered. "The arrangement I made with Camilla … it's off. She's sending another vampire to procure the grimoire and … I worry that you may be in danger."

I searched for an appropriate response but came up blank. What did he mean I was in danger? Surely it wasn't anything *he* couldn't protect me from.

"I don't know what to do," he breathed, taking my head in his hands and peering his dark brown eyes into my green ones. "I have never felt so helpless. Before I met you, Emma, love was merely something I read about. In over five hundred years, I honestly didn't think I was capable of it. But when I look at you—" Andre stroked my cheek gently, never taking his eyes off mine. "You've changed everything, Emma. You've tamed me."

It was hard to concentrate on global marketing tactics and trade barriers with everything going on in my life. Painting my nails a different color each day had been a coping mechanism I'd recently developed. Today my hands were Pleasantly Plum. I had this constant worry looming over me and Andre's relentless coddling didn't help matters. According to him, Camilla wasn't one for a sneak-attack; that wasn't her M.O. Instead, she'd probably have one of her minions threaten me first or, if I were just that lucky, maybe she'd do me the honor of gracing me with her ethereal presence. After all, I was simply dying to see how her lotus pose was coming along.

"Emma?" I heard my name and suddenly, there I was, back in class with everyone gawking at me.

"Yes?" I answered meekly.

"The 4 P's. Name them, please."

"Oh." I gaped at Mr. Wentworth as though he were wearing a bright pink tutu when Andre suddenly dropped his pen and whispered the word "price" on his way down to the floor. I stared at him uncomprehendingly and then back at our professor. *Umm.*

"Well?"

"The 4 P's. Of global marketing." It finally hit me what the professor was asking me and I felt dumber than I must have looked at that very moment. "Umm, price, product, place. And ... promotion?"

"Very good, Ms. Dresden. It seems your juvenile daydreaming hasn't fully impaired your aptitude for business. Now, who can tell me some disadvantages of global marketing as a whole?"

The attention was finally off me and I let out an inaudible sigh of relief. I wasn't behind in my classes, but I wasn't giving it my all; that's for sure. Considering my life had recently been threatened, I'd say I was doing pretty well in school as a whole.

Jaq and I decided to spend the early part of the afternoon in Blackstone, a serene, park-like area with a cluster of cherry blossom trees where students gathered to study or clear their heads. I was awed by how breathtaking this place was. We sat on a bench by a large weeping cherry tree reading *Cosmo* and *Interview with the Vampire,* respectively. The pale pink flowers swallowed us up and it felt like we were blanketed in a sheet of sweet cotton candy.

"No, he's definitely not that," Jaq beamed. "Tristen seems like he'd be more comfortable at a sports bar eating hot wings and watching a football game. Strangely enough, I find it kind of sexy."

"Leave it to the dignified debutante to find hot wings and beer sexy," I chuckled.

"I know, right? Who would have thought? I mean we did meet over a game of beer-pong. I wasn't exactly expecting operas and pâté."

"I'm just glad you finally found someone who can keep up with you."

"And to think, he almost didn't come to the Sigma Phi house that night. He had so much going on at home. Still does. His dad's all worried because he thinks someone wants to steal something from his study. It doesn't really make any sense. Who would want a dusty old book, anyway?"

Piece by piece, I began assembling the puzzle in my mind. The all-powerful mage Andre had mentioned was named Alexander *Valgard*, as in Tristen Valgard. How had I not put two and two together before? On our second day of class, Tristen had revealed to us all that he came from a line of Viking's. Did Camilla go to Tristen's father in the hopes that he would give her the grimoire? Had she threatened him? Or had Andre been the cause of his anxiety? After all, my boyfriend could be quite intimidating when he wanted to be. I'd seen that side of him firsthand on the night we met.

"Did Tristen happen to mention what the book was about?" I asked trying to keep the conversation flowing. Though I already knew the answer.

"No, just that it's really old and it's been in his family for, like, generations."

I'd figured as much. "Did he at least say who wanted it?"

"Apparently, his father received an anonymous phone call right before school started. The person said if he didn't give up the book, Tristen and his little sister would be held responsible. That's why he wasn't in class on the first day."

"Well it's been a few months since then. Has the person called back?"

I'm sure that after a thousand years, a few months were nothing to Camilla. But it still made me wonder what she'd been up to this whole time. Had she put all her eggs in one basket and simply expected Andre to follow through? Or was Andre the one who made the threat in the first place? All of these unanswered questions were starting to give me a headache.

"He said someone showed up at his sister's school last week. The craziest part is that she doesn't remember who spoke to her. She can't even remember if it was a man or woman! Jessica just came home and told her father that Alexander's debt shall be paid in full. Whatever the hell that means."

His debt to whom, though? His debt to Camilla? To Theron? What about the debt owed to Alexander for his wife's untimely death? Who was responsible for paying *that* debt?

"Well, whoever's threatening his family will get what's coming to them. The Valgard's don't exactly seem like the docile type. They are Vikings after all."

"Yeah. I've just never seen Tristen so … troubled, *chérie.* There's no other word to describe it. He thinks his family is in some kind of serious trouble. I just wish there was something I could do to help, but he says there isn't. Jessica's been on house arrest since the thing at her school and I have a feeling Tristen's next. And he can't afford to miss any classes. It's already the end of the semester and he's barely getting by as it is."

"Everything is going to be fine. Tristen's tough and from what I've heard about Mr. Valgard, he is too. I'm sure there's nothing to worry about."

I hated lying to Jaq. She was one of the only people I could confide in without being criticized in the process. She was the voice of reason in my complicated life. And yet, I couldn't tell her how I really felt. I couldn't begin to describe to her how I scared I was for us all. For Tristen and his family. For Andre. For me. I knew that if I went down that path, my fear would take over completely and there would be no going back.

"He's a descendent of Alexander Valgard's," Andre whispered. "If I could simply compel him to get me the grimoire, things would have been a lot easier for everyone. But it's virtually impossible to execute any form of compulsion on a mage."

Well aren't we lucky?

Quinn kept looking at us with probing eyes as I feigned my most innocent smile. I shifted in my seat and tried to think logically. Tristen was the key to obtaining the stupid grimoire but we couldn't just ask him for it.

"We need to tell Jaq." The idea came at me with such force that I almost jumped up in front of our entire class.

"Umm ... no."

I wanted to stomp my foot like a child but restrained myself. I already felt like a total adolescent given I was multiple centuries younger than my boyfriend. I sat and wondered if I could even call him my *boy*friend. He was technically older than my dad. *Creepy.* I gave him a sidelong glance and giggled to myself. He looked at me confused but grinned nevertheless and shook his head. I attempted a different approach at getting him to listen. For once in my life, I tried reasoning to get my way.

"I'm serious!" I murmured enthusiastically. "If there's any way to get this damn book, Jaq can help."

I knew I was right. This wasn't just about Andre anymore. This was my own life and Tristen's and Jessica's that I needed to worry about as well. I decided right then and there that Jaq needed to know and she needed to know soon. Telling her was our best shot at getting out of the supernatural mess we had all inadvertently stumbled into.

After some mild coaxing that gradually got more and more forceful with my limited patience, Andre finally agreed to tell Jaq about the grimoire as long as he was permitted to compel her not to reveal his nature to anyone. Ever. I felt bad about him using compulsion on my best friend but this was a secret so big, he needed to take all necessary precautions. Andre was nowhere near willing to divulge every detail of his life story but just enough to fill her in on what was going on and find out whatever vital information we could. I brewed three cups of coffee and sat down on my little bed beside Andre as he began telling Jaq about Tristen's connection to the grimoire and what happened the night Camilla met us at the lighthouse.

"Do you remember Tristen ever mentioning any old family heirlooms?" he asked her gently, like a detective would act when questioning an innocent victim. Jaq looked at Andre dumbstruck and I started to question my bright idea of getting her involved.

"Not that I recall," she said honestly.

Come on, Jaq, you've got to know something!

"Anything about his ancestors? Family history?" I added, hoping for some minor detail to get the ball rolling.

She sat Indian-style on the floor, sipping her oversized mug and stared more through us than at us. After a few frustratingly long moments, she began to reveal to us whatever she knew of the Valgard lineage.

"Just that his ancestors were Vikings and his father's some big collector of old stuff. Weapons, books, you name it. That's all I really know. I mean I never really dug too deep into Tristen's family life. I just figured he would tell me more when the time was right."

"The entire Valgard estate is sealed off to vampires," Andre informed us. "Meaning, even if Tristen were to ask me inside, a spell more powerful than his invitation would ultimately block me out. The grimoire could be anywhere. It could be in a safe or through a hidden doorway; the possibilities are endless. And since there's no way for me to get inside, I have no idea what we're up against. It's really rather frustrating."

"That house is the oldest standing residence in the entire state," I recalled vividly. "I read about it when we came here for the campus tour. Remember, Jaq? We drove by it on our way back home and you said something like how it reminded you of *Gone with the Wind*. I bet they've had a lot of time to vampire-proof the property since it was built in the Stone Age."

Andre couldn't help but smile at my remark, since he too was born a trillion years ago, give or take. I threw my arms around him playfully and planted a big wet kiss on his cheek. He acted so shy sometimes, especially around others. When we were alone, he put his guard down as much as he could manage, but with others, PDA was still very new to him. I sometimes wished he were more affectionate in public. For someone who could be such a caveman when it was just the two of us, in front of people he was uncharacteristically reserved.

"And that is why," he continued. "For now, all we need is for Jaq to do a little reconnaissance work and scope out as many rooms as she can." He turned to look at the anxious little girl on the cerulean carpet holding her giant mug. "Will you do that for us, Jaq?"

She nodded hesitantly and sipped her drink.

After about a week of recon, Jaq had managed to go to Tristen's house three times. The only piece of valuable information she could offer was that his father had a locked study where he kept his many trinkets and heirlooms. When Tristen attempted to show her an old high school football trophy, his father immediately sent them away before she had a chance to look inside.

"At least we know ballpark where it is and that Tristen has access to it," I said trying to stay positive.

"I just don't know how much longer I can keep inspecting his house." She looked at me like a lost puppy and I felt her sadness reach the pit of my stomach. "I'm really falling for him, Em. He may look like a Viking but he's got the biggest heart in the world."

Poor Jaq. Here she was, finally connecting with a boy she genuinely cared for, and I had to go and throw lies and deception into the equation. *All for the greater good,* I kept reminding myself.

"I'm sorry. I know how hard this must be for you. And I wouldn't have asked for your help had there been any other way."

"I know. And I wouldn't have done this had it been for anyone else. But all in all, it's not so bad. It's not like I'm looking under his mattress or anything. If snooping around Tristen's house is going to help keep you all safe somehow, it's the least I can do. Besides, there's no way I could handle getting a new best friend *and* a new boyfriend right now," she smiled and I could tell her moment of guilt had dissipated. "So if Camilla's getting someone else to steal the book, why is Andre still after it?"

Leverage? Revenge? Security?

"If Camilla gets her hands on that thing and manages to bring Theron back, who knows what'll happen? She's not exactly resurrecting a saint, you know. Theron is dangerous and the two of them together, lethal. We can't risk it."

"I didn't think of it like that." Jaq stared at me for a few moments and I saw her grief had resurfaced. "You'll always be in danger as long as Camilla's alive. Well, you know what I mean. Undead. Whatever."

"Hey," I whispered. Placing my arm around her shoulder, I pulled her in for a tight hug. "It's not over yet. Andre thinks that if we can get the grimoire, we may be able to cast the same spell Alexander did and trap Camilla in her own amulet. And if it works, he would ultimately give her what she's always wanted, to be with Theron for eternity."

A lifeless body is in the center of an abandoned tower. The wind is ruthless and I wish I dressed warmer. My dress is torn and dirty and I can't remember where I am. There are eight candles lit in between each pillar. This doesn't feel right. I apprehensively approach the body and notice a silver ring on the middle finger of the man's hand shining brilliantly in the flickering candlelight. *Something is definitely wrong. Before I can get a good look at his face, Camilla stands before me smiling. She looks stunning in a white strapless dress that goes all the way down to the floor. Her amethyst eyes have that usual menacing blaze that studies every inch of my face.*

"I see you've come to join in on the festivities," she says, *that sultry gleam radiating like wildfire.* "Fortunately for you, this is only a warning."

I have this urge to tell her that my entire life has become one big cautionary tale, but I remain quiet. If I keep her talking, I'll be safe.

"I see Andre has taken a liking to you," she continues indifferently. "What he doesn't understand is that in a few decades, your pretty little petals will wilt like a flower and you will cease to exist." *She pauses for a moment, relishing in her words.* "He has walked beside me for over five hundred years, child. We have hunted together, explored the world together, and even loved one another in our own way. I see why he wants his freedom; I have kept him to myself for far too long. But for him to vulgarize that freedom by spending it with a human, that is something that as his maker I cannot allow."

"You don't think hurting countless innocent people is a vulgarization of your freedom?" I ask her, feeling a jolt of courage. "You survive on the life force of others, unable to truly pass on so you walk through eternity in neither heaven nor hell. This is your everlasting purgatory, Camilla."

"You are too bold in your words," she whispers coolly. "A symptom of adolescence." She walks over to the body and admires her choice. "Naturally, I want Andre to be happy, but permitting him to love you would be scandalous, even for us. All those years have taught him nothing."

"Andre is strong and compassionate. He is nothing like you."

Her smile doesn't reach her eyes. "That may be so, but he is still my creation. Without my gift, he would have died old and frail." She looks disgusted by the mere thought.

"He did die," I breathe, holding back the tears in my eyes. "You killed him."

"He was reborn, child." I see a flash of rage and can't help but shiver. "He came back as a hunter, a god," she says vehemently. "He watches the weak expire and lives on forever. Do you know how many of your kind

would sell their souls for a gift like that?" She gathers her composure and continues. "You, little flower, are the prey. Just think of yourself as a casualty of the supernatural food chain. You can't really expect me to allow my best soldier to consort with you. I mean, how would that look?"

"Once Andre gets you the grimoire, it won't be your choice to make."

"Andre will never get his hands on the grimoire so his freedom will be mine until I say otherwise. As for my settlement, I plan on draining you dry before that time ever comes. It will be my reward for being so patient with him. Goodnight, little flower."

I woke up in a panic, sweaty and parched. The clock on my nightstand showed twenty past four. After getting a drink out of our tiny refrigerator, I sat back down on my bed and tried to calm my racing heart. My nightmares had been less frequent lately, but this one was almost too real. When I took a sip, I tasted something warm and metallic that made my stomach churn. I spat it out onto the floor and switched on the table lamp. Afraid to look down, I wiped some of the liquid onto my finger and stared at it for a second. Water. *I'm officially losing it.*

Six

Inside Chapel Hill's crowded cafeteria, Jaq and I sat quietly at our usual table, each lost in thought. As I was idly munching on a grilled cheese sandwich, I saw Tristen walking over to us. I felt the air get all warm and tingly as soon as she noticed him approach. He gave her a light peck on the cheek and joined us with a cheeseburger in hand.

"So, Tristen," I began my interrogation. As far as I was concerned, it was long overdue. "You've been dating my *gorgeous* best friend for quite some time now and we barely know each other." I shook my head at him wryly. "That just wont do."

"You're right," he nodded and shot me a friendly but challenging grin. "Well, I may have just the solution to our little problem. My parents are hosting a party in a couple weeks and I'd be honored if you two ladies would accompany me. And Emma, you can invite Andre too if you want," he quickly added. "It's going to be a bunch of my parent's stuck-up friends and I'd definitely appreciate some people my age around."

Perfect. Maybe this is my chance to find the book and finally end this nightmare.

I caught Jaq's lips turn up into a slight smile and did my best not to laugh.

"I'd love to come. I'm sure it'll be an unforgettable evening."

Talk about the understatement of the century.

From the look on Andre's face I could sense an argument coming on. I silently brewed myself coffee and him a cup of green tea as he sat pensively on my bed. After a good three minutes, I couldn't hold it in any longer.

"It's like it just fell in my lap!" I exclaimed. "And it'll be a party so that means lots of distractions for any security."

Andre didn't look as pleased as I felt. "That means tighter security, Emma," he said dryly.

"Oh, come on! I thought you'd be happy."

"This puts you at risk." He paused for a brief moment and I felt his anxiety clouding the entire room. "And I can't protect you in there."

"I'll be fine. I promise," I whispered, trying to soothe the tension building around us. "Vampires can't get in so I'll be safer in there than out here anyway. Besides, this is a great opportunity to get the grimoire. It may be our only shot."

"Hypothetically, if you were to go, which I'm not saying you are," he added that last bit deliberately. "You wouldn't know the first thing about getting upstairs past security, possibly picking a lock or entering a security code. It's too dangerous," he said shaking his head. *The man has a point.* Nonetheless, my mind failed to see it.

"I'm not a child," I whined proving otherwise. "I've made up my mind. You can either help me brainstorm or not. Your choice."

He looked surprised by my impassioned reaction and, after a long silence, finally nodded.

"If you can't access the study or if there's some passcode you need, go back to the party. And I mean go immediately. Do you understand?"

"Yes, sir!" I lit up like a Christmas tree and threw my arms around him. He took my head in his hands and kissed my forehead tenderly.

"We should go on a double date," I suggested. "I think we all deserve a night out. A night with no mention of any grimoire or immortal psycho bitch."

"What do you have in mind?"

"Dancing."

We'd all been so caught up in the paranormal suspense film that was our lives that one carefree night was essential if any of us had any hope of keeping our sanity intact.

"There's a lounge over on Kings Street that could be fun," I recommended. Jaq and I had walked by it a few times and the place looked pretty incredible from the outside. I had wanted to check it out for weeks, but with everything going on, it didn't seem practical.

"What's it called?"

"Marquis."

As we walked up to the entrance, I fumbled in my purse for my fake ID. Jaq and I had been using the same ones since we were sixteen and they worked every time. *One of the many benefits of knowing spoiled rich kids.* I was less than two years away from my twenty-first birthday and since I wasn't much of a drinker to begin with, I didn't see any harm in going to a lounge to hang out with my friends.

The line was especially long and I was in a pair of the excruciating six-inch heels I had bought with Olivia a month back. Tristen and Andre failed to notice the horde of people waiting to get inside and walked right up to the bouncer. A few seconds later, we were all ushered inside and I was enveloped in the sound of techno. There wasn't much room to walk around without bumping into someone so it was a relief to see the boys lead us to a secluded table in the VIP section.

"This is fancy for Rhode Island," Jaq shouted in my ear over the repetitive beat. I could see by the smile on her face that this was just what she needed.

The walls of the lounge were a dark violet and the bar was embellished with gold leaf around the edges. Little booths with black leather tufted seats were on both sides of the large room and I saw replicas of works from Caravaggio and Peter Paul Rubens. The current owners had obviously attempted to recreate a Baroque-like ambiance but hardly took the time to open up a history book to compare. I found it a bit gaudy for my liking, to be honest.

Andre ordered a bottle of Johnnie Walker Blue Label for the table and asked me what I wanted. Since Jaq and I weren't big drinkers, we decided to make things easier on everyone and just had what the boys were having. The slender brunette cocktail waitress came back with a tray that was larger than she was and placed four glasses, a bottle and one small ice bucket on the table. She poured us each a bit of Johnnie, barely looking at the glasses below her. Jaq kicked me under my seat and grinned, showing me she saw exactly what I had. The provocative bar wench couldn't seem to keep her eyes off of our men. When she finally came a hair from spilling the whiskey, I graciously took the bottle from her, thanked her for her services and finished the job myself. I couldn't keep the smug look off my face as the flustered girl walked back to the bar. Andre and Tristen both looked amused.

"To an unforgettable year," Tristen shouted over the music.

"To an unforgettable year," we repeated in unison, clinking our glasses together with an undeniable realization that this will, in fact, be an unforgettable year for us all. *To say the least.*

As I downed the first bit of whiskey I'd ever had, I saw a look of pride on Andre's face. I noticed Jaq beside me, gasping for air, and quickly realized why. Apparently, he hadn't thought me capable of holding a straight face after swallowing a mouthful of Johnnie Walker. Tristen was literally force-feeding Jaq a bottle of cold water when I noticed Andre's hand had casually landed itself on my upper thigh.

"In public? Why, Mr. Talon, I'm shocked," I said in his ear playing coy.

"Indeed, we are," he smirked. "But it's dark and you look absolutely stunning in that dress, sweetheart. Have I ever told you that you're quite the vision?"

Slowly, his hand ascended to the point where my leg met my hip. I was stunned at how affectionate he was being. I'd only seen this side of Andre when we were alone in his apartment or in my dorm when Jaq was out. I placed my hand on top of his and squeezed it gently.

"Not often enough."

I was starting to feel the effects of the alcohol and my entire body was getting tingly. I turned to my friends and noticed they had left the table. Jaq must have been tipsy already because I spotted her all over Tristen about ten feet away.

"Dance with me," he commanded, bringing my attention back to more pressing matters.

The small dance floor was packed with people all bumping and grinding to the throbbing beat. We managed to find a spot away from the boisterous crowd and Andre put his hands on my hips, swaying us from side to side with the rhythm. I never knew the man had moves.

The music had slowed to something a bit more sensual and I felt Andre grab me by the waist. He pulled me into his chest tightly until there wasn't so much as an inch between us.

"Thank you for giving me tonight," he whispered softly in my ear.

I got up onto my tippy toes and pressed my lips against his. What started out as a tender kiss quickly turned heated. The forcefulness of Andre's mouth was so inviting that all I wanted was more. More of his tongue caressing mine with the tempo of the track. More of the feel of his hands gripping onto my hair. As if the music was composed specifically for this moment, his hips dug into mine and I felt the anticipation consuming us both. We'd never been so passionate in public before and it was thrilling.

Rudely interrupting our fervent moment, a young man stood next to us grinning. It was eerie how similar he looked to Andre. They both had dark hair and dressed in black shirts with jeans. I noticed they also shared the same luminously pallid skin tone and wondered if he too was a vampire. The man was about half an inch shorter than Andre and the only major distinction I saw in the dim lighting was that the stranger's eyes were a slate grey as opposed to Andre's intense dark brown. He unexpectedly took my hand to shake it and I realized that that stupid grin hadn't left his face the entire time.

"Caden Locke. Pleasure," he roared to me in a thick English accent. The man then turned to Andre and gave him a hearty slap on his back. "How are things, mate?" he asked him as if they had known each other for years.

"What are you doing here, Caden?" Andre looked much less sociable than he had a minute ago.

I didn't quite know if it was because the man disturbed us or if there was another reason for his atypical standoffishness. Caden motioned for him to get off the dance floor and come outside where there was more privacy. We walked passed the exit and stopped around the corner of the building. It was already after midnight and the streets were empty.

"Who's the broad?" he asked as if I wasn't standing right there.

"Emma, this is Caden Locke, an old friend. This is my girlfriend, mate," Andre indicated with an English accent of his own. His British twang came out periodically and it still managed to puzzle me when I heard it. It was a though he had multiple personalities when he talked like that. "What the hell are you doing in Rhode Island?"

"Camilla sent for me. Obviously. What else would I be doing in this sleepy little town?"

"I assumed as much. You're here for the grimoire?"

"Indeed. She's promised me quite the reward for my troubles."

"Release?"

"Only thing worth the trip," he said with his customary grin.

"Have you drafted your best laid plans then?"

"In due time, mate; in due time. I just wanted to stop by and say hello before it was business as usual. After all we've been through, I thought I owed you that much."

"Yes, well, it's been a pleasure, Caden." I could tell he was being uncharacteristically insincere when he said it. "Good luck."

With that, he grabbed my hand and escorted me back into the club before giving Caden a chance to respond. We sat back down at our table and Andre took another shot of whiskey.

"Has Johnnie been treating you well?" he asked me with a seductive smirk.

"He's been my saving grace," I replied vivaciously. "How do you two know each other?"

"Johnnie and I have been friends for a long, long time."

"You know what I mean!"

Andre suddenly looked troubled as he thought back to what I could only assume was his history with the man. He poured another round for each of us and raised his shot glass. "To a bright future, sweetheart."

We clinked the little glasses and I downed my second shot like a champ. The alcohol was making me impatient and I started to become somewhat exasperated that he was dodging the question. "How do you two know each other?" I repeated.

"He's kin," he said glumly. "I didn't expect to see him here. I apologize. I'm just a bit taken aback is all."

They were *related?* Well, at least I couldn't complain about never having met Andre's family.

"How is that even possible?" I asked stunned.

"Let's say goodbye to our friends and go back to my place, shall we? I'll tell you about Caden but a conversation like this shouldn't be had over this damned cacophony of sound."

I gave Jaq a quick hug and kissed Tristen chastely on his cheek before we headed back to Andre's apartment. He lived within walking distance of Marquis but my sky-high heels were getting the best of me. Every muscle in my feet was aching for relief by the time we reached his door. I removed my shoes as soon the elevator doors sprung open and walked down the hallway barefoot.

When we got inside, I threw myself onto his plush charcoal grey sofa. Andre handed me a glass of ice-cold water and sat beside me. I took a large swig of what I thought was the best tasting drink I'd ever had in my life and placed the half empty glass atop his antique mahogany coffee table. It had the most magnificent ornate patterns etched into the dark wood and I sat there for a moment admiring the craftsmanship. I felt the whiskey leaving my system and was starting to feel like my old self again.

"Better?" Andre asked considerately.

"Much."

"Good. So, about Caden," he began. "I had a sister, Natalia. She was the most beautiful girl, blonde with the biggest and brightest blue eyes. Her face was so round when she was a baby that I called her Luna, which is "moon" in Russian. Natalia married some lad a few years after my disappearance and they ended up having six children."

"Six? Wow," I breathed. I thought about how painful it must have been for her back then with no epidural to soothe her. I'd always pictured myself having one boy and one girl. Two labors seemed grueling enough, but six? God bless her.

"Back then, people didn't have birth control as they do now. Nor did they have any safe means of abortion. Many women died in childbirth; it was a miracle Natalia survived. I visited her in her old age, just before she died. It was a bittersweet reunion for us both."

"How did she react when she saw you?"

"As any sane person would. At first, she thought I was a ghost. She marveled at how young I looked and asked me if we were in heaven. I could never lie to my sister. Had Natalia not been frail, I'm sure she would've run off right then and there. After a few minutes of talking to her, though, she calmed down and we chatted for a while like we used to when we were kids. She told me about her children and her late husband and how much she'd missed me all those years. Everyone thought I'd been murdered and she said it was God's final gift to her to see me well. I made her a promise that night that for as long as I walk the earth, I'd look out for our family."

"So when did you end up meeting Caden?"

"I was living in London in the late 1800s and by then, many of my relatives had immigrated there. One

October night, just a couple years after the Tower Bridge had been built, I decided to take a walk along the Thames. The river was shining so brilliantly below the waning crescent moon. I wish you'd been there, Emma. You would have loved it back then. The culture. The decadence. It was magnificent."

I sprawled across the sofa and rested my head in his lap, feeling like a child listening to a bedtime story.

"Anyway, as I turned to leave," he continued. "I could hear a woman's screams reverberating in the distance. I had been keeping tabs on all my descendants over the years and realized the sound was coming from a home I once visited about a decade earlier. When I reached the window, I saw a boy, pale and feeble, fast asleep with whom appeared to be his mother at his bedside. I understood instantly that these people were my family and felt this sudden urge to help them. I don't know why I did it, but I summoned Camilla. It was the only thing I could think to do at the time. She arrived a week later and when I told her the situation, she offered to turn him vampyr and save his life."

"Why didn't you do it yourself?"

"I don't have an answer to that, sweetheart. I wish I did, but I don't. She offered and I accepted. If I could do it all over again I would have left well enough alone. This kind of existence shouldn't come without choice. By then, Caden's days were numbered and he was too weak to give his consent. I made the decision for him and it's something I'll always regret."

"What's so bad about being what you are?" I asked feeling myself starting to doze off.

"Oh, Emma, there aren't enough years in your precious human life to make you truly understand why what I am is the ultimate curse. One day, I'll try and explain it to you but for now, let's get you to bed."

As much as my mind relished these little story sessions we'd have from time to time, my body was playing a different tune. I was exhausted. Andre lifted me into his arms and carried me off to his bedroom. He placed me gently onto the bed and crawled in beside me, wrapping his arm around my waist. It must have taken me all of six seconds before I was propelled into my favorite sort of dream world, envisaging London and Andre and the countless memories my precious human life had yet to form.

Seven

I awoke in a pair of sweatpants and an oversized t-shirt, feeling perfectly content in the shelter of Andre's arms. With everything that had been going on, any logical person would've sprinted back to New York to be as far away from this melodramatic escapade as possible. But there, in the refuge of Andre's little two-bedroom apartment, I felt like a normal college student, a girlfriend; I could actually be myself for a change.

We'd been an item since school started but he had yet to take me further than second base. By all means, I wasn't a harlot, but part of me wondered why he hadn't tried anything yet. Aiden was my first and only and it took him a good short month before the pressure was on for me to give up my virginity. At the time, I thought we'd be together forever. Looking back, it was naïve of me, but how much common sense could one really have in high school?

Andre's place wasn't huge by a long shot but definitely had enough space for one man, vampire or otherwise. He hung paintings all along the hallway that led to the master bedroom. I recognized a Van Gogh, a Monet and a Degas, letting out a quiet giggle at the idea of them being real. As much as I loved European history, I had an equally passionate love affair with art.

A large bookshelf stood in the corner of Andre's bedroom with a variety of classics and newer works. I could see a few volumes that had to have been at least a hundred years old. All that time spent seeing the world and to have kept so little, I considered. Why hadn't he kept more things? I turned over to face him and Andre looked down at me smiling.

"Morning, beautiful," he whispered and kissed me lightly on my forehead.

"Good morning," I grinned like a schoolgirl. "Hey, I have a question."

"Shoot."

"How is it that with everywhere you've traveled and the length of time you've been around, your place is so bare?"

"I guess it just desperately needs a woman's touch," he chuckled.

"I'm serious. Why haven't you gathered a small mountain of stuff over the years?"

I thought of my own bedroom at home. In a box hidden away under my bed, I kept ticket stubs, photographs and old love letters from my childhood. I convinced myself it wasn't technically hoarding if it was all contained in one small space.

"I don't know; I don't think it's bare. I mean I was originally going to be here for only as long as it took to find the grimoire. But now that I've been given a reason to stay for a while, you have my permission to redecorate."

"I have every intention of putting a little life into this place," I said looking around at the rooms potential. "But where is all your stuff?"

"I have a flat in London where I keep anything of value. There's also the little cottage in the Cotswolds, the house in Seville, another flat in New York, the cabin in Big Sur and, let's see, I have a small waterfront home in Fernando de Noronha, Brazil." *You have* got *to be shitting me.* "But all in all, when you've lived as long as I have, sentimental things become harder and harder to hold on to. I've learned to make peace with the fact that anything tangible may eventually get lost in the crossfire." He ran his fingers through my hair and noticed my eyes peering up at an old painting above his writing desk.

"My mother," he said. "I painted it from memory a few centuries ago. She would have absolutely adored you."

"Was it completely unbearable, losing everyone you've ever loved?" I asked.

"Not everyone," he smiled and tenderly kissed me on the mouth. "You find distractions. The thought of your family and everyone you've left behind never truly goes away, but I guess I've just learned to divert my attention elsewhere. Some vampires focus on business, others on knowledge, sex, anything really." He was visibly saddened by the onset of painful memories. "For a long time, I felt like I was just existing. I had no path, no hope for an endless future. Nothing was exciting anymore. I thought I'd seen all there was to see." He pulled me in closer and rested his chin on the top of my head. "And then I remember hearing the sweetest voice. I remember looking up and seeing your timid, beautiful face; you had so much *life* in you. And that's when everything changed."

"I vote for the blue one!" Olivia shouted as I held the final two options up for the girls to see. There seemed to be a consensus among them and I eyed the little navy-blue and silver checkered number curiously. Jaq had already decided on a shiny emerald dress that hugged her in all the right places. Isabel and Olivia had also chosen their respective outfits for Tristen's party and I was the only one left.

"The blue one it is," I obliged, not wanting to spend another minute shopping for a party that Andre wouldn't even be going to. *Damn those stupid mages and their spells.* I had to admit the dress looked pretty good on me. I took out my credit card without giving myself a chance to second-guess my decision and headed over to the register. There was only a week to go until the party and we still had no idea how we were going to get the grimoire.

"So how's Andre?" Isabel asked me somewhat suspiciously as I signed the receipt, shaking my head at how ridiculously overpriced one piece of fabric could be. "I heard he isn't coming Saturday."

"He's great; he just has some things he needs to take care of so he won't be able to make it. Are you bringing anyone?"

I tried to divert her attention elsewhere as any more probing would lead to more questions I couldn't answer truthfully. Isabel was a nice girl but there was something off about the way she acted around me sometimes.

"I can't believe I haven't told you guys!" she exclaimed. "I met the hottest guy last week. He's *so* perfect."

Olivia stood there silently and I could tell she felt out of place since she was the only single one of us left.

"He's the total package," Isabel went on. "Tall, dark and handsome. We'll all have to go out sometime."

"I'm really happy for you," I told her genuinely. "Now we just need to find Olivia a cute boy. Hey, what about Chris?"

Olivia's cheeks were suddenly flushed and she smiled bashfully as we started walking back to campus.

"Oh. He's really nice. But I don't think he'd go for someone like me."

"C'est du n'importe quoi!" Jaq shouted. Her native language always came out when she was riled up about something. "Nonsense! If he wouldn't go for you, Olivia, then he's obviously blind. If we were in New York, Emma and I would have introduced you to dozens of eligible bachelors by now. I'll talk to Tristen and see if he knows anyone worthy of you."

"You really don't have to." From the vehement glare Jaq shot her, Olivia knew it best not to argue with the French. "Okay … if you insist." And knowing Jaq, she did.

"I see," Andre uttered to the voice on the other end of the call. "And you'll be here on Wednesday? Good. Anything else I should know?" He hung up the phone without saying goodbye and looked at me pensively. I stuck out my tongue to ease the noticeable tension in his face and he smiled. "My friend Blake will be visiting us soon."

"Is he also a vampire?" I asked.

"Mage. He thinks he may know of a way to unbind the confining spell. I'll know more when he gets here but for now, it's something at least."

"I thought vampires and mages don't get along?"

"We normally don't, but Blake and I have a long history. I helped him out of a messy little predicament once and he owes me."

"So what do you want to do now?"

I crawled over to his side of the sofa and straddled him. His dark eyes grew bloodshot as he cupped my butt in his hands and lifted me toward him until my breasts pressed against his rock-solid chest. He gave me another, more fervent, smile and I saw his fangs had extended. *Could tonight be the night?*

"Why must you ask questions you already know the answers to?" he whispered sensually in my ear, nibbling playfully.

"Show me."

Andre started to pull my top up slowly over my head until I was in nothing but my black lace bra and jeans. He kissed my stomach from my navel up to my ribcage and nuzzled his head in the center of my chest. I felt heat surging through my core and traveling downward. I wanted him. I wanted him more than I'd ever wanted anyone in my life. Wrapping my legs around his waist, he carried me into his bedroom and placed me carefully on the bed like I was made of porcelain. He climbed on top of me with his elbows at my sides and began grazing my neck with his teeth. He parted my legs, pushing his lower body against mine and let out a deep moan as I grabbed his ass.

He was the first man to ever make me feel like this. Aiden had never taken his time with me. He was a selfish lover and usually left me disenchanted at best. With Andre, I felt like my satisfaction came second to none. He was studying my body intently and somehow knew exactly which buttons were aching to be pressed.

With one hand behind my back and the other gripping my hair, he unhooked my bra strap in one fell swoop, ever the pro. He removed it in half a second and I lay there, half-naked, watching him expectantly. He tugged gently at each of my nipples in turn and I felt sparks shooting from my breasts all the way down to my upper thighs.

"Are you sure?"

"Please," I breathed.

He kissed me passionately as one hand continued to support my head while the other unbuttoned my jeans. Andre's soft tongue caressed mine until we developed an idiosyncratic rhythm. He ventured lower until he was right above my zipper and pulled it down, taking his sweet time. He pulled my jeans off and threw them across the room onto the floor.

"Please what?" he whispered.

"Sir."

I couldn't think. My responses were automatic. I was frozen on his bed, unable to move or say anything else remotely coherent. Andre removed his t-shirt and jeans until he was left wearing nothing but a pair of black boxer-briefs. His body was perfectly toned and chiseled, every muscle in its right place. He parted my legs once more and kissed my inner thighs until I was ready to combust.

"Please," I repeated.

He yielded to my request by taking off my panties and planting his lips in between my legs. I let out a soft moan as his tongue brushed against me in little circles, driving me crazy. I was delirious under his touch and pushed myself into his mouth harder until I was almost there; I was so close. Just before I could let go, he stopped, looking up at me pleased with himself. I whimpered, pleading for more, and he made it clear he wasn't quite finished with me yet. He wriggled out of his underwear and thrust into me as I screamed.

"Like this?"

I pleaded with him shamelessly and unintelligibly. Nothing I said was an actual word or phrase anymore. Just sounds.

He let out a loud groan and plowed into me harder, faster, until there was no option left but surrender. He was relentless and dominating in his motions. I exploded all around him and he soon followed suit, both of us bellowing so loud I thought the neighbors would have surely called the cops on us.

He collapsed on top of me and I ran my fingers through his hair, stroking his bare back with my free hand. I was spent and utterly sated. He looked down at me after a few moments and grinned slyly.

"Please," he muttered teasingly and turned me over as we went for round two.

If all vampires shared similar features like pale skin and lean figures, the same couldn't be said about mages. Blake was the polar opposite of Tristen. He looked like he was in his mid-thirties and was only a few inches taller than me. Being that I was petite to begin with, that made him far less than six feet tall. Blake had almond-shaped hazel eyes, coffee-colored brown hair and was more than a few pounds overweight. His pearly-white smile seemed genuine and I immediately took a liking to him.

"It's such a pleasure to meet you, Emma. I wish I could say Andre's told me so much about you, but as we both know, he's a man of few words," he greeted courteously extending his hand.

"It's nice to meet you too, Blake."

"Now that you two have been formally acquainted, may we get down to business?" Andre asked rather impatiently.

"Of course," Blake answered like his father had just chastised him for dawdling. Odd, since Andre looked like he was more suited for the role of Blake's much younger and furthermore, much fitter, cousin. "I've done a bit of research and called in a few favors. I have a spell that should be able to unbind the confining enchantment placed on the grimoire, but it can only be performed by a mage. Since you can't get into the Valgard house, how do you suppose we're going to do this?"

"Emma has recently been invited to a party being held inside the Manor this weekend. You will accompany her as her date and she'll lead you to the grimoire. Do you think once you're inside the room, you'll be able to find it?"

Blake was evidently dumbfounded by such a query, his confidence in his abilities transparent.

"Oh, I'll find it. I'll just conjure up a locator spell and it should be easy as cake. But how do you suppose we'll get past the guards?"

"Vampires are obviously forbidden from entering so I don't think they'll be as cautious as they ought to be. It should be standard security with no more than five men to worry about. Let's hope they underestimate a vampire's tenacity," Andre grinned.

"Someone threatened Tristen's sister not too long ago but she can't remember who it was. Do you think it was a vampire?" I asked, remembering I'd totally forgotten to fill him in on that little tidbit. Andre's grin swiftly faded and he became Mr. Serious again.

"What do you mean she was threatened? How?"

"Jaq told me someone came to his sister's school and told her to deliver a message to her father. Something about Alexander's debt being paid in full? Does that make any sense to either of you?"

"Smell's like the workings of one blonde vampire, if you ask me. This has Camilla written all over it," Blake noted.

"No," Andre said pensively, pacing back and forth in his living room. "Camilla's already made an appearance. It's unlikely she'd go to the girl herself. She has a personal vendetta against Emma, which is why she stuck around for as long as she had; but not with the sister. She surely sent someone else to do her dirty work. My money's on Caden."

"That old chap? He's in town too? Why, it's a bloody family reunion!" Blake seemed intrigued that Camilla had sent reinforcements. "Interesting. So I guess this grimoire must be pretty valuable then. What time is the party, love?" he asked me. If Andre were human, he'd have probably flinched at the term of endearment aimed my way. Instead, he glared down at Blake ominously. "I mean, Emma," the plump man quickly corrected himself. I shot

Andre a glare of my own and then kindly smiled Blake, trying to make up for my possessive boyfriend's pointlessly rude behavior.

"It's Saturday at eight. Will you be picking me up?"

"No," Andre cut in. "I'll drive you both there myself. The last thing I need is for you two to get mauled before the party even begins. Blake may be powerful in his own way but he isn't nearly as strong as I am, especially not against a vampire. No one will be after him, though I'd bet my fortune that no less than a few pairs of eyes will be on you, sweetheart," he said looking at me grimly.

"Then it's settled. I have a test I should be studying for so, Blake, I'll see you on Saturday. It was lovely to meet you. Andre, I'll call you later."

I gave Blake a polite nod, kissed Andre on the cheek and left the boys to their plotting.

Tristen's party was right around the corner and Jaq was a nervous wreck. Her guilty conscience was getting the best of her. Sorting through dozens of dresses that looked like they had taken over the entire dorm room, she turned to me and sighed.

"I hate lying to him, Em. I just have this feeling that he's going to find out about my snooping. What would I even say?"

"When caught in a lie, deny, deny, deny."

She let out an overly dramatic groan and continued her search for the perfect outfit. From the looks of our room, a tornado could have hit Newport. Clothes were scattered all across the floor and on each piece of furniture. If we happened to remain unemployed after college, there was always the option of opening up a boutique. We had already bought dresses for the party but Jaq was still undecided.

"What we need to be focusing on is the grimoire," I said rationally. "I'll need you to keep everyone distracted while Blake and I try to open the door to Mr. Valgard's study. Do you remember what the lock looked liked?"

Jaq stared into space for a few seconds trying to recall. "I'm pretty sure it was one of those skeleton key locks. It looked pretty old and secure."

"Well there goes my hairpin and credit card idea." Never in a million years had I thought I would be searching the Internet for ways to pick a lock. In all honesty, I didn't really think I'd be dating a vampire either. Since Andre was probably around since before the skeleton lock was invented, he'd be the one to know how to break it, unless Blake could manage to work some of his juju. "Once we're inside, I'll grab the grimoire and leave with Blake immediately. You can tell Tristen I'm sorry and I wasn't feeling well or something."

I tiptoed through any open area I could find and sat on what may or may not have been my bed. Jaq looked noticeably worried and who could have blamed her? We were as close as sisters and I knew she was anxious about my safety. If Blake and I failed, I could be in some serious trouble with a group of exceptionally powerful mages. If we succeeded, Camilla could be right around the corner ready to attack. However the night played out, just as I told Tristen a couple weeks earlier, his parent's bash was surely going to be unforgettable.

A knock came at the door and I took one last look in the full-length mirror before turning the knob. The expression on Andre's face made me feel more beautiful than ever before. He surprised me, showing up in a dashing black tux and leather oxfords. Jaq had left early to help Tristen's family prepare and do a bit more recon before the guests arrived.

"You look stunning," Andre whispered and kissed me seductively on the mouth. I saw his eyes turn bloodshot and it was all the confirmation I needed to grasp that he was more than satisfied with my outfit. When he turned to go, I pulled him back into the room and kissed him passionately once more.

"You wore a tux," I grinned in disbelief.

"Well, for once I won't be overdressed. Besides, I wouldn't dare escort you in jeans and t-shirt. I mean, look at you."

He stared at me with a burning flame in his eyes and I realized how much I'd rather have stayed in. After running the idea by him, it was all too clear he felt the same way.

"You know I want nothing more than to have you all to myself, honey. But with Camilla on the loose, we need to stick to the plan. As much as I wish we didn't have to. Besides, Blake is in the car and it's impolite to keep him waiting. Not that I really care, truth be told."

I was disappointed but I knew he was right. "I'll message you as soon as I get this stupid book. And when we have it, make sure to save me a dance somewhere. Maybe we can crash some swanky gala at the country club and forget about our responsibilities for just one evening."

"Sounds like a plan. After you," he motioned me out the door.

Andre drove a newly acquired black Range Rover the short distance to Valgard Manor and promised he would be waiting close by. The plan was simple. Once Blake and I retrieved the grimoire, he would be right outside and play getaway driver. As I went for the handle to open the car door, he took my hand.

"Blake, step outside and give us a moment," he commanded. The man quickly did as he was told and left us alone in the car. Out of his pocket, Andre pulled out a small blue velvet box and handed it to me.

"The sapphires belonged to my mother. I had them carved into smaller stones and mounted in platinum. I hope you like it."

My heart started to race as I saw what rested inside. It was a beautiful tennis bracelet made of sapphires and diamonds. It looked as if it were intentionally made for my dress. When I went to unclasp it, I noticed he had had it engraved in the back. *Semper tuus ero.*

"I am forever yours," he translated. Andre took the bracelet and delicately wrapped it around my slender wrist. "No matter what happens tonight or any night for that matter, I want you to always remember that."

I looked down at my gift and then up into his piercing brown eyes. My heart hadn't slowed a single beat. As I placed my hand upon his cheek and shifted in the leather seat to reach his ear, I whispered, "I love you," and made my way toward the party.

"Welcome. You must be Emma," greeted a radiant woman in a bright red ball gown. Her auburn hair was secured in a formal chignon and she wore diamond chandelier earrings that nearly reached her shoulders. "I'm Tristen's mother, Valeria. You'll most likely find Jacqueline dancing with my son in the great hall straight ahead. I do hope you enjoy the party."

"Thank you, Mrs. Valgard. It's a pleasure to make your acquaintance. This is my friend, Blake."

"Pleasure, ma'am," Blake said taking her hand and giving it a light, courteous peck.

Everything was so extravagant. From the outside, Valgard Manor looked like an especially large plantation home. On the inside, however, I may as well have stepped foot into some European palace. The interior was covered in the finest French wallpaper and a series of intricate tapestries led each guest to the great hall. I was consumed by the decadence around me, admiring the antique furniture that seemed as though no one had ever touched it. When I looked up, I noticed the ceilings were decorated with images of clouds and angels painted within ornate golden frames. Being the oldest residence in all of Rhode Island, they clearly did more than simply vampire-proof the house.

The double staircase in the foyer was swarming with people. I silently prayed that everyone would eventually disperse and give us an opportunity to find Mr. Valgard's study undetected. When I saw Jaq standing with Tristen, feelings of doubt began to set in. It was all really happening and I had come too far to turn back now.

"Hello, Tristen. Thank you so much for having me. You have a beautiful home."

"Emma! I'm so glad you could make it," Tristen said warmly. His eyes shifted to Blake and he suddenly looked confused. "Where's Andre?" he asked.

"He had a last minute family thing he needed to take care of but he told me to thank you for the invitation. This is my friend Blake."

"It's cool. Nice to meet you, man. Welcome."

"Pleasure's mine, mate. I never knew Rhode Island could be so refined."

Tristen admirably brushed off Blake's backhanded compliment and told us he would be back in a flash with some drinks. I saw Olivia and Isabel on the other side of the room chatting it up with some well-dressed men twice their age and convinced myself that there wasn't enough time to say hello. I was discernibly tense and tried my best not to implode before the evening's festivities really began.

"I want you to take some deep breaths and calm down, *cherie,*" Jaq instructed me. "Everything is going to work out fine, okay?" She quickly led Blake and me to the other side of the expansive room and through a long corridor. At the end of it was another staircase. "Okay, take this all the way up and once you reach the top, turn right and count three doors to your left. That's Mr. Valgard's study," she muttered quietly. "Now I have go back to the party before Tristen starts looking for me. If he asks where you went, I'll tell him you had a girl issue and you're in the ladies room. *Merde!*"

"I'll need it. Thanks, Jaq. You really are a life saver."

"You can thank me later, Mademoiselle Bond," she grinned playfully.

Eight

Just as we reached the top of the staircase, I could hear two men speaking clandestinely. From what I was able to make out, one of the men was heavyset and middle-aged and the other had to have been Tristen's dad or maybe his uncle. The resemblance was uncanny.

"She's come back, Henry," Tristen's possible father whispered angrily. "That blood-sucking bitch threatened Jessica and told me that if I don't give up the grimoire she'll start hunting us one by one, starting with Tristen."

"We can't take her threats seriously. Camilla knows you're her only chance at getting that ancient prick back. She wouldn't risk it, Alex."

"And how can you be so sure? Camilla knows I would never gamble with my family's lives, no matter the consequences. If I give her what she wants, she'll leave us all alone."

"If you give her what she wants, you can expect a body count in the fucking thousands," the plump one said a bit louder than I was sure he'd intended to. "Maybe more. What I've gathered from the history books is that Theron wasn't exactly stable. The boy was a vile monster, through and through. No humanity. None. Are you prepared to have that much blood on your hands?"

"Oh, Henry, am I left with an alternative? I will not have my children thrown in the middle of this. They're just kids for Christ's sake!"

"Listen, don't do anything rash. We already know vampires can't enter this house. Our ancestors made sure of that. So for the time being, we're okay," he assured him. "Let's go back to the party and we'll deal with this nightmare in the morning."

"As you wish, cousin."

My stomach started to churn at the thought of them heading in our direction. By some twist of fate, the men decided to use the main staircase instead and marched down the hall, giving us a chance to get to the room unseen. Tristen's father had known about Camilla all along. The nauseating sensation in my gut began to wane as I realized we were all on the same side.

Taking a leap of faith, Blake and I counted three doors on our left and stopped right outside the purported study. I tried to turn the knob and just as we had expected, it was locked.

"Don't fret, sweetness," Blake said with a sly grin. I guessed that without Andre around, the mage was much more comfortable around me. I stood guard as he began faintly chanting some unintelligible mumbo-jumbo. A few seconds later, I heard a click come from inside the brass doorknob. "Like I said, easy as cake."

He opened the door and as we crossed the threshold, I peered around the room filled with countless trinkets and artifacts. It felt as though we were in some sort of history museum, looking through protective glass at remnants of the past. The walls were covered in elegant red velvet wallpaper with golden details all along the edges. There was a heavy black and gold desk in one corner and a sitting area in another. An entire wall was devoted to a collection of literature that no one person could read in a human lifespan. Each glass piece exhibiting the lovely mementos was as polished as the items themselves.

Between two wooden batons at least two and a half feet long sat a large book with pages made of worn sheepskin leather and vellum encased in a thick glass box. The manuscript was untitled but I could make out a small inscription on the bottom right corner. *A. Valgard.* When I examined the glass, I realized there was no lock or lever with which to remove the grimoire. If we broke the glass, an alarm could easily go off. The doors would likely seal shut and we would be trapped. Maybe I'd seen one too many heist films, but I nevertheless stared at Blake sullenly as if we'd failed.

"Just watch," he whispered to me calmly.

Blake placed his hands above the glass and started reciting some more of his indecipherable mage-talk and the glass miraculously started to fade away. In less than a minute, the grimoire was lying uncovered right in front of us. He stopped chanting and grabbed the book as if it were his and tucked it into the inner pocket stitched inside his tuxedo jacket. When I turned to look back at the spot on the table, the empty glass box had suddenly reappeared.

"Time to go," he said, hastily pulling me out the door and back to the already thriving party downstairs.

We spotted Jaq and Tristen dancing in the great hall and swiftly headed for the exit. I saw three guards by the front door and tried to look queasy so they wouldn't think twice about us leaving so early. Just as we were steps from the large mahogany double doors, Isabel caught sight of us and crudely yelled out my name for everyone around us to hear. I forced a smile and reluctantly gave her a big hug.

Perfect timing, Is.

"Who's your friend?" she asked me bewilderedly.

"This is a friend of Andre's. Because he couldn't make it to the party, Blake was kind enough to escort me. Blake," I turned to my accomplice. "This is Isabel. Isabel, Blake."

"It's nice to meet you Isabel," he grinned. I could see in his face that he no longer felt the urge to leave the party in such a hurry. He looked at Isabel like she was an angel brought from heaven and my feigned nausea started to resurface. However this time I didn't have to fake feeling queasy after all.

"It's nice to meet you too, Blake. I didn't know Andre had such handsome friends," she gushed.

Oh, God. Really?

"I'm not feeling too well," I quickly intervened. "I think I must have eaten something that didn't agree with me."

"Oh, no!" she exclaimed. "You can't leave *now!* The party's barely begun. Please say you'll stay for just a little while," Isabel pleaded more to Blake than to me.

"We really do have to get going," he said as if he were just as disappointed. "I would love to take you out some time if it's not too forward of me, sweetness."

You're kidding me, right?

"I'd like that," she beamed.

I had seriously had enough of this. "Blake, I'll give you Isabel's number in the car. I'd really like to go now," I said more callously than I had planned to.

He gave her one last smile and we were out the door. I could've punched him right then. Unfortunately for us all, we weren't at the Valgard's party to have a good time. He'd just have to flirt with Isabel later. I saw Andre parked across the street waiting for us and I bolted into his arms like he was a safe haven. And in some strange way, to me he was.

We dropped Blake off at a nearby inn and drove back to Andre's apartment. We rode in silence as I contemplated everything that had just happened. I couldn't believe we actually had the grimoire. It all seemed too good to be true.

"So. What now?" I asked groggily as we entered his living room.

"I'm so proud of you, Emma. I can't believe you would risk so much to help someone like me."

"Someone like you? Andre, you mean the world to me. I would do anything for you."

Was it really so surprising that I would help the man I loved? I'd have broken the glass with a sledgehammer if that were what it took to get that damn book for him, for us.

"I just hope you understand that I never wanted this for you. If there was an easier way—"

"Hush."

I quickly put one finger on Andre's lips to silence him and kissed him gently.

"And by the way, I love you too," he murmured in my ear.

We were dressed as if we belonged at some formal charity ball and Andre walked over to the entertainment area to put some music on. He sorted through a bunch of old vinyl records and chose "Someone to Watch Over Me," by Ella Fitzgerald.

"I believe I owe you a dance, Miss."

I took his hand and placed my arms around his neck as he swayed me from side to side in accord with the slow, sensual beat. He studied me thoughtfully and I once again saw the adoring glint in his eyes that he had when he first picked me up for the party. By the time we reached the middle of the song, Andre tenderly caressed my neck with his mouth and whispered, "I am forever yours."

He kissed my palm and then leisurely made his way to my shoulder until he reached my lips. We stood there for a while, embracing each other raptly, as if this was our last night on earth. Even having the grimoire in our possession, Camilla was still a threat. I buried my head in Andre's chest and felt his hand reach for the side of my dress. He looked into my eyes to make sure what he was doing was all right. I just smiled at the gentleman before me as he pulled down my zipper and the lovely checkered gown fell to the floor. As exposed as I was, I couldn't have felt safer. I began unbuttoning his shirt as he led me into his bedroom.

I sat on his bed expectantly and hooked my fingers inside the waistline of his slacks. Andre slowly positioned himself on top of me and I noticed his fangs had protracted, eyes tinged with crimson. He removed his shirt in record time and stroked my neck with his cool fingers.

"I want you to," I whispered breathlessly.

He was clearly taken aback by my reaction and hesitated at first. I could sense his resolve finally wavering and without another word, Andre lowered his mouth upon my neck. His subtle, sweet kisses traveled down to my collarbone and then back upward until I felt a sudden sharp sensation as his teeth pierced my skin firmly. It was the polar opposite of how I'd imagined it would feel.

A rush of ecstasy consumed me and I let out a muffled sigh. He was moaning softly and relishing in the warm life that poured from out of me. It all lasted but a moment until he forced himself to stop. I could feel his memories entering my mind. The power. The torment. The intense love he felt for me. Everything was made clear to me at once.

When I awoke, Andre was examining every inch of my naked body. I could feel the devotion in his eyes as he stroked my back. *He is forever mine,* I reminded myself. And I wouldn't have had it any other way.

"Normally I would be the last person to point out anyone's walk of shame, but you really had me worried last night!" Jaq roared irritably. "I couldn't sleep!"

"I'm so sorry, Jaq. It all happened so fast and I didn't think to text you. I'm sorry."

She looked at me with a blend of frustration and curiosity. "You're telling me! After you broke into Mr. Valgard's study, the entire party was sent home! Everyone was asked to leave due to an unexpected family emergency. If you would've gotten caught—"

"But I didn't. That's all that matters. I know you were looking forward to spending a nice evening with Tristen so again, I'm sorry."

Jaq could see the sincerity in my face and calmed down slightly. It was hard for either of us to stay mad at each other for long.

"It's okay, *chérie*. I was actually the only person who didn't get sent home," she told me with a triumphant smirk. "Tristen's dad didn't want him involved in anything and for obvious reasons he wasn't allowed to leave the house, so we just watched movies in his home theatre while the adults dealt with the *family emergency*. The night didn't end so badly after all."

She paused for a minute and I considered that all the chaos was ultimately due to our own little master plan. "So?" she went on. "Were you able to get the book? I couldn't tell what happened because Mr. Valgard was super secretive, but I wasn't sure if he was mad because someone tried to steal it or because someone actually stole it."

"We got it. I keep thinking, though. I overheard Mr. Valgard and his cousin talking about Camilla and how if she succeeded in bringing Theron back, countless lives would be lost as a result. I'm starting to worry that maybe stealing that thing from a vampire-proof home wasn't the smartest move on our part."

"Listen, you have to take care of yourself first and foremost. From you've told me, Prim, uh, Camilla, is not someone you want to mess with."

"You're right."

After so many years of wishing my life were more interesting, I found myself praying for just the opposite. I actually wanted things to be simpler. Worrying about finals and getting a part-time job were all insignificant notions after everything I had been through since my arrival in Newport. I carefully hung my dress in the closet and took off the oversized t-shirt and sweatpants I was wearing. It was time for a well-deserved hot shower.

As the water poured onto my skin, I replayed the events of last night in my head. The grimoire was finally in our possession. We'd succeeded in our highly improbable objective. If everything seemed to be going according to plan, then why did I feel so miserable?

Jaq and I were heading to Chapel Hill when we noticed a crowd forming next to the large bronze statue of Benedict Arnold. When we saw what all the commotion was about, I froze in my tracks. Olivia was sprawled out on the ground, bloody and motionless. She was still wearing the dress she wore to the Valgard's party. I didn't need a paramedic to tell me she was dead. Dean Turner ran to the scene and commanded us all to return to our dorms immediately. I couldn't believe it. Olivia was the sweetest, most kindhearted girl I'd met in school. Could one of the older men I saw her and Isabel talking to last night be responsible? Someone was obviously sending a message; otherwise they would have gotten rid of the body. Instead, Olivia was put on display for all to see like some beautiful fallen angel. Whoever did this was clearly losing patience and something in my gut told me Camilla was behind it all.

"But you got the stupid grimoire," Jaq cried when we made it back to our room. "Why would that evil bitch kill Olivia? That girl had nothing to do with any of this! She was innocent."

"I don't know, Jaq. I just don't."

There was no rhyme or reason for Olivia's death. The poor girl had no idea what we were up to and even if by some improbable chance she found out, what could she have done? Gone to Dean Turner and told him vampires and mages were lurking around Newport? It didn't make a lick of sense. If Camilla was trying to get my attention, it worked. If she was trying to scare me away from Andre, I was sorry to say her efforts were sadly ineffective. If anything, seeing my friend's lifeless body made me realize how much I truly couldn't bear the thought of losing him too.

Olivia's murder gave me the strength I needed to fight. We couldn't let her get away with this. I didn't care how powerful Camilla was. Our friend would be avenged no matter what it took. I turned on my cell phone and dialed Andre's number. He picked up my call after just one ring.

"Good morning, beautiful," he answered none the wiser. "How did you sleep?" After a long silence from my end, his casual tone became serious. "What happened?"

"It's Olivia. She's been murdered."

"Something's wrong," Andre announced as he brought Jaq and me some coffee and breakfast about an hour after we hung up. He took out a binder from his leather satchel and turned to a blank page. "This is a copy I made of the grimoire. After reading through every single spell, I've found absolutely nothing that could be used to stop Camilla." He paused for a moment. "But then I noticed this." He lifted up the blank page for us to see.

"It's blank," Jaq pointed out as if no one had come to that realization.

Thank you, Captain Obvious.

"Yes, Jaq, it is," Andre said with a bit more patience than I'd had before my morning brew. "But the better question is *why* is it blank?"

I remembered reading stories about ghostwriters and invisible ink as a child and an idea came to me.

"What if the spell was made hidden in case the grimoire was stolen by the wrong people?" I suggested. "The Valgard's seem like they've had lots of experience keeping this thing out of reach. If there was a spell to bring Theron back, I'd bet my life they'd do anything to make sure nobody, not vampire nor human, could get to it."

Andre's eyes widened. "But a mage could. And something tells me that the spell to bring Theron back and the one used to entrap him in the amulet is a reversal enchantment written on this page."

"A reversal what?" Jaq asked visibly perplexed.

"The incantation used to entrap him is the same one to free him, only reversed," he explained. "Reversal enchantments were particularly common among mages in

175

Alexander's time. The catch is that it can only be cast by someone of the same bloodline as the initial architect of the spell. It's the only way to ensure that a vampire couldn't make friends with just any mage and convince him to undo the spell that's been cast."

"Like Blake," I noted.

"Precisely. So, Jacqueline, if you're still willing to do anything it takes to save Emma and the Valgard's, we're going to need you to call your boyfriend."

"But Tristen doesn't know anything about magic!" Jaq squealed. "He watches ESPN and goes to sports bars with his friends. He's never even been out of Rhode Island! What good could he possibly do in a situation like this?"

"Magic isn't something you learn, Jacqueline; it's innate," he countered. "You can recite a spell a thousand times and chances are, I won't levitate or grow a tail. You either have it or you don't, as it were. I'm not talking about high school girls with a fascination for love spells and séances. Whether Tristen Valgard believes in his power or not, he has it. He's had it since the day he was born."

"Can't we ask Blake to figure out what it says?" I asked.

"Blake's already done more than enough for us. I've sent him home. Even if he deciphers the spell, he's still no Valgard."

"Why don't we ask Tristen's father to help us instead?" Jaq asked. "Emma overheard him talking about the grimoire the night of the party, so he's definitely much more aware of all this than Tristen is anyway."

"That may be so, but have you forgotten what I am? The Valgard's *hate* vampires. They don't care who I am or what my intentions are. Tristen has been lucky enough that his family sheltered him from my kind's existence. It makes for a clean slate. Tristen only knows me as his friend and right now, that's exactly the type of person we need on our side."

We both knew he was right. Mr. Valgard would try and kill Andre the first chance he got. Tristen was our only hope. Jaq went into her purse and reluctantly grabbed her cell phone.

"Mrs. Valgard? I was wondering if you'd seen Tristen. I need to speak with him." A moment later, she hung up and had a troubled look on her face.

"He's not at home," she murmured uneasily. "His mother hasn't seen him since early this morning and from the sound of her voice, she seemed worried."

"That's not good. That's not good at all."

Just then, Andre's phone began to buzz. "Talon," he answered harshly. "What have you done?" The call ended almost as soon as it began. "She has him. Camilla."

"What? We have to do something! Oh no, this is so bad. He didn't do anything!" Tears started to pour down Jaq's perfectly bronzed cheeks as she sat there helpless.

"She wants the grimoire."

"Then give it to her!" she screamed. "How are you so calm about this? My boyfriend's been kidnapped by a crazy psycho bitch and you're not even upset!"

I saw the horrified look in her eyes and tried my best to pacify the situation. "Jaq, please. I'm sure Andre is just trying to think about how we can get him back. Right?"

"I think I may actually have an idea. The page we need is blank, right?"

Jaq just stared at him expressionlessly.

"So even if she has the grimoire," he continued. "It wouldn't be much use to her. She'd go through it as I did and come to the same dead end. But if we carefully remove the page we need and you two bring it to Tristen's father, he'd more than likely be able to sort it out. In the meantime, I'll give Camilla the grimoire sans spell and get Tristen home safely."

"I'll bring Mr. Valgard the spell alone. The last thing he needs is to hear that his son's girlfriend is involved with vampires. No offense, babe."

"And what exactly am *I* supposed to do? Should I just sit here and do homework while my boyfriend is held hostage?"

She was fuming. I had never seen Jaq this distraught in all years I'd known her. What if the tables were turned? What if Andre was taken? I shuddered at the thought. I took Jaq's hand in mine and looked at her intently.

"That's exactly what you should do. There's no reason to get any more involved in this than necessary. We'll handle it. Besides," I smiled compassionately, trying to lighten her solemn mood as best I could. "Don't you have that French final to study for?"

As I walked up to Valgard Manor, bundled up in a long brown pea coat and purple scarf, I wondered if what I was about to do was a huge mistake. Would Tristen's father be able to help us? Did he even practice the kind of magic needed to trap a centuries old vampire into a little amulet? Taking risks was something I had become all too familiar with in the past few months. When I kissed Andre goodbye,

I couldn't help but think it could be the last time I'd ever see him. It was a dreadful thought and I swept it away immediately. He was on his way to make the exchange with Camilla and who knew what would happen? *Doubt is not an option*, I convinced myself.

When I got to the entrance, an intimidating man dressed all in black was standing at the gate and looked at me suspiciously. "What can I do for you?" the tall, burly guard asked.

"I need to speak with Mr. Valgard," I said with a coquettish smile. If batting my eyelashes was what it'd take, I was prepared to lie on the charm, and thick.

"He isn't taking any visitors today. Would you like for me to deliver a message?" he asked me in a much too friendly tone for a security guard I'd assumed was paid pretty damn well to protect the Manor.

"It's urgent," I frowned. "Please tell him that it's Emma. Tristen's friend."

He pushed a few buttons on the chrome keypad next to him and in a matter of seconds, the large metal gate opened. I mouthed a quick "thank you" and made my way toward the house. Tristen's father was waiting for me before I made it to the door. He had bags under his eyes as if he hadn't slept all night.

"Emma? What can I do for you? Have you any idea where my son could be?"

"Hello, Mr. Valgard. May we speak in private?"

He led me to the spacious sitting room where one of the housekeepers handed me a cup of tea. Once we were finally alone, I started to explain the purpose of our impromptu meeting.

"Tristen is with Camilla. He must have left home at some point this morning and she took him. She wants your ancestor's grimoire, but you already know that."

He looked at me bewildered and I'm sure he didn't want to believe what he was hearing. Though I sensed a large part of him knew I was telling the truth.

"How do you know all this?" he asked me warily.

"That's not important. All that matters is that we get Tristen back safely."

He studied me briefly and eyed the exquisite china sitting in front of him untouched. "Well, I don't have the grimoire. But something tells me you already know that."

Here goes nothing.

"We kept trying to think of ways around giving it to her, but it was no use, Mr. Valgard. She threatened us and we thought that if we did what she asked, she'd finally leave us all alone. So the night of your party, I was the one who stole it, thinking maybe there was a chance we could cast the same spell that was used to entrap Theron on Camilla. I am *so* sorry that we went behind your back and took what belonged to your family. But we were left with no other choice."

His expression was a combination of utter shock and admiration. I couldn't tell if he was ready to throw me out of the house or offer me a position at the Manor.

"The problem," I went on. "Is that the page needed to perform the spell is blank. We think it's a … reversal enchantment? I brought it with me and my boyfriend is on his way to give Camilla the grimoire in exchange for Tristen's life."

"And once your boyfriend brings my son back, what makes you so sure I'll help you deal with Camilla?"

"Because once she realizes the spell is missing, we won't have much time before she kills me and most likely a bunch of people you care about. You and I both know you wouldn't risk it. Besides, sir, Tristen's barely had a chance at life. You can't lock him inside this house forever."

After a long pause, Mr. Valgard broke the deafening silence. "You're smarter than you look. Jonathan!" he shouted. "Bring me a glass of scotch and my journal. It should be resting inside the nightstand by my bed. As for you, Emma, give me the spell and get yourself back to school. I'll work on deciphering it and call you when I have something."

"How can I be sure that if I give you the spell, you'll help me?"

"You can't. But what you can be sure about is that I will do anything it takes to protect my family and the citizens of this town. Seeing as how you need a Valgard to bind this reversal enchantment, you'll just have to trust me," he asserted with a knowing smile.

It was late in the afternoon by the time I left the Manor. I didn't fully trust Tristen's father but knew that I didn't have much choice in the matter. Walking along Main Street, I caught myself admiring the simple lives of my peers. Girls were casually sitting outside a café drinking cappuccinos and discussing their upcoming finals. Some high school kids were throwing a football around in the middle of the street as they talked about their rivals, West Warwick, and how badly they were going to defeat them next season. Everyone seemed to be acting so normal, caught up in their trivial dramas and completely oblivious to the imminent chaos that was so unbelievably close to each of our doorsteps.

As I turned to cross the street into a nearby alleyway, taking a shortcut back to campus, I noticed a tall man going in the same direction. Normally it wouldn't have bothered me, as we all knew it was the fastest way to the dorms. But with Camilla being on the loose, Andre not answering his phone, and everything else that had been going on lately, I was understandably apprehensive. *Only a minute walk until the end of the alley,* I reminded myself as I quickened my pace. When I looked back, the man was gone.

I breathed a quiet sigh of relief and shook my head. *I really am losing it.* As I turned to take my next step, he was directly in front of me and I clumsily bumped into his firm chest. Only he wasn't just a man; he was a vampire. I saw Caden's porcelain skin; his perfectly chiseled features that looked so much like Andre's. His lustrous dark brown hair shone in the sunlight and he looked down at me with his customary grin.

"Ello, love," he purred in a thick English accent. "A little birdie told me you have the grimoire Camilla's after. Is that true?" He held up his long pale finger. "Before you answer, I must warn you. I don't take well to liars."

"No. It's not," I said through clenched teeth.

"Interesting. You're telling the truth. Well, where is it then?"

"I don't know exactly." Well, that was partly true.

A throbbing fear coursed through my body when I saw the threat in his bloodshot eyes. "What are you going to do with me?" I murmured, fully aware that I looked as scared as I felt.

Caden must have found his effect on me amusing because the grin never left his striking face. He looked as evil as Camilla had at the lighthouse. I let out a deep breath. After all I'd recently been through, a part of me knew there was no way my journey would end in some narrow alley in Rhode Island. That single thought calmed me down slightly and gave me the courage I needed to narrow my big green eyes at him in contempt.

"I think I like you, Emma. And I don't like anyone, really. You have this fire blazing within you. That's a rarity for a human."

"I wish I could say the same."

"You're bold," he chuckled. "You know I could kill you at any moment and yet you address me so audaciously. I think when all is said and done, I'll keep you for myself."

"You can die trying," I said in a voice so husky, it could have come from someone else entirely. "I'm spoken for."

"But I'm already dead, love. And as for your holier-than-thou Andre, we shall see which of us speaks for you in the end."

"You're right. We shall," I agreed coldly.

He smirked playfully as he took me by my wrist and placed it upon his lips. "Yes, we shall," he repeated. I felt the sharp prick of his fangs and then everything slowly faded away.

Nine

I awoke in an unfamiliar bed. Candles were lit inside embellished silver sconces suspended amongst a handful of abstract paintings that hung along the royal blue walls. The furniture was a blend of both contemporary and antique. Some pieces were made of leather and metal while others looked like they belonged in Valgard Manor. I noticed a white Barcelona chair in the corner and nearly slapped myself for admiring the décor in my chic prison. I looked down and saw my clothes had been changed. I was wearing an elegant pale green nightgown made of weightless silk.

"I thought it went well with your eyes, love," came a voice from the other side of the room.

"Where am I?"

I wasn't sure I was even prepared for his answer. I wanted to see Andre. I would've given anything to be in the safety of his strong arms. Where had my valiant safe haven gone?

"Don't worry, Emma, you're completely safe here. I'd say I don't bite but that would be both cliché and untrue," Caden grinned.

I wanted to slap that stupid grin right off his face.

"It's already dark out." The curtains were drawn back and the large floor-to-ceiling windows revealed a bright full moon hovering in the black sky. "I ... I need to be somewhere. Please, let me go," I pleaded.

"You need to be where exactly?" he asked raising one black, neatly shaped eyebrow.

I was at a loss for words. My mind went blank and I shut my eyes tightly in the hopes that when I opened them, I would be in the comfort of Andre's warm bed and these last few minutes would simply have been a terrible dream.

"No response? Well, if it pleases you, I've arranged for your supper. I didn't know what you prefer as I don't generally eat," Caden smirked. "So I had my chef prepare an assortment of just about everything. I've always rather enjoyed options."

"Somehow that doesn't surprise me," I responded sardonically. "Oddly enough, I don't seem to have much of an appetite this evening."

"Listen, love, as unfortunate as it is for us both, you are human, which means you must eat."

"Why not just have me starve? Why bring me food and keep me locked up in your bedroom when your friend has every intention of killing me?"

"Let's get a few things straight, shall we?" he began slightly more peeved than before. "If I wanted you dead, you wouldn't have left that filthy alleyway alive. Secondly, Camilla is *not* my friend. She's a means to an end. I'll admit, when she told me about you, I didn't think twice about killing you myself. But that was before I had the pleasure of meeting you firsthand. I see now why Andre fancies you so. Who could blame him? I mean, God, look at you." His expression made me uncomfortable and I shifted on the bed.

"Those brazen green eyes," he went on indulgently. "That long blonde hair, ravishing figure. You'd have been much more appreciated in the fifties. Everyone's so gung ho about brunettes these days but I can't seem to fathom why. If you ask me, blondes get a bad rap nowadays. I'd have taken Marilyn over Audrey any day of the week."

I felt like I was going to throw up all over his overpriced duvet.

"I *didn't* ask you," I pointed out with frigid hostility. "So you're not going to kill me?" Well, there was a shocker, not that I complained.

"If it were up to me, love, I'd have you killed, turned and feeding on some charming schoolteacher by the night's end. However I, unlike most of my kind, believe in choice above all else. It's something I wasn't given. So until you agree to spend an eternity vampyr, no, I'm not going to kill you."

"Then why am I here? I certainly didn't *choose* to be here."

"Because when I caught sight of the fire in your eyes, I was bloody titillated. I'd like to get to know you, Emma."

Well that answer surely wasn't what I had expected.

"I already told you, I'm spoken for."

"And where is this Andre who speaks for you? Camilla set him free just a few hours after the exchange was made. Has he called? Has he whisked you away on his chariot? No, he hasn't. For five hundred years, all Andre wanted was his autonomy from his maker. Do you really think he was falling for some college student in Rhode Island? The moment he handed her the grimoire, Camilla released the Viking boy and your Prince Charming was liberated. Your little scheme worked perfectly according to plan. And yet, he's made no effort to find you, love."

I felt my heart drop. It couldn't be true. Not Andre.

"You're lying."

"You can call me a monster or a demon or the devil incarnate, but I do not lie. He'd do just about anything to escape her. And who could blame him? Imagine following around a woman you hated for half a millennia. In fifty years, he'll still be young and vibrant. He'll have the world at his altar just as he's had it since before you were born. Christ, since before your great-grandparents were born. In fifty years, you'll witness yourself decay. How would a twenty-year-old boy look beside a woman of nearly seventy?"

His words reminded me so much of Camilla's in a dream I had not long ago. As much as it hurt me, I realized they both had a point. I would grow old and senile, that was, if I survived the next few weeks, and he would stay just as handsome as ever before. Maybe our relationship really was doomed from the start.

"Why are you doing this?"

I never allowed myself to think too deeply about my future with Andre. I had been taking things one step at a time. But what if Caden was right? How ridiculous would we look arm in arm fifty years from now? I was so focused on getting past the semester that I never stopped to think that far ahead.

"I didn't mean to upset you, love. I just don't want someone so beautiful, so passionate, to put all her eggs in the wrong basket, as it were. Now enough of this dreary banter. You have to eat something. I'll go ahead and check on your supper."

And just like that, Caden was out the door and I was left miserable and alone in the confines of his expansive bedroom thinking of all the reasons Andre and I could never work as a couple. I got up warily and walked toward the door, trying to turn the knob. Locked. I turned back and sat in the plush armchair by the window overcome with despair.

Caden couldn't have been telling me the truth. Andre loved me. He was forever mine. He told me so himself. He even gave me his mother's sapphires, taking the time to engrave the quote so that I'd never forget it. We had made love. Andre saved me from those drunken idiots on the first night of school. Was I just another girl he met along the way, a human pet to play with as he conspired to earn his freedom? Was I nothing but a means to his end?

I did manage to befriend Tristen and get an invitation to his family's party. I entered the house when Andre was unable to. How could he love me? I wasn't a vampire, only a silly human girl completely in love with a man I thought I knew. How could I have been so naïve?

A knock at the door startled me and I went to answer it thinking Caden had returned with some food. To my surprise, a little old lady stood before me smiling. She was wearing a long black dress with a white collar that reminded me of my headmistress at Astor. She had thinning white hair neatly pulled back in a tight bun and handed me a large garment bag.

"Mr. Locke requests your presence in the dining room, ma'am," the woman said politely. She had such kind eyes that it felt wrong to be discourteous to her, regardless of the asshole she chose to work for.

"Please tell Mr. Locke that he can request whatever he likes. I'll be right here just as he left me."

If he wanted to kidnap me, there wasn't much I could do about it. I already checked for all possible escape routes and came up blank. I was up on the second story of a large mansion that looked just as lavish as Valgard Manor if not more so. The windows wouldn't budge and even if they had, there was no balcony or fire escape for me to climb down from. I was stuck in that house and though he'd succeeded in keeping me captive, I had no intention of listening to a single command he planned on giving me.

"He told me you might say that," she grinned sweetly. Did his stupid grin rub off on everybody? "He said if you don't come downstairs, I won't be given my supper this evening, ma'am."

Son of a bitch!

The dining room table was covered in a variety of entrées. I was given three types of wine to choose from as well as cheese plates, salads and about four different kinds of potato dishes. There were no other dinner guests and I was free to indulge in every delicacy available. As much as I wanted to be my usual stubborn self, I was famished and everything looked too good to pass up. If I was going to be here a while, I might as well build up my strength. I placed a tender chicken breast on my plate and poured myself a glass of vintage red wine. It was Romanée Conti, 1956. *Impressive,* I thought.

About fifteen minutes into my meal, Caden walked into the room and sat at the other end of the table with his own glass of red liquid in hand. Whether it was a dark wine or blood, I had no idea. He wasn't given a plate or utensils, only a finely woven placemat for his drink.

"Is everything to your liking, love?" he asked far too sincerely for my liking. "I wasn't sure what you ate so I just told the staff to go mad."

Was it too much trouble to tuck away his grin at the dinner table at least?

"Everything is fine, thank you."

I couldn't believe I had just thanked the man who was holding me hostage. I needed another sip of my costly, delectable beverage.

Perhaps I'll get too sloshed to be good company and he'll just want to kick me out. Either way, I might as well make the most of my incarceration.

"Just fine? Oh, come on now, love, you could do a little better than that. You're drinking the finest grapes money can buy. Any other girl would be fucking wrapped around my finger by now. Then again," he considered. "You come from wealth so I guess I'm not too surprised."

"I'd be happy to trade places with any other girl if you'd like."

His grin got wider. Yes, this was all very amusing. I wouldn't have minded wrapping a stick of dynamite to his fucking finger right about now. Ignoring my comment, he looked around at all the dishes in front of us.

"You know, sometimes I see how pretty it all looks laid out on a fine porcelain plate and miss the days when I was human. In my time, though, the food was much more limited; meat and potatoes would just about cover it."

"Meat and potatoes still pretty much cover it for most people. Why am I here, Caden?" I asked getting to the point.

"I already told you," he groaned as if I should have known better by now. "I want to get to know you. It's not often I meet a lady who holds my interest. Let alone a *human* one."

"Andre's your family. How can you betray him like this?" I asked completely dumbfounded by the absence of loyalty between them.

It was one thing to try and steal a stranger's girl for yourself, but one who was clearly dating your own flesh and blood? I didn't even consider Jaq's boyfriends men, let alone scheme to take them away from her. And she wasn't even technically family to me.

"Andre shares my blood and that's where our ties end. I have no allegiance to that man."

His eyes were bloodshot and his expression icy. The playful grin had finally left his face and a part of me kind of wished it came back. An angry vampire wasn't exactly the best kind of vampire to be around, especially with no means of escape in sight. Changing the subject was the only thing I could think to do to ease the tension in the room.

"Is your loyalty to Camilla then?"

"That cunt?" He burst out laughing. I was glad the sinister look on his face was gone but the sound of his wholehearted guffaw was the last thing I expected to hear. "Oh, bloody hell! Sorry, love. That was just too funny. No, my loyalty is not to Camilla. Like I said, she's a means to an end. Being a vampire has its disadvantages, makers being one of them. I just want to be released is all. So, does your room have all the necessary amenities or would you like for me to have my assistant bring you something else?"

"Why are you being so nice to me?" I asked, finishing the last few bites on my plate.

"Not this again," he sighed in exasperation. "Let's just say you remind me of a girl I once knew. Besides, is it so wrong of me to want to indulge in a bit of pleasant conversation? There are few people in my circle that I care to speak with freely."

"If you don't care to speak with them then why are they in your circle?"

Caden stood up and walked toward me. He was wearing a snug black t-shirt and light denim jeans, seemingly acclimated to modern times and looking so much like my beloved. I couldn't help but admire the vampire's perfectly shaped figure. It was just as toned and muscular as Andre's. Andre. God, how I missed him.

"All these questions. It's my turn to ask a few," he said, extending his hand. I ignored it but followed him into one of the sitting rooms where he refilled my glass with more wine. "Now why would a girl as delightful as you leave a lively metropolis to come to a quiet town in Rhode Island? Someone your age should want to be out experiencing all life's little pleasures in the city that never sleeps, as it were."

I took a sip of my wine and sat down on the plush burgundy sofa. "I spent my entire life in that lively metropolis; it was time for a change. I've always preferred a lake house to a penthouse anyway. I guess walking along crowded streets to even more crowded restaurants and rowdy nightclubs didn't seem fun anymore," I answered honestly. "I just wanted to spend some time in a place that wasn't swarming with skyscrapers and angry cab drivers. I wanted to see stars."

"You really are fascinating, Emma Dresden. Next question. Why art?"

"How do you know so much about me?"

I didn't understand how a total stranger had gathered that much information about me and why.

"It isn't polite to answer a question with a question. Why art?"

"I've always loved art," I began hesitantly. I had to remind myself that I wasn't making small talk with a new friend. I was a prisoner here. Nevertheless, it was a subject I enjoyed discussing so I indulged us both to pass the time.

"I've been painting since I was a little girl," I admitted. "I guess I'm captivated by the story even more so than the image itself. One of my favorite paintings is Jan Van Eyck's *Arnolfini Wedding Portrait*. It isn't just a pretty picture to me. Everything on that canvas serves a purpose. The fruit by the windowsill meant the couple was wealthy enough to afford such luxuries. The dog signified loyalty. The candle lit inside the chandelier depicted God's presence within the room." It was so nice to be able to discuss art with someone other than Andre who actually seemed interested in what I was saying. Jaq certainly didn't care for Monet or Mucha. "When I paint, I tell a story that only I can fully understand. A lot of it comes from my dreams. Nightmares, really." I felt slightly embarrassed at my rambling. "You probably think I'm crazy."

Caden's eyes hadn't left me even for a moment. He was analyzing me, figuring me out. I took another sip of my wine and suddenly it dawned on me that I didn't have my cell phone. How could I have known whether or not Andre had called, or Jaq for that matter, if I didn't have it? I was finally starting to calm down and part of me truly enjoyed talking to Caden. But this was all too bizarre and I started to get irritated.

"Where is my phone?" I asked him suspiciously.

"In safe keeping," he smirked.

"Safe keeping? How can I trust what you say about Andre? How can I trust anything you say if you're keeping my own property from me? I want my phone back," I roared.

"It's on your nightstand, Emma. But please, if your distrust for me is so great, feel free to believe I've deleted all the *hundreds* of missed messages from your darling Andre. I've had enough of this conversation. I hope the meal was to your liking."

Before I could respond, Caden was gone in a flash. I walked up the long staircase back to my room and shut the door behind me. When I looked to the nightstand by the bed, I saw my little white phone resting just where Caden said it would be. I immediately turned it on and found about twenty missed calls from Jaq. Andre hadn't tried to reach me a single time. Nothing made sense anymore. I guessed my dark knight had gotten what he wanted in the end. The sad realization hit me like a brick when I knew what he wanted wasn't me after all.

I'm back in the same tower, only this time I'm wearing the green nightgown Caden had given me, covered in blood. Over a hundred white candles are lit all over the damp grass and Andre is lying in the middle of it all. He is dressed in a three-piece suit, unconscious and wearing Theron's ring. In the corner of my eye I see Mr. Valgard, chanting in a language I don't understand. When I run to him, pleading with him to bring me home, he doesn't move or even notice my presence. When I turn to run as far as my feet will take me, Camilla stands in my way blocking the exit.

"Little flower, so glad you could make it."

Camilla's eyes are scarlet and though I know I'm dreaming, I feel frightened. "It seems you've been making friends in all the right places," she continues. "I've made a promise to Caden that I won't harm you in exchange for our sweet Andre. You see I'm going to use him as a vessel for Theron. Once his soul is returned to me, he'll need a body, of course."

"But you promised Andre his freedom," I mutter as timidly as a mouse.

"Andre detests what he is," she answers with a hostile undertone. "He's hated his nature since the moment I turned him. He thinks our kind is an abomination. I never received a thank you or any sort of appreciation for giving him the gift of immortality. Once the spell is complete, he will have earned his ultimate freedom. He'll have the death he's always longed for. I thought bringing you here to watch, just as I watched my dear Theron as he was taken from me; I thought it would be rather ... poetic."

I run to the unconscious body just a few feet away and cradle Andre like a doll.

"Wake up. Andre, please wake up," I beg. "Wake up! Please!"

I was jolted awake by the familiar sound of my alarm. Jaq was sitting at the edge of my bed waiting for me to open my eyes. I sat up as she stared at me incredulously. There was a steaming cup of coffee on my nightstand and my phone was characteristically on its charger as it was every morning. *What the hell happened last night?* I was so confused. Could Caden have been nothing more than a bad dream?

From the expression on her face, Jaq was clearly furious. "I must have called you a million times, Emma! Where the hell have you been? Why couldn't you at least text me back and tell me you were okay? You can't worry me like this, *chérie*. It isn't right!"

"I'm sorry." It was all I could say and I felt like I'd had to apologize to her way too often lately. "It's been a rough night. Have you heard from Tristen?"

She let out a deep sigh and I could feel her anger turn to grief. "He's still missing. I've stopped calling the house because every time I do, his mother just gets more and more upset. I can't handle the sadness in her voice. It's too much. She said she'd let me know as soon as he's back."

I took a deep breath and braced myself before asking my next question. It was the only one that truly mattered to me at that moment. "And Andre? Have you heard from him?"

A swarm of butterflies crept into the pit of my stomach, as I wasn't sure I was prepared to know the answer. He hadn't tried contacting me to see if I was all right. Should I have even cared if it were obvious he didn't? Logic clearly wasn't my strong suit lately.

"I haven't heard from him, *chérie*. I would have told you if I knew anything."

My heart felt like it was slowly being ripped out of my chest and tears began streaming down my face.

"I know," I mumbled with a small, contrived smile. A few moments later, my phone began to buzz as a text came through. I secretly hoped it was Andre but when I looked at the message, it was from an unknown number.

Unknown | 8:03am: I'm sorry about how we left things last night. Please meet me for coffee at The Annex to explain. 2 o'clock? Caden.

"So *another* vampire wants to meet you for coffee? Haven't you had enough supernatural drama?" Jaq justly chastised.

She was totally right; what was I doing? The heart-wrenching ache I was feeling over Andre should have made me think twice about seeing Caden. After all, he did abduct me and keep me prisoner in his home. If all that even happened in the first place. But there was something about him. I didn't think Caden would hurt me. He had this rough exterior with something undeniably charming and innocent on the inside. He reminded me of the guys I dated before I fell in love with Andre. Always a sucker for the bad boy, I never failed in bringing out their gentle side, no matter how deep down it was hidden. I loved a good challenge and eventually, my curiosity always got the best of me.

Convincing myself I might be able to get some much-needed answers from Caden, I took a quick shower and put on a bronze silk blouse with a pair of white slacks and tan stilettos. If I was going to get my mind off of my absentee boyfriend, why not do it in style?

It was way too cold to walk all the way to the café so I called for a cab. I made it there about fifteen minutes late and couldn't have cared less about my tardiness. When I stepped inside, I immediately noticed the entire place was empty. At the far corner, I spotted Caden sitting by himself in a white button-up and jeans. He looked so much like Andre it hurt. I took one deep breath and walked over to him. As he saw me approach, Caden stood up at once and pulled out my chair.

Why couldn't human guys be this courteous?

"You look incredible. Thank you for coming," he greeted me with a smile.

I could feel my cheeks begin to blush, which backfired as I did my best to hide my steadily growing embarrassment. As much as every part of me knew it was a bad idea, I couldn't help but stay and hear what he had to tell me.

"What did you need to talk to me about?" I asked hoping he wouldn't notice my puffy tear-stained eyes.

"I wanted to apologize for my abrupt departure last night. I'm hotheaded by nature and, unfortunately, our human traits are only heightened as vampires. Our last conversation regrettably brought out that side of me." He looked as if he were telling the truth. "I also wanted to try and make amends with the girl I can't seem to get out of my head. I never meant to upset you, love. I never wanted to give you the wrong idea about me."

"And what exactly is the right idea about you, Caden? You stole me like a handbag and kept me locked up inside your home until you were ready to let me go. Is that what you typically do to the girls you can't seem to get out of your head?" I should never have come. I knew this was a big mistake.

"If I met you in that alleyway and invited you for tea, would you have come willingly? No. But I've told you repeatedly that all I want is to get to know you. Initially, when I spoke with Camilla, she made you out to be some kind of bloody strumpet, undeserving of love or mercy. I'll admit I followed you yesterday afternoon to find out where the grimoire was. But it was when I really allowed myself to see you. When I looked into your eyes. I couldn't help myself." He paused for a while, deep in thought. "You were so much ... more."

My face was reddening again. Why wasn't he less attractive? Why couldn't he have been the ultimate friend? I had so many male friends back in New York. They took me to the movies and listened to my Aiden troubles. They were always there when I needed to be rescued from a date gone wrong. Eventually, one by one, they all fell for me. But those first few months of what I thought was real friendship were so lovely. Those boys made me feel so beautiful without the pressure of giving them my whole self.

"You could have asked me to sit down with you. You could have invited me for a drink. You didn't know what answer I'd give."

"But I did. I knew from the moment I met you at that little lounge how enthralled you were by Andre. I felt your emotions, love. I felt that you belonged to someone else, someone unworthy of you. I just wanted one evening.

I wanted one proper, uninterrupted conversation with you. I'd have regretted it for the rest of my existence if I hadn't given myself that opportunity."

He looked disappointed at the notion of having to steal me away in order to spend time with me. It didn't seem like that was something he was used to in all his years, human or vampire. Considering how handsome he was, I could understand why it must have been an unfamiliar feeling for him. It would have been so much easier had he known I might have obliged. Of course, out of common courtesy, I would have run it by Andre first. But I knew there was a pretty big chance I would have gone voluntarily, if only to learn more about Andre's family and the reason behind their apparent feud.

Andre's sudden disappearance clouded my mind again and I did my best to conceal my emotions. If he felt them the night we met at Marquis, he'd surely sense my anguish now. I let out a long sigh.

"Next time you decide to go and kidnap someone, how about you ask them first before coming to your own conclusions? The answer may have surprised you."

"Perhaps, but I don't fare well with rejection, love. And the look in your eyes when you saw me yesterday was far from fondness."

"I didn't know you, Caden. You stalked me in an alley and if I remember correctly, you bit me. What fondness could I have for you then?"

He stared at me as though he understood where I was coming from and then looked down at the ivory tablecloth, deep in thought. When I saw his face, he looked like a shy little boy who had just been reprimanded for some childish misconduct. How could he be so intimidating one moment and then so innocent the next? When the waitress came by to ask us what were having, he quickly ordered a double espresso and one large iced Americano. Caden knew what I wanted without asking.

"There are many apologies I owe you this afternoon," he muttered as the girl went behind the counter to fetch us our drinks. "I sincerely hope you'll give me a chance to redeem myself. The awful behavior you saw yesterday was unwarranted and I am sorry. Life has an interesting way of bringing two people together, don't you agree?"

"Listen, Caden, you seem like you're being honest and I appreciate that. If you're looking for an apology then I forgive you. But getting to know me is a bad idea. My luck with men, especially lately, hasn't been the best."

"Then let me change that," he whispered with a glimmer of hope in his eyes. "Let me make it up to you somehow. Andre doesn't realize what he's lost."

I lowered my gaze and wondered what he meant by that. Had Andre really lost me? Had he disappeared once he gave Camilla what she wanted? I couldn't bear the thought of our relationship coming to an end so abruptly. The waitress returned with our drinks and I twisted the tall glass around in circles, unable to put anything into my stomach. I worried about Andre and whether or not he was safe. Caden was handsome, smart, powerful, all the things any girl would want in a man. But at the end of the day, he wasn't mine. And I knew that at this particular point in my life, he couldn't be.

"How do I know he's not locked up somewhere in Camilla's evil lair? How do I know he hasn't been trying to reach me this entire time? Given how we met, I'd say I trust you about as far as I can throw you, Caden."

"You have every right to question my motives. But I told you once before, I'm no liar. Camilla and I spoke an hour ago and she assured me she released Andre as soon as he brought her the grimoire. If she was dishonest with me, I can't say. Perhaps she's holding him hostage. I really have no idea. She knows now that the spell is with the boy's father. She thinks the elder Valgard is much more capable of unbinding the reversal enchantment than his son is and she isn't willing to take any chances with Theron."

"So she still has Tristen too. She's holding him for ransom," I ascertained. It's what I would have done if I were some psycho bitch vampire lady.

"Nothing escapes you, love. It's one of the many things I adore about you." His customary grin appeared right on schedule. I had to admit, it was growing on me.

"I apologize for telling you otherwise last night but she changed her tune last we spoke," he admitted. "Maybe she was rooting for us all along and wanted you to think Andre had abandoned you. I know I secretly wished he had. But yes, she still has the boy. And just as well, for her sake. Otherwise, his father would never have helped her. The moment the old chap figures out how to do the spell, she'll know about it. She has eyes and ears all over town, that sly fox. I believe she's even compelled one of your mates. Isabel, was it? The girl's been keeping tabs on you for months."

I *knew* something wasn't right about Isabel from the moment I met her. She asked too many prying questions in the time that I'd known her and there was always this kind of glossy look in her eyes. I'd just always attributed it to her being nosy or that she hadn't gotten enough sleep. Everything about her strange behavior suddenly started to make complete sense.

"I had a dream the other night," I recalled. "I vaguely remember Camilla trying to use Andre's body as Theron's vessel. Do you think that's true?"

"Camilla's always been physically attracted to Andre. In order to bring Theron back successfully, she would need a body in which to house his soul. A vessel, just as you said. I think if she had to select a vampire with which to resurrect Theron, Andre would be her prime choice. Your dream may be more of a foreshadowing."

I felt a surge of fear and rage all at once. How dare this woman think she could take Andre and swap his soul for Theron's? Who the hell did she think she was? I remembered waking up and praying that my dream was nothing but a nightmare but now I knew it was much more than that. I took a sip of my drink, feeling the caffeine begin to stimulate my body. Of course Andre wouldn't have ignored me purposely, I realized. I buried my head in my hands and felt my eyes start to water.

"We have to do something," I cried.

Caden couldn't miss the genuine sadness written all over my face. Regardless of what he felt for me, my expression made it all too clear that my heart belonged to someone else. Reluctant as he was, he agreed to help me rescue him.

"There's an old mansion on the outskirts of town where Camilla's been staying. I'll try to convince her to find another vessel. I don't want to make any promises I can't keep but I give you my word that I'll do what I can to bring him back to you. I truly wish we met under better circumstances, Emma. Things would have been different. I suppose you would have liked me."

Before I realized what I was doing, I bolted out of my seat and wrapped my arms around the vampire. He was as stunned as I was when I finally let him go and saw the startled look on his face. The waitress in the corner was eyeing us with a blend of envy and curiosity. She probably saw me there with Andre a few weeks ago and wondered how I managed to keep such good-looking company. With half a smile, he rose from the table, slid a twenty under the ivory sugar bowl and walked out of the café.

Ten

Quinn went on about longships for what seemed like an eternity as I willed myself from dozing off in class. Simply getting out of bed had been a struggle and it took Jaq a good thirty minutes to rouse me from my deep sleep. Things at school were already back to normal and everyone seemed to have forgotten about the death of one of our classmates. It sickened me how nonchalant the faculty was being about the whole thing.

Sure, we were offered a few counseling sessions to deal with the tragedy, but no one really cared. They all just assumed she was drunk and followed some crazy person back to campus for a night of sex and depravity. I could feel the energy around everyone and though they believed it was all very sad, Olivia's death hadn't affected them personally. Isabel took advantage of the few mental health days they gave her and I hadn't seen her since the funeral.

The seat next to me was vacant and as I stared blankly at it, I remembered all the humorous looks I had exchanged with Andre when one of our classmates said something silly or when our professor went off on a tangent.

It was our final day before winter break and we'd all handed in our final exams over forty minutes ago. Every other teacher let us go as soon as we were finished, but Quinn wanted to milk us for all we were worth. I could see Jaq's head turn to the empty seat beside her every few minutes, longing for her own absent boyfriend just as sadly.

Once we were finally back in our room, I crawled into bed and tried my best to shut myself off from the outside world. My first semester at Newport University had come to an end and winter break was upon us. I would be back in New York in just a few days time. I thought about how much I missed my family and part of me was relieved that I would soon be home.

I loved spending Christmas in the City. Ice-skating in Rockefeller Center, admiring the enormous tree that lit up like a giant ball of fire; it was a slice of familiarity I very much needed. It was comforting to know I would see my brother and we would all have dinner as a family again.

Holidays and birthdays were the only times we would ever really sit down together at the dinner table. My father was constantly working and Liam had his own life now. I was excited to bake my famous plum tarte tatin for the people who loved me unconditionally and who wanted nothing in return. I missed my mother most of all. She was the one person aside from Jaq that I could talk to about anything. She understood my mood swings and had always been there for me through every lapse in judgment and every bout of heartache.

Just as I closed my eyes to fall asleep, I heard my phone begin to buzz. Though all I wanted to do was throw it across the room, I knew there was a small chance it could be important. With my eyes still shut, I said a quick prayer, hoping it was Andre.

Caden Locke | 12:03pm: Spoke with Camilla. You were right. I'll be downstairs at half past seven. Dress warmly. Yours fondly, Caden.

Caden was waiting for me in his pitch-black Audi Q7, dressed in another one of his simple t-shirts and a pair of dark colored slacks. He greeted me cheerfully and asked me how I was holding up.

"I've seen better days," I muttered, filled with a sense of false hope that I wished was true.

The ride didn't last long and we listened to some jazz, which only reminded me more of Andre. Rows of oak trees lined the street that led to Camilla's mansion. I noticed a crow fly by us just as we entered the towering black iron gates with intricate swirls of gold upon them.

"They never get hit," Caden said, as if reading my thoughts. "As close as they come, those bloody creatures *never* get hit. Lucky bastards," he chuckled.

"Why are you helping me?" I asked him somewhat suspiciously.

"Not this again. Emma, I would love to turn this car around and take you to my house, keep you confined until you realize I'm worthy of you. But you're unlike any woman I have ever met. You deserve more than that. When the time comes, when I rescue your Andre, I want you to remember the man who stands before you. I want you to make that choice for yourself."

"You once said you weren't given a choice," I remembered vividly. "Did you mean about being turned? Is that why you hate Andre so much?"

"I don't hate Andre; I very much dislike him. For a heap of reasons. But yes, that's why we don't get on well. I should have died in 1896, love. Instead, I've watched everyone I've ever cared for pass on while I'm stuck in this godforsaken hellhole for eternity. I'll never forgive him for what he did to me. Rather, what he allowed Camilla to do to me."

"But why don't you resent Camilla then? She was the one who turned you, not Andre."

"Because aside from being the one who physically did the deed, she had nothing to do with it. Andre is the one who summoned her. He's the one who chose this life for me."

I sat there quietly until we arrived at a little road leading up to the mansion. When we finally reached the entrance, the place looked like an old French hunting lodge with its brown bricks and white roughcast. There were large, intricately carved sculptures of cherubs at the foot of the property, which only added to its spookiness. Small wrought iron gates a few feet high sat against each of the second story windows and the lush greenery added some life to the exceptionally eerie gothic residence.

Low-profile lighting fixtures illuminated the long, narrow path as the SUV pulled up to the entrance. I noticed a bright red Ferrari resting peacefully outside and struggled to contain my laughter. *How inconspicuous,* I thought to myself smirking. We were on a mission to save Andre, though, and Camilla's taste in automobiles was neither here nor there. Caden parked right beside the flashy vehicle and opened my door in lightning speed before I ever realized he'd left the car.

"My lady," he gestured holding out his hand.

As we walked up to the front door, I noticed at least five cameras taping every inch of the vast perimeter.

"She's big on security," Caden grinned.

Before he managed to ring the bell, an old man in a custom-tailored suit stepped out to greet us.

"You must be Emma," he smiled.

His teeth were so crooked that I did my best not to stare. The man must have been around since well before braces had been invented and a trip to the orthodontist would have helped him a great deal. Dental insurance was obviously not part of the list of benefits he received from his psychotic boss, if there were any to speak of at all.

"Good evening, Mr. Locke, ma'am," he graciously said with a nod. "Please, do come inside. Miss Camilla has been expecting you both."

"He's been compelled, love," Caden whispered too low for the man to hear. Judging by his age, he could have probably kept his normal tone and the guy wouldn't have overheard him anyhow. "Good evening, Mr. Greyson," he greeted much louder and with his usual charm.

Mr. Greyson led us through a dark hallway filled with framed photographs of family members from the turn of the last century until present. I especially admired the old wedding pictures, wondering if I'll ever get to take any of my own someday. As soon as the thought crossed my mind, Caden looked down at me knowingly and smiled.

The old man took us down a renovated wooden staircase into an abandoned cellar where dust and cobwebs grew like weeds in an unkempt yard. Before I reached the last step, he said, "This is as far as I'm allowed to go, sir."

"Very well. Thank you, Mr. Greyson."

As he turned to go back upstairs, Caden twisted the knob and we entered the murky room. Everything seemed so old and untouched. He didn't let go of my hand for a second, knowing danger was lurking in every corner.

"Caden, how good of you to make it. I was getting lonely here all by myself," came a voice at the end of the room. "I see you've brought supper."

"How predictable you are, Camilla," he answered without a shred of civility in his voice. "Release your captive before I remove that pretty little head of yours. And you know I will, or die trying."

"Oh, Caden," she sneered. "Always so needlessly melodramatic. We'll see what Theron has to say about your attitude when he's been awakened."

"Where is Andre?" I asked frigidly.

"Why don't you come with me and see for yourself. I've made a deal with the Viking. He's made sure all will go according to plan."

My nightmare was coming true. The evil bitch had Andre and she had no intention of letting him go.

"Take me," I snapped, clenching Caden's hand with all the strength I had in me. He didn't even flinch.

"Can we not find anyone else to act as Theron's vessel?" Caden asked suddenly. "Is there no one worthy of this bloke's spirit other than bloody Andre?"

I glanced at Caden and saw an inextinguishable fire that glared red once we made our way toward her. There was something so unbelievably menacing that ventured from his spirit. The energy in the room was vehement and I winced when I looked back and forth at the two vampires before me. His crimson eyes were haunting when he let go of my hand and grabbed Camilla by the neck.

"Tell me where he is before I rip out your lifeless heart."

All the woman did was smile. Caden didn't scare her in the least. She was about a thousand years older, give or take a hundred or so years, making his threats trifling at best.

"Let go of me, boy," she warned. "We both know I'd end you before you even had a chance. My amulet is with Valgard in the old tower. He's with Andre and waits for my arrival. Please, do join me," she invited him with an ear-to-ear grin.

"It would be my pleasure."

We pulled up about three blocks away from the Old Stone Mill and walked the rest of the way. Caden took my hand protectively and assured me that everything would be all right. Camilla didn't take her ostentatious sports car but somehow she had gotten there even before we did. She was watching Mr. Valgard as he stood chanting something vaguely familiar.

"Sólveret anima. Adducite anima retro."

Everyone always joked about the pointlessness of Latin and I could've kicked myself for taking French in high school.

When I saw what he was standing over, my heart sank. White candles were lit beside every pillar and an unconscious Andre was in the center of it all, just as he had been in my nightmare. Only this time, I was fully aware that I wouldn't wake up to the sound of my alarm ringing or the smell of coffee on my nightstand. This was real and it was happening. I felt helpless and for the first time in my life, wished I were a vampire. I would have pounced on Camilla and ripped her heart out myself before Caden even got the opportunity. I let go of his firm grip and ran to Andre, cradling his head in my lap. He was out cold.

Mr. Valgard was still chanting when I noticed Isabel and then Jaq and Tristen next to her. There were numerous bite marks on each of their necks and they looked so weak and frail in the dim lighting that I could have screamed. They were sitting between the glimmering candles with glazed looks in their eyes. Tristen was the only one who looked semi normal, though the sadness in his face was palpable. He had his arm around Jaq and stroked her hair as if to calm her, even though she seemed to be completely unfazed.

"Jaq!" I screamed. My best friend didn't even glance in my direction. "Jaq!" I repeated louder. Nothing. They had obviously been compelled.

"They won't listen, little flower," Camilla scoffed. "Scream all you like. How long is this going to take?"

Ignoring her question, Mr. Valgard continued what he was doing as Caden burned a hole through Camilla with his gaze. I petted Andre's head like he was a small puppy and my tears dampened his face one by one.

"Why are you doing this?" I cried. "You could've used anyone! Why him?"

Camilla leisurely approached me with Alexander's grimoire in hand and threw it onto the floor beside me.

"This is why!" she exclaimed, her thunderous shriek making me wince. "You thought you could fool me, child? You thought I wouldn't realize what you were up to? I have spent over five bloody centuries with this sorry excuse for a progeny and you think I wouldn't have noticed that he was betraying me? You really are quite dense.

"How could I release him knowing he would just come after me once I let him go?" she continued in a more matter-of-fact tone. "Andre is without doubt one of the strongest vampire's I've ever encountered, even if he is half a millennia younger than I. *You* did this. If you hadn't come into his life, he would have procured the grimoire and I'd have sent him on his way. That or he would have failed and went on as he always had, focused on his work and nothing else. Instead, he fell in love with a little human girl and look where that got him!" She pointed her long, perfectly manicured finger at the beautiful man resting peacefully on my lap.

She was right; it was all my fault. I was the reason for all of this. Had he never met me, Andre wouldn't be in this mess. Neither would poor Jaq, or Isabel for that matter. Olivia would still be alive. I looked over at my oblivious friends, sitting calmly only a few feet away and shivered.

"Then take me," I pleaded. "If this is my fault then take me! Turn me and use *me* as Theron's vessel. I'll do it willingly. Just please, leave everyone else alone!"

Camilla and Caden looked at me incredulously at my offer. Then a tiny smile began to form on the woman's lips.

"A human offering her soul in exchange for a vampire? Oh, this is rich. Little flower, as pretty as your petals are, I'm afraid not. I have another purpose for you and your little friends. Theron will need blood once he's awakened, and lots of it. But it's quite lovely to hear that you're volunteering your services."

She put her hand on Mr. Valgard's shoulder as a flash of bright light ignited the air around us. He ceased his chanting when Caden unexpectedly flung Andre across the tower and through a gap in between the pillars. He fixed himself directly in front of the mage just as another spark shot out from the man's hands and inadvertently struck

Caden's heart. He let out a subtle whimper and fell to the ground with a thud.

"No!" Camilla screamed. "You fool! What have you done?"

Just then, I saw a very much alive Andre, apparently having had regained his composure in those few seconds away from Mr. Valgard's influence. He quickly planted himself directly in front of me to shield me from what came next. What would have been a lethal blow to my skull merely yanked him slightly off to the side until he spun around and seized Camilla by the throat.

She tried fighting him off but it was to no avail. He was ferocious in his attack, as if combat was something that came naturally to him. It was startling to see someone who was once so tender with that much hatred radiating from his entire being. Andre looked like a fierce warrior in that moment and from the arctic glare in his crimson-stained eyes, the much older vampire had every reason to be frightened. He lifted her off the ground, one hand still firmly gripping her neck, and effortlessly ripped off her head as if she were a ragdoll, never giving her a chance to speak another word.

I couldn't contain my screams at the sight of her once lustrous flaxen hair rolling across the grassy floor like a bowling ball. The compulsion she had on Jaq and Isabel broke instantly and they joined me in my high-pitched shrieking. Tristen held on to his girlfriend stringently and put his hand over her eyes, forcing her to look away from the gruesome spectacle. The formerly gorgeous woman whose beauty I once secretly envied was now nothing more than a withered argentine corpse.

Andre came to my side at once and pressed my head against his chest, murmuring assurances I wasn't ready to grasp. When I finally pulled away to check on Caden, I saw Jaq crying over Isabel, who was lying there stiff as a board. At first I assumed she had fainted but when I got a closer look, I saw the blood dripping down from her neck.

Mr. Valgard had his arm around his son and tears were trickling down both of their cheeks. I ran to Isabel and tried to locate her pulse but found nothing. She was gone. Jaq and I hugged each other for what seemed like hours while the remaining men did away with the bodies in case the cops showed up. I didn't care that my face was blotchy and I looked like a ripe pomegranate. I didn't care about anything anymore.

Two of my friends had lost their lives and it was my fault. I deserved their fate, not them. If anyone had to die it should have been me. I did this. I was responsible, not them. Andre kneeled down until we were at eye level and sympathetically put his hand on my shoulder. I let go of Jaq and stared at him blankly. I should have been happy to see him. I should have been relieved to know he was safe. But I was too lost in my own grief to let myself feel anything else. I hadn't known such overwhelming sorrow in my entire life. What reprieve, what absolution could I possibly hope to attain when it was all for nothing? Isabel was dead. Olivia was dead. Caden …

"Where's Caden?" I stammered to my feet, looking around for the man who had risked his eternal life for me. "Where's Caden?" I shouted as if by raising my voice he would magically appear. Andre looked down at the ground, unable to look me in the eyes. He handed me Camilla's amulet and stared off into the distance.

"Caden's gone, Emma."

"Then let's go find him!"

I didn't understand why Andre was just standing there. We needed to find Caden and make sure he was okay. Mr. Valgard looked at me more compassionately than I thought possible given his usually stoic demeanor. He took my hand in his and squeezed it gently.

"The reversal enchantment was successful, dear," he grimly informed me. "Caden is no longer. The man you will find, should you ever find him that is, won't be the same person you once knew."

"No," I breathed, trembling as the realization hit me like a brick.

"Theron has been awakened."

Eleven

I sat on my bed holding Camilla's amulet, studying its countless swirls of caramels and browns. It seemed surreal that Caden's soul was locked inside the little gemstone mounted in silver resting in my hands. I kept replaying bits and pieces of my conversations with him in my head. I imagined his customary grin and the childlike innocence he sometimes bared when he looked at me. Caden gave his soul in exchange for Andre's life, a life he didn't much care for. He did it for me. He gave up his life for a silly little girl, a human girl no less, in love with another man.

I put the amulet around my neck and looked out the window broodingly. There wasn't a single person in sight as most of the other students had already left for winter break. The leaves had all fallen, leaving only stark branches to adorn the tree trunks. The entire world below looked so peaceful, almost too peaceful considering how much hatred and violence it really encompassed. *It's all a ruse*, I thought bitterly. Nothing was ever quite how it seemed. Not here. Not anywhere.

"The cab is here, *chérie,*" Jaq announced, bringing me out of my reverie. "Are you ready?"

I grabbed my suitcase and we headed downstairs silently, both of us still shaken by the ungodly details of the night's past. Jaq's wounds were slowly healing and she caked some make-up on her neck to cover the marks from her parents. Andre had offered to take us to the airport but I needed some time away from him. It seemed irrational for me to blame him for the untimely deaths of my friends or for Caden's horrid fate. But I couldn't look at him the same anymore.

So much had happened since we first met. I needed normality in my life right now and being with a vampire was far from it. I told him I would call him as soon as I landed but the usual anticipation to hear his voice or feel his touch wasn't quite there. It wasn't that I fell for Caden or that I didn't love Andre anymore. I just needed some time to process everything.

As we touched down at LaGuardia Airport I already felt calmer. I was in the comfort of my own city now and I would be seeing my parents momentarily. We could have driven as New York was only a few hours away, but the thought of concentrating on the road seemed impossible. My mother and father waited patiently for us holding bouquets of flowers and a big "Welcome Home" sign. I felt my worries begin to slowly fade away as I saw them across the room beaming at us.

"Emma!" my mother shouted enthusiastically. I could feel the tears trickling down my face as I ran into the shelter of her arms. "Emma, I missed you so much." She kissed my cheek and then my head and held on to me as if she hadn't seen me for a year. The man beside her cleared his throat impatiently.

"Papa!" I yelled and hugged him next. "Why aren't you at work?"

He squeezed me tight and laughed heartily at my observation. He was always at work.

"And miss seeing my girls? The company can do without me for a few hours."

Jaq's parents rarely showed up to anything that wasn't some kind of charity luncheon or other overpriced gathering. My mom and dad gave her the warm affection she lacked from her own family and she cherished their love for her wholeheartedly. Mrs. Avignon was probably out getting her nails done while her father was holed up in his expansive office on Lexington Avenue. My best friend was a prime example of how money could never truly buy happiness.

Our driver, William, dropped Jaq off at her apartment, only a few blocks from our own. When I opened the door to my childhood bedroom, I noticed that everything was just as I had left it. My California king bed with its white tufted headboard was neatly made and my desk still had a framed photograph of Aiden. I picked it up and threw it in an old box where I kept the last remnants of our failed relationship. I turned on my phone and texted Andre to let him know I made it home safely.

Once I unpacked my clothes and took a quick shower, I changed into a pair of sweatpants and went into the kitchen where my mother was slaving away at the stove with our housekeeper, Rosa. They had developed their own system, each doing the things they were best at. Mama handled the entrées while Rosa was responsible for salads and appetizers. I was assigned desserts, as that had always been my specialty.

"Where's Liam?" I asked the two women, adorably dressed in matching polka dot aprons.

My spoiled friends growing up always treated the people who worked for their families with such callousness. I never understood why they spoke to them as if they were lesser human beings than they were. Rosa had been with our family for over two decades and I regarded her with the same love and respect that I would an aunt. Even William received birthday cards and little presents from Liam and me every year since I can remember. I took treating others how I expected to be treated very seriously. After all, karma was a bitch and a half.

"He'll be here in a bit, darling. Just doing some last minute Christmas shopping. You know your brother."

I could barely contain my excitement. I last saw Liam in late August; right around the time I started packing for Rhode Island. He took some new job in Boston and I rarely got to see him even though he was only an hour and a half away by car. Liam was some hotshot attorney now and our family couldn't be more proud. Well, my dad not so secretly hoped he would take over his company someday but given his winning trial record, he knew his son had chosen the right profession. Seeing as how European History had no real future according to my beloved father, his sights were now set on me eventually running Dresden International. I didn't have the heart to break it to him that heading a major conglomerate wasn't on my immediate to-do list.

I started working on my tarte tatin, peeling a handful of ripe plums, and nearly cut myself when I heard the front door open. *Liam!* I ran out of the kitchen and pounced on my older brother. He caught me effortlessly and gave me a big kiss on the top of my head.

"I missed you too, Em," he chuckled.

Seeing him brought back a flood of memories from my childhood, sitting on his floor and watching Liam study as I played with my Barbie's just as diligently. He had a bunch of shopping bags with him and a large suitcase that William helped carry upstairs.

"Whatever you guys are cooking smells amazing," he gushed. "When's dinner? I'm starving."

"Go on and get settled, dear. Dinner's in an hour," my mother said as she came out to greet him. "William, would you like to stay and eat?"

"No, ma'am, thank you," William answered as politely as ever. "The Mrs. has something planned for us this evening. It's our fortieth anniversary."

"William! Why didn't you say anything?" I chided. "I would've gotten you two an anniversary gift!"

That was just like him, keeping his private life private in the hopes of saving himself the embarrassment of accepting any more of my presents. I loved surprising him and Rosa with little trinkets, even if it did make them uncomfortable. They had been in my life for far too long for any of that to matter, though. I considered them family and treated them as such.

"Oh, Miss Emma, because I know you too well," he smiled coyly. "Mrs. Dresden, is there anything else?"

"No, William. Thank you. Go on to your family. We've kept you long enough for today."

After placing my tarte tatin in the oven, I sat on the floor of Liam's bedroom just like old times and studied him as he unpacked his things. My brother always dressed to impress and brought with him what would have been a typical guy's entire wardrobe. Liam loved shopping and had the kind of build that everything he wore looked flawless on him. Jaq would especially love coming over when he was around if only to gawk. Sadly for her, Liam looked at her just as she was, his little sister's best friend and nothing more. Nevertheless, she still flirted with him shamelessly and it was hilarious to watch.

My phone started ringing and when I saw who was calling, I quickly got up and walked into my bedroom. Liam eyed me suspiciously but continued what he was doing.

"Hey," I answered.

"Hey, sweetheart. I'm just checking in. How is it to finally be home with the family?" Andre asked hesitantly.

He was still a bit cautious with how he spoke to me, trying not to overwhelm me after I'd asked him to give me some space.

"A breath of fresh air. How's Newport?"

He paused for a moment, thinking how best to approach his coming answer.

"I'm actually in New York. I thought with you being gone, there wasn't much reason for me to stay. But don't worry," he quickly added. "You won't even know I'm here … unless of course you want me around."

Andre was acting as if we were in middle school and I couldn't help but find his unusual bashfulness endearing. I did ask him for space, but hearing him speak like that only made me want to see him more. Christmas was just a few days away and I wondered where he would be spending it. I'd assumed he would spend the holidays with my family since his was long gone, but with all that had happened, I forgot to invite him.

"Would you like to have dinner with us tonight?" I asked, unsure what his answer would be.

"Are you sure? I wouldn't want to impose."

I could tell he was nervous. I guess even after five hundred plus years, men were still boys.

"I'm sure. Dinner's in a half hour. Is that enough time?"

"I'll see you then."

I walked up to my mother who was discussing the dangers of salt with Rosa and let her know we would be having a guest this evening. She was thrilled to meet Andre. I told her things here and there about him throughout the semester and she had been counting the days to meet Aiden's replacement. It wasn't often I'd speak so highly about another man, so she was justifiably curious.

"What kind of family does this Andre come from? What's his background?" My father was always interested in a person's upbringing, as he considered it to be the basis for one's character.

"Oh, Papa," I sighed. "Andre's family comes from Russia but he spent most of his life in London. He lost his parents a few years ago."

"A few" wasn't exactly accurate, but it would do. I couldn't exactly go into detail about Andre's past and, at least this way, they wouldn't expect to meet them for brunch.

"How tragic," my mother uttered. "Oh, Wesley, do be nice to the boy. Your daughter really likes this one."

"I'm always nice," he said with feigned disbelief.

"Well *I* don't have to be. I'm the older brother so I can be as critical as I want," Liam added chewing on a warm biscuit. I playfully punched my brother in the arm as I heard the doorbell ring.

Andre brought two bouquets of a dozen red roses and handed one to my mother and the other to me in true gentlemanly fashion. I could hear Liam snicker when he saw the man he undoubtedly deemed unworthy of his little sister. I knew Andre noticed my brother's discourteous reaction considering his hearing rivaled that of an owl. Even still, he extended his hand and shook Liam's with much less force than he would have liked had he been anyone else.

"It's a pleasure to meet you, Liam," he greeted courteously. "Emma's told me a lot about you."

"All lies," he grinned.

Next came the real hurdle to overcome: Papa. They shook hands and Andre gave him a bottle of vintage cognac. *Sold.* My father happily accepted his gift and I knew right then that they would get along.

"Frapin, my favorite. I see my daughter has chosen well," he smirked. "This is a rare vintage, Andre. How did you manage to get your hands on this beauty?"

"Emma told me you appreciated fine cognac so I made sure to verse myself well before meeting you. I have some friends in that region of France and they all recommended this blend above all."

"Hmm."

Dinner went off without a hitch. I was surprised at how well everyone was getting along. It all seemed too ordinary being that we were hosting a vampire for supper instead of the other way around. Andre was joking with my father about shoddy investments and Liam even laughed a few times. The entire evening was lighthearted and it made it easy to forget about the craziness of the past few months.

I decided to show Andre my bedroom after my mother, Rosa and I finished cleaning up. He spotted some of the canvases I painted as a little girl and praised me repeatedly, making me blush like a schoolgirl. I loved how uncomplicated the night turned out to be and part of me became nervous that this simplicity would be short-lived. Brushing the negative thoughts aside, I smiled up at my boyfriend, the man I sincerely grew to love, and wrapped my arms around his waist. He tenderly kissed the top of my head and whispered in my ear, "Thank you."

"For what?" I asked.

"For everything. For introducing me to your family, for allowing me into your home … for giving me your heart. I still hope that last part is true." He began to look as nervous as he'd sounded on the phone earlier. "I know I've done wrong by you. I put you in danger and that is something I'll have to live with forever. But please know that I love you. I love you more than I ever thought possible. You mean the world to me, Emma. Without you, I have no purpose."

"I love you too, Andre. And don't ever thank me for any of that. I gave you my heart the moment you rescued me. I just didn't know it then."

He lifted me up and kissed me sweetly. I missed the taste of him so much. It had been too long since I last got the chance to feel his mouth on my skin. I kissed him back fervently and pressed my body against his like we were two magnets unable to pull apart. I wanted him. I wanted him in my own bed in the comfort of my own home. My two safe havens were in the same place and it amplified my longing for him tenfold. I started to undo his zipper when he pulled my hand away.

"Your parents will hear us," he whispered.

"Then I guess we'll have to be extra quiet, won't we?"

Andre smiled and softly placed me on my bed, never taking his eyes off of me. He removed my shirt and grazed his teeth against the cups of my bra. I moaned quietly and he instantly put his finger against my lips to hush me. I opened my mouth and let his finger enter, licking it like a sweet candy.

In true vampire form, he rapidly turned me over and kissed the nape of my neck all the way down to my tailbone. I felt his hands at my waist as he took off my tight slacks in no time at all. I was sprawled out on my stomach, half naked with my face pressed into my pillow. Andre then grabbed me, positioning me on top of him until I was straddling him in nothing but my bra and panties. I could feel his bulge beneath me and pushed myself down until I heard a faint groan come from deep within his throat.

I undid the buttons of his shirt and threw it on the floor. He was just as beautiful as I remembered, every muscle toned and powerful. I recalled how strong he was when fighting Camilla. He was commanding in his efforts as if it were something he had done countless times. He was a true warrior through and through. The thousand-year-old vampire never stood a chance.

With remarkable precision, he unfastened my bra and it landed in the small collection of garments below us. I unbuttoned his pants and added them to the pile. I could tell he was admiring my figure because his gaze was set on my breasts and then my abdomen until it stopped at the only article of clothing I had on. He hooked his fingers through my red lace panties and drew them apart until there were two pieces of fabric left in his hands.

"I'll be sure to replace those."

He had successfully destroyed the nicest pair of La Perla panties I had ever owned, and the most expensive.

"But they were my favorite," I pouted.

"And you are mine."

He pulled me down toward him, locking his lips with mine as I felt unabashed sensations of pure, ethereal warmth invading my entire body. Nothing had been forgotten in the nights we spent apart. Andre knew exactly where I wanted to be touched, to be kissed. He schooled himself brilliantly, learning every gesture that I yearned him to make by my unconscious reactions alone. He felt every tremor, every quiver and responded accordingly. It was as though he read a manual penned specifically for my pleasure and mine alone.

"I am forever yours," he whispered in my ear as he entered me slowly.

I heard a knock at my door, waking me from my tranquil sleep. No nightmares. No dreams of any kind. I was at peace and fully rested. It was the first time in weeks that I woke up without fear or worry of any kind. The sound of my mother's angelic voice made the morning that much better. I loved being home.

"Darling, you have a package. I'm leaving it by your door."

A package? I wasn't expecting anything. Had Andre thought up some pre-holiday surprise I was unaware of? I got out of bed smiling and opened my door to find a small UPS box with my name on it. I took it over to my desk and opened it eagerly, expecting to find some cute little knickknack inside.

When I opened the package, I saw another, neatly wrapped box inside with a card. The penmanship on the envelope was unfamiliar so I knew right then that it wasn't Andre's doing. I opened it to discover a note addressed to me in a lovely cursive script.

Dearest Emma,

It seems we have yet to be formally acquainted, but all in due time, I suppose. It has come to my attention that you are to blame for the greatest loss of my existence. The only person I have ever loved has been taken from me and I have only you to hold responsible for her fate. I have waited a thousand years to be at Camilla's side and you, little girl, have ruined everything. Please know that I will find great pleasure in taking your loved ones from you, one by one, just as you have taken from me. I do hope you enjoy your gift. I assure you, there will be more to come.

Theron

"No," I breathed.

I set the note down and felt so naïve for thinking my life was finally getting back on track. I slowly opened the door to my bedroom and walked into the hallway, leaving the small box unopened on my desk. I couldn't unwrap it. If I looked inside, I knew everything would become all too real. I needed to check on my family to make sure they were all right first. I couldn't bear the thought of seeing them hurt.

My father was already at the office while my mother and Liam ate breakfast reading *The New York Times* and discussing foreign affairs. They arched their eyebrows simultaneously when they saw me enter the dining area.

"What's wrong?" Liam asked. "You look like you've seen a ghost."

"Nothing. Can I see the Style section?"

I had to stay calm and act normal if there was any chance they would let me see Andre without raising suspicion. Knowing it annoyed my mother to no end, I hid my phone under the table and covertly sent Andre a text message asking him to meet me for coffee down the street in an hour.

I brought the note with me as well as the unopened gift from Theron tucked away in my purse. He got there shortly after I did and looked at me warily. I couldn't hide my apprehension from him even if I tried.

"What happened?"

I handed him the letter and waited until he finished reading it, which took no longer than two grueling seconds. He crumpled it up into a tiny ball and stuffed it in his coat pocket.

"What gift?" he asked after a moment of silence.

"I don't know what it is. I wanted you here when I opened it."

I took out the little box and set it on the table between us. He immediately took it and removed the silver wrapping paper. When he saw what rested inside, he closed the box and eyed me pensively, unsure whether or not I could handle knowing its contents. "Well?"

"Oh, Emma," he sighed shaking his head with eyes cast down.

"Well?" I questioned a bit louder this time.

"I'm so sorry."

I couldn't take the suspense anymore. I grabbed the box and opened it myself. I suddenly felt a thick lump start to form in my throat and my eyes welled up with tears. *No!* This wasn't happening. Jaq's Fleur-de-Lis necklace; she wore it everywhere. Its chain was broken and there was dried blood on the pendant.

I last saw Jaq yesterday afternoon when my parents dropped her off at home. She was wearing it then. I didn't even think to call her and check in, assuming she would want to be left alone to spend time with her family. How could I have been so stupid? I should have known better. Andre took my hand and stoked my palm tenderly. I recoiled and held my hands together in my lap. I didn't want to be touched. I didn't deserve to be shown any sort of affection when this, as so many dreadful things were lately, was clearly my fault.

"Do you think? Is she?" I couldn't form the words but Andre knew what I was asking. He didn't answer for a while and when he finally spoke, he chose his words carefully and my worst fears were realized.

"I think she might be," he said sorrowfully.

"No!" I screamed and stormed out of the café. The people around us were probably looking at me like I'd lost my mind but their flabbergasted expressions didn't concern me in the least. Andre came after me and stopped me on the sidewalk. He restrained me with no effort at all and I was unable to break his hold on me. I was in hysterics. My best friend. My sister for all intents and purposes. She was gone. I didn't believe him; I couldn't. This was all some sick joke, some horrible nightmare I'd surely wake up from in a minute's time. But a minute turned into two and then three until I felt my legs give way and I passed out cold in Andre's arms.

Twelve

When I opened my eyes, I found myself in a strange room with a cool towel on my forehead. Andre was sitting on a chair beside the bed and stared at me miserably. We were in his apartment and I noticed it was much bigger than the one he rented in Rhode Island. We were on the top floor of colossal skyscraper. His bedroom was spacious with floor-to-ceiling windows and a glass door leading out to a snow-covered terrace. I put the damp compress on his nightstand and sat up on my elbows. I wondered if by some miracle, all that had happened this morning was a bad dream. Judging by the grim look on Andre's face, I knew that wasn't the case.

I slumped back down on the bed and threw the covers over my head, thinking about a myth I'd once read about ostriches burying their heads in the sand when frightened. If they could refuse to confront their problems, so could I.

After a few moments hiding under the soft sheets, I stuck my head out and saw Andre still looking at me with the same bleak expression. The bloodstained necklace was real and Jaq was in danger, if she was even alive. I couldn't think like that. If Theron wanted to play his nasty game, I'd play it better. I wondered if there was any leverage I had over him. Camilla was already dead and that left me with little to work with. I was at a loss.

"What are we going to do?" I asked drearily.

Andre moved to sit beside me on his bed, cradling my head in his lap and stroking my hair. I could tell he was deep in thought. It wasn't often that he found himself in a position where he didn't have the right answer. I knew seeing me like this bothered him to no end. Feeling helpless was a distinctively unfamiliar feeling to him. He didn't know how to make me feel better and the whole situation was clearly making him uneasy.

"I'll think of something," he assured me staring off into space. "I promise."

Andre's words were comforting even though I knew he didn't have a solid plan just yet. Somehow I had faith that we would find a way to rid ourselves of the monster that had been awakened. We had to. When Jaq's life was on the line, failure was not an option. I was not about to let another thousand-year-old vampire head case control my life and threaten the people I loved most. I let out a deep breath and prayed that Jaq's necklace was merely a warning and Theron had only intended to scare me. From everything I'd heard about him, though, he was rash and cruel, devoid of any humanity. The thought brought a cold shiver down my spine.

I turned onto my side and Andre covered me up to my shoulders with a heavy blanket. He lay down behind me and wrapped his arm over my waist, burrowing his head in my hair. All I wanted to do was go to sleep and shut the world out. It was too painful to stay awake. I had nothing more to offer. There was nothing to do but wait. I didn't know Theron's whereabouts and had no clue how to get in touch with him. I dreaded the possibility that my next package would contain something that confirmed my best friend was dead. At this rate, I was either going to pass out again or throw up. Neither option appealed to me in the slightest and I decided I had better get some rest if I was going to face Theron head on.

I remembered the very first time I met Jaq, when she spoke broken English and how all the stupid kids at Astor had made fun of her for her thick accent. I thought about our trip to Europe and about all those nights she spent consoling me as I cried for hours over things that all seemed so inconsequential now.

In high school, we believed every little crisis was the end of the world as we knew it. We must have shared a thousand pints of Ben & Jerry's ice cream and watched just as many romantic comedies since then. Jaq had always idolized Scarlett O'Hara and I could swear she had perfected her English by watching *Gone with the Wind* repeatedly.

I missed her so much that the idea of being run over by an eighteen-wheeler sounded more pleasant than a life without her in it. Who would I spill all my secrets to? Who would give me valuable advice on dating or reprimand me for accidentally pairing navy blue with black? Who in the world would be the maid of honor at my wedding if not for Jaq? My best friend was the voice of reason when I was too caught up in my own naïveté to think clearly. I wallowed in my grief, my eyelids growing heavy with each passing memory. I felt the wetness of my tears streaming down my face and saturating the pillow. The last words I heard were Andre's, whispering, "I love you more than you will ever know." And just like that, sleep took hold of me and I lost myself in the somber, murky abyss of my mind.

"Okay, what the hell is up with you, Em?" Liam demanded to know. "You've been totally out of it lately."

Oh, nothing. My best friend may or may not have been murdered by a fucking vampire. Would you mind passing the salt?

"Nothing. I'm fine. Tell me about Boston. How are you liking the new firm?"

"It's not bad, I guess. I work with a bunch of tools but that's to be expected. I mean, let's face it, there aren't many lawyers as badass as I am," he grinned. I had to give him that. I didn't know many lawyers but the one's I did know were way more uptight than my brother was.

"Any girls in your life, darling?" my mother chimed in as she filled her plate with some scrambled eggs. "All my girlfriends are already grandmothers, you know."

Liam let out an exaggerated sigh. "Oh, Mom. We both know you have no interest in being called Grandma any time soon."

"That's not true! I would absolutely love a little one around the house. It's been ages since I changed a diaper."

"In a few more years you can change Dad's," he smirked. "To answer your question, Ma, no. There aren't any girls in my life. I'm saving myself."

"For what?" I asked. "A sugar momma?"

"Exactly. Besides," he gave our mother a big smile from ear to ear. "You and I both know Emma's going to give you a kid way before I decide to settle down."

At the mention of me giving my mother a grandchild I started to choke on my fruit salad.

"You all right there, champ?"

"Fine. Can we talk about something else?"

I needed to steer us away from such a depressing topic of conversation. If there was one thing I learned from the movies, it was that vampire's couldn't bear children. If Andre and I had any kind of future together, it would have to be one without the pitter-patter of little feet running around the house.

"Of course, dear. You are way too young to be thinking about having kids right now anyway. How is Jaq? Is she having a nice time with her parents?" I felt my stomach churn at the mention of her name.

"Jaq's fine." *My word of the day.* "I haven't really spoken to her much since we got back. I wanted to give her some space. It's been a while since she's seen her family, you know?"

"That's very thoughtful of you. And Andre? What a charming young man. Even your father has taken a liking to him. And we all know that's saying a lot."

"Andre's fine—"

"If you say fine one more time I'm going to chuck my eggs at you," Liam sneered.

"Andre is *great*. Better?"

"Much. Is the *charming* young man planning on spending Christmas with us?"

"Mom? Would that be okay?" I asked uncertainly.

"Oh, that would be wonderful! Of course he can spend the holiday with us. I'll ask Rosa to set an extra plate," my mother beamed.

Just as I was finishing up the last bits of food on my plate, the doorbell rang. A few moments later, Rosa handed me another package. I couldn't believe I'd be getting another one so soon. Some part of me was relieved because maybe it would give me some information as to where Theron was or how I'd be able to get in touch with him. Another much larger part of me wanted to hurl. It was the moment of truth I had been waiting for.

I excused myself from the table and carried the box to my room. Tangibly, it was light, but the hefty load it brought on my heart augmented the physical weight of its contents. I couldn't decide whether to wait for Andre this time or to simply take a deep breath and open it alone. I chose the latter option and would just call Andre as soon as the deed was done. It wasn't like him being there would have changed anything.

I grabbed a razor and sliced the tape. There was another note written in the same handwriting as well as a carefully wrapped box, a bit larger than the last one. I inhaled sharply and told myself that no matter what happened, everything would be all right in the end.

Dearest Emma,

I sincerely hope your new necklace was to your liking. I hadn't had much time to shop but I assumed even a secondhand gift would suffice. After all, you don't seem like a pretentious sort of girl. This next offering is truly from the heart. We'll be seeing each other very soon. I promise. Send my regards to Andre. He and I have much to discuss.

Theron

P.S. Merry Christmas

I hated his cryptic little messages. There wasn't a single piece of helpful information in the entire letter. Hoping the contents of the larger box would give me some answers, I took another deep breath and forced myself to open it. When I saw what lay inside, it took all of my self-control to keep from shrieking at the top of my lungs. I shut the box instantly and called Andre. He barely understood what I was saying as the growing lump in my throat felt like a giant boulder. I just kept mumbling random words incoherently until he'd finally had enough and hung up the phone midsentence.

Less than ten minutes later, Andre was sitting on my bed next to me, holding me firmly in his arms. He knew instantaneously what the box contained. His acute vampire senses could smell the fresh blood inside without having to open it.

"Jaq's?" I garbled like I'd just downed an entire bottle of vodka.

He only nodded, knowing that saying the word would only make it worse for me. *This next offering is truly from the heart.* In a plastic Ziploc bag laid my best friend's no longer beating heart. My confirmation had arrived.

Christmas dinner was brutally long and tedious. My family attempted to bring me out of my miserable funk by showering me with a variety of gifts for the holiday. Liam surprised me with a brand new iPhone while my parents opted for some clothes and a handbag big enough to carry a few textbooks for the upcoming semester. I appreciated the effort but material goods were about the last thing on my mind. Andre showed up with two full shopping bags worth of presents for everyone.

He got my parents a pair of tickets to the latest Broadway play as well as another bottle of vintage cognac and a large box of Cuban cigars for my dad. My mother received a stunning chiffon wrap and Liam was given a variety of elegant silk ties to wear in the office. He even remembered to bring something for Rosa, who got a beautiful Swarovski necklace. Her plump cheeks got so red the moment he handed her the little box. After three admirable attempts at refusing his generosity, her resolve weakened and she finally accepted his offering.

For me, Andre custom-ordered an exquisite ring with a small tiger's eye gemstone mounted in a band of platinum. He had Blake charm it with a protection spell to shield me from any supernatural influence. Considering I was unable to be compelled for whatever reason, I didn't see the point in him going to all the trouble. Nevertheless, my concerned vampire boyfriend determined that he could never be too careful when my tenuous life was at stake.

It took me a full month to decide on the perfect gift for the man who had everything. I opted for a handmade Christmas card and two plane tickets to the Cotswolds. It was ultimately a present for us both, but also an incentive to make it out of this mess unscathed so we could have a peaceful week to ourselves in the English countryside. I made sure the dates were open so we had free rein to go whenever we got the chance. I had always been interested in seeing the rolling hills and magnificent little churches and thought, what could be better than to explore the quaint villages with the man I loved? Andre had once told me that vampires have been around since long before Jesus Christ, Moses, or any other religious prophet, so any sort of holy institutions were completely safe for him to enter.

I sat at the dining table picking at my food while the rest of my family and Andre were trying to make the best of the festive occasion. They discussed politics, business, even the latest celebrity gossip, as I willed myself to keep the tears at bay. The Avignon's called me numerous times asking if I had any idea where their daughter was and I played dumb, unable to be bearer of bad news.

As much as I resented Jaq's parents for their selfish tendencies, their only daughter had been murdered and it felt wrong of me to ruin their Christmas with the news of her passing. Until we successfully avenged her death, I thought it best to spare them by simply letting them believe she was just being a rebellious adolescent. I couldn't allow them to involve the cops, who would have undoubtedly forced me to sit inside a stuffy police station for hours, poking and prodding me with questions regarding her mysterious disappearance. The guilt I felt for Jaq's death was excruciatingly painful, but no good would come of hurting her already despondent family with an assortment of inconceivable notions that couldn't be proven.

"Emma?"

"Yes?" I answered weakly, blinking back the flood of tears that threatened to spill down my puffy face. I was starting to get used to the swollen features I'd donned as of late and wondered how in the world Andre still found me attractive when I looked liked like that.

"Hey. It's Tristen. Have you heard from Jaq? I've been calling her for days. She didn't even answer when I tried to wish her Merry Christmas yesterday. Do you know if she's mad at me or something?" he asked anxiously.

"Oh, Tristen."

I couldn't handle this conversation right now. It was selfish of me to want to tell him that Jaq was fine and that she wasn't mad at him or at anyone else for that matter. She wasn't anything anymore. But I owed it to him to be honest. If I couldn't tell her parents, I'd make sure the one other person she loved besides them and myself would know the truth. After all, Tristen had been brought into this chaotic disarray because of me.

"We need to talk," was all I could come up with. It was the only response I deemed appropriate given the tragic circumstances. Wasn't that what people said right before they shattered someone's hopes and dreams? And that was exactly what I was about to do.

"Okay," he said hesitantly. "I'm listening."

"Not over the phone." I couldn't bear telling him the news of Jaq's death without the common courtesy of doing it in person. It was the least I could do. "Please come to New York. I need to see you."

Tristen didn't feel the need to ask me why or what happened. From the tone of my voice alone, he knew what I had to say was urgent and no doubt serious. He agreed to hop in his car immediately and meet me at Andre's place as soon as traffic would allow. I had remarkably convinced my parents to let me stay at Andre's for the night and they were kind enough not to push for answers since they were all privy to the pained expression I wore as of late.

My face was blotchy and barely recognizable by the time Tristen arrived. It was already past ten and my body was slowly shutting down. I strained to stay awake and was extremely grateful to Andre for brewing a pot of robust coffee to help keep me up. He propped my feet up on his black ottoman and bundled me up in a thick blanket. The pungent aroma of coffee beans filled the entire living room, reminding me of my little dorm and all of the entertaining nights Jaq and I shared chitchatting about anything and everything with our respective mugs in hand.

"Are you okay?" Tristen sympathetically asked me as soon as he saw the atypically large bags under my eyes. "No offense, Em, but you look like shit."

"None taken. I feel like shit too."

"Care for some Columbian blend?" Andre offered his guest politely, ever the well-mannered host.

"Sure, thanks," he assented taking the steaming cup. "So what did you need to talk to me about? Where's Jaq?"

"I think you'd better take a seat, mate," Andre suggested.

"Okay," he sat down on the couch and looked at each of us in turn. "Well?"

"Remember how that night in the Old Stone Mill your dad said the reversal enchantment was successful?" I began.

"Yeah …"

"Theron. He's back. He … he …" I couldn't do it. The words just wouldn't come out no matter how many times I practiced saying them in my head. Andre put his hand on my shoulder supportively, letting me know he'd handle it.

"I'm so sorry, Tristen. Jaq is gone."

The perplexity on Tristen's face was palpable. He didn't seem to comprehend. That, or he simply didn't want to.

"What do you mean she's gone?"

"Theron got to her the night she arrived in New York. He killed her."

Talk about not beating around the bush, babe.

Tristen just sat there holding the coffee cup in his hands staring blankly ahead. Nothing was on television but he was engrossed in the black screen. We all sat in silence for what seemed like ages until Andre finally spoke up.

"Is there anything else I can get you? Some water?"

"Yeah. You can get me that son of a bitch's head on a platter. You think you can do that, vampire?"

"Stop it!" I exclaimed. "This isn't Andre's fault, Tristen. We're all upset here, okay? I'm not sure if you remember but *I* was the closest person to her. If anyone wants Theron's head on a platter, it's me."

263

"Sorry, Andre," he said. "I just need a minute to take it all in. It all seems so surreal, you know? I fucking loved that girl. She was the only one who really got me."

"We understand. Emma, how about we give Tristen some time alone?"

Andre picked me up and carried me into his bedroom, leaving Tristen to mourn his loss in as much privacy as an apartment could offer.

"He'll be all right," he assured me as he crawled into bed next to me. I rested my head on his chest, silently praying that it wasn't really Jaq's heart in the box. Maybe Theron had killed a bear or even some poor, defenseless deer instead. I'd never been one for animal cruelty, but it sure beat knowing my best friend had been murdered in cold blood. Sadly, deep down I knew that Andre's senses were unparalleled and if he said it belonged to her, I had no choice but to believe him, no matter how much I wished it weren't true.

"What are we going to do?" I asked for probably the umpteenth time, hoping he would miraculously have some viable answer. "Theron is blaming me for Camilla's death and I have a feeling Jaq was just a warm-up."

"He has his talisman back, making him exceedingly difficult to kill. I'll need to wear the amulet if we have any hope for a fair fight."

"It wouldn't be a fair fight, regardless," I countered. "Isn't he much stronger than you?"

"Yes. But that hasn't stopped me before," Andre said stroking my back soothingly. I thought back to how easily he had ripped Camilla's head off and felt slightly more relieved. "If we can get Tristen involved somehow. If he's willing to learn some magic, we may have a chance at reversing the spell and maybe, if it works, we could even get Caden back."

I hadn't told Andre about Caden's ungentlemanly attempt at getting to know me better. Possessive as he was, I figured it would only upset him and for the time being, I needed him focused and free of any unwarranted anger. If Andre were pissed off for the wrong reasons and at the wrong person, it would only hinder our plan. That is, if we ever managed to devise one in the first place. I intended on telling him when the time was right and I knew deep in my bones that it sure as hell wasn't right now.

It seemed so bizarre that the small amulet I kept in my jewelry box had Caden's soul trapped inside it. He was able to see and hear all that went on around him, but was helplessly confined. I knew what Caden felt for me and made sure I only wore it when Andre wasn't around. It would have been torturous to allow him to be a part of the intimate moments we shared with one another or hear the tender words we so commonly exchanged. If I were in his position, I would have expected the same courtesy and as flippant as he often acted, I knew in my heart that Caden would have been just as considerate had the tables been turned.

After about fifteen minutes, Andre and I went back into the living room to find Tristen sitting in the exact same position as before. He was still staring at the blank screen, though his coffee cup was now empty. We joined him on the plush sofa and I took his hand in mine sympathetically. I could feel my droopy eyelids fighting to stay open and forced my fatigued body to comply with the demands of my mind.

"Have you ever done any magic?" I asked him.

Tristen looked at me like I'd seriously lost my mind in the short while that we were gone.

"No," he muttered.

"Andre says it's in your blood."

"It's true," Andre concurred. "You're a Valgard, a mage by birth. Whether you've practiced magic or not, it's

266

within you. And I believe that with a bit of practice, you'll be able to harness your powers and avenge Jacqueline's death. That is, if you're up for it."

"If I'm up for avenging my girl's murder? I'd do anything to kill that bloodsucker. No offense," he swiftly added after I shot him another scolding look.

"None taken. Good. First off, we'll need the page with the reversal enchantment your father deciphered. I'll have Blake go through it as well as the rest of the spells I've copied from the grimoire and try to find something in it that can help us. Do you know where it is?"

"Actually, I brought it," he said unexpectedly as he took out the piece of vellum from his back pocket. "Emma sounded really off on the phone so I kind of took it from my dad's study without telling him. Just in case something really bad was happening. I guess I did the right thing."

"Yes, you did," Andre agreed, still utterly stunned at Tristen's contrivance. "Next, you'll need to do a bit of studying with Blake. Just saying the words won't work against a vampire. He's much too powerful for a simple incantation to be of any use. There's a certain panache that goes with proper magic. You'll need to feel the intent and channel it, but Blake will explain all that once he gets here."

"Okay, I'm down. What else?"

"Finally, we'll need to find Theron. I'll make some calls and see if I can find out if there were any sightings of newly turned vampires lurking the streets. Chances are if we can get to the baby vamps, Theron won't be too far behind."

"Got it. So when's this Blake guy coming? Wait, the guy from my parent's party? He's a mage too?"

Andre nodded in agreement as he put his arm over my shoulders and let me rest comfortably against him. I was getting more and more exhausted by the second and hoped this conversation would reach its end as quickly as possible. I was nearly at the end of my rope.

"Blake's a good man," he continued. "I've known him for a long time. I'll give him a call first thing in the morning. It may take a day or two for him to get out here but you two can start practicing straightaway once he's in the City. In the meantime, you and Emma look like you're about to pass out so how about you take the guestroom and we can talk more once you've had some sleep?"

"Sounds good, bro. Hey … Andre?" Tristen paused in the hall on his way to the extra bedroom.

"Yes?"

"Thanks."

Andre smiled and gave him a quick, understanding nod.

"Goodnight, Tristen."

"Night."

"Three! Two! One! Happy New Year!"

Andre pulled me in for a long, affectionate kiss and lifted me off the ground until I felt like I was floating on air in his strong arms. We clinked our crystal flutes filled with Perrier-Jouët and I was already experiencing a slight buzz from the bubbly champagne. A new year was upon us and I couldn't help but feel a twinge of disappointment that Jaq wasn't there to celebrate it with us. It was the first time in five years that we weren't together, counting down the final seconds until the ball dropped and confetti covered the streets of Times Square.

"She should have been here," I sighed.

"I know, baby. I know. Come, I have a surprise for you."

He took my hand and led me out the front door of the restaurant into the bitter chill of New York's infamous winter gloom. The only other person outside was the valet and I didn't understand what he was trying to show me. I looked at my positively beaming boyfriend bewilderedly as he took out a pair of keys from his pocket and handed them to me. *What the hell is he grinning about?* He looked like a cheerful schoolboy and I couldn't help but smile up at him.

"What are these for?" I asked, still confused as ever.

"Happy New Year," he whispered in my ear and then brushed his lips over mine.

"Happy New Year to you too. What's going on?"

Just as the words left my mouth, I saw the emblem on the car keys he gave me had matched the brand new black Porsche 911 Turbo parked right in front of us.

You have got *to be shitting me.*

"You got me a *Porsche?* Have you completely lost your mind?" I shouted loud enough for the valet to flinch at my blatant moment of hysteria.

"School's starting again soon and you don't have a car," he muttered as if my reaction wasn't at all what he'd expected.

"Andre, I can't accept this." I tried to give him back the keys but he quickly recoiled, unwilling to take them from me.

"You don't like it?"

He looked like I'd just thunder stormed on his parade. The exultant smile abruptly left his face and I saw that he was dumbstruck, undoubtedly wondering if he made the wrong choice.

"I don't think there's a single person on the planet who wouldn't like a Porsche. But it's too much! What am I supposed to tell my parents?"

"Just tell them that your remarkably generous and devoted boyfriend got you a car. Who the hell cares what make it is? I won't have you driving around in anything unsafe, Emma, and honestly, I think this car suits you."

I shook my head knowing that there was no way I was going to win this battle and shrugged my shoulders in defeat. I was now the proud owner of one of the most beautiful vehicles I had ever laid eyes on. Turning on the ignition, I glanced over at Andre in the passenger's seat and mirrored the childish grin he wore when he first handed me the keys to my outlandish present.

"So, you really like it?" he asked me with the eyes of an expectant twelve-year-old boy. "Because if you'd rather drive something else, I can always exchange it."

"I don't really like it."

"You don't?" The poor guy's face fell yet again.

"I *love* it," I chuckled as I grabbed him and brought his soft lips to mine.

"You know I'd do anything for you, right?"

"And I for you, my love. I'm speechless. No one has ever done anything like this for me. I don't deserve it."

"You deserve the world, Emma. And I'll make sure I do all that is in my power to make sure you get it."

"You know I've never asked you how you manage to afford all these things," I said as we pulled out into the street for a quick cruise around the block. "I know you've been around forever and all that but I've never seen you actually work. Are all vampires just wealthy by default?"

It always puzzled me how Andre was able to keep so many properties and buy such extravagant gifts without ever once having attended a single business meeting. For all I knew, he could have had countless offshore accounts and secret investments. We never really talked about his fortune or how he'd acquired it. It didn't really matter to me any which way, but I was curious nevertheless. It seemed rather strange that we had been through so much together and yet he never felt the need to mention his profession, if he even had one.

"I own Plasmacorp. It's the world's largest blood bank," he revealed. "We supply hospitals in the States and most of Europe and South America. It's a pretty lucrative business since both our species need blood to survive."

I remembered seeing Plasmacorp on the blood bags in Andre's cooler. He normally kept it under lock and key, but I'd sneak a peek inside whenever he got thirsty and opened it. So, the man who never worked was actually an entrepreneur who controlled an international conglomerate that dealt, quite fittingly, in the business of blood. I no longer felt so bad about accepting my over-the-top new gift.

"I had taken a leave of absence while procuring the grimoire for Camilla. I still get calls here and there when things get messy but my staff has done pretty well at taking care of the company while I've been away."

I was stunned. No wonder he and my father got on so well. They were both heads of major corporations and had much more in common than I initially thought possible.

"My primary focus these past few decades has been researching ways we can generate synthetic blood," he continued. "Not only would it save countless human lives, but also it would give vampires easier access to blood bags. We currently have only so many human donors and our resources are mediocre at best. I've heard so many people talk about what kind of footprint they want to leave on this planet when they're gone. It really made me sit down and think about my own mark on the world. It's always been my dream for blood to become universally available. And I decided long ago that when my time here is up, I'd like for that to be it."

As Andre spoke of his altruistic ambitions, I fell in love with him all over again. It was as though I were seeing him for the first time. Forget the bracelet or the car or the ring or any of our overpriced dinner dates. I'd always been surrounded by pretty little things and was lucky enough to want for nothing in my life, at least in the material sense. Listening to him go on about aspiring to help others and leave his mark on the world made me realize how much I truly respected him as a person. There was so much more to him than met the eye.

It was all I could do not to put the car in park and pounce on him right then. Andre was the most generous man I had ever met and his benevolent aspirations only cemented my adoration for him.

I am forever yours.

His words played over and over again in my head and I felt my resolve waver as I changed course and headed straight for his apartment to show him just how much he really meant to me.

Thirteen

Tristen and Blake were going at it for hours casting simple incantations like moving objects around Andre's coffee table and zapping crumpled pieces of paper until they went up in smoke. I had to admit it was fun to watch for the first hour or so, but after a while I became jaded. I knew deep down that everything they were doing was supposed to be leading up to a much more intricate sort of magic, but I nevertheless grew uninterested in their little study session.

They had been practicing for two weeks already and it felt like they weren't any closer to advancing to the next level. We were set to be starting the spring semester in just a few days time and I was getting a bit worried that such little progress had been made. Andre assured me that they were making headway and I had nothing to worry about. But it was easier said than done and since I hadn't had any other messages from Theron, it only made me feel tenser. We didn't know what kind of tricks the treacherous vampire had up his sleeve. Apprehension often clouded my thoughts and I needed to clear my head before the new semester started.

I said goodbye to the boys and hopped into my new ride, which I dotingly named Shadow. My family was as taken aback as I was when they first saw it sitting in one of our parking spaces. Liam immediately offered to swap cars with me since I always joked about commandeering his candy apple red Camaro when he least expected it. It was the ultimate muscle car and he cared for it as if it were his only child.

I explained to everyone that Andre's parents were very wealthy and left their fortune to him in their will. It was the only feasible justification I could think of for a twenty-ycar-old to be able to spend that much money on his girlfriend. Explaining to them that he controlled most of the world's blood supply didn't seem realistic. I made sure to mention that Shadow was solely registered on Andre's name and he could take her back whenever he wanted. That made them somewhat less uptight, but not by much.

Shadow was the first car I ever considered mine since I never really needed one living in the City. New York's venerable underground subway system as well as its countless yellow taxicabs had always been sufficient forms of transportation to get me wherever I needed to go. As I sluggishly crossed over Broadway on my way back home, I laughed at the memory of Jaq's first attempt at taking the train.

We purchased her very first MetroCard together on the day we met and I showed her what buttons to press on the vending machine so she would be able to do it by herself in the future. The simplified map I drew her of all the important station stops popped into my head and the concerned look on her face was priceless. For most people, the subway grid seemed daunting at first glance. It was only until they actually took a leap of faith and gave it a go that they understood how uncomplicated it really was. I supposed that if over ten million commuters managed to use New York's transit system on a daily basis, my foreign friend had no excuse but to figure it out.

I hated driving in Manhattan because the ride was always tediously slow and unnerving. The cabbies were intimidating, maneuvering around the narrow streets like they were in competition with one another to see who could get from Point A to Point B faster. They swerved and cut people off like it was some special skill to be mastered and the one-ways on every other block were unbelievably irritating. By the time I made it home, I felt like I'd been on the road forever and wanted nothing more than to slip into a pair of sweats and unwind. Rosa informed me that I received no new packages and I was relieved to know that there weren't any more body parts to discover, at least in the immediate future.

Liam went back to Boston about a week ago and the apartment felt emptier without his witty sarcasm. I asked him to text me every day to let me know how he was doing and he made good on his promise. My brother never was the sentimental type but he kept me in the loop of how boring the new firm was and how much he wished the female lawyers in his office paid more attention to how they dressed.

"I don't think a low-cut blouse ever hurt anyone," he messaged me a few days ago, making me giggle shamelessly. The only thing Liam was currently saving himself for was a hot piece of ass.

Just as I put on my Newport University t-shirt and matching sweatpants, a knock came at the front door. Lately I had been getting nervous any time we had guests, whether they were expected or not. I tried to shrug off my uneasiness and convinced myself it was probably nothing. As I flipped through the myriad of channels for something mind-numbing to entertain myself with for the next few hours, I heard another knock coming from right outside my bedroom. When I opened the door, two police officers were patiently waiting for me in the hallway.

"Good afternoon, Miss Dresden. I hope we aren't disturbing you. My name is Officer Carroll and this is my partner, Officer Romero. We'd like to ask you a few questions regarding the recent disappearance of your friend, Jacqueline Avignon."

My stomach was churning as I tried to remember everything Andre and I had practiced. We knew this day would come sooner or later and he coached me on the right answers to their typical line of questioning.

"Sure," I consented; silently praying they wouldn't sense the tension radiating throughout my entire body. "Would either of you like a cup of coffee or some water?"

"No, thank you, ma'am," the tall, dark and handsome African-American policeman declined politely. "Can we talk in the living room?"

"Of course. Right this way."

They sat across from me on my parent's teal velvet sectional and crossed their legs in unison. They seemed to mirror each other's movements in a way only genuine friends could. They must have been partners for a long time judging by how comfortable they were with one another.

Seeing them like that reminded me of how things used to be with Jaq and it only made me feel more on edge.

"This is just standard procedure, ma'am. We're questioning anyone who might have any useful information regarding Miss Avignon's whereabouts. When was the last time you saw her?" Officer Carroll asked as if he were reading lines off of a script.

He appeared to be in his late forties and must have done this too many times to count. The monotony of it all had them both visibly unfazed. I sort of expected them to be more pushy and cynical but instead they just seemed bored. We could have been discussing the weather by the looks on their faces and I had to admit their nonchalance made what I was about to say much easier.

"My parents and I dropped her off at home as soon as they picked us up from LaGuardia," I began as they each started jotting some notes down on pads of paper. "We're on winter break right now and I wanted to give her some time with her family. She barely ever gets to see them anymore since we started college."

"And at what point did you realize Miss Avignon had gone missing?" the baby-faced Latino man asked me matter-of-factly.

"I honestly thought she was just taking a break from everything and hanging out with her mom, going shopping and stuff. It wasn't until Mrs. Avignon called me asking me where she was that it even occurred to me that Jaq could be in trouble."

"And you told Mrs. Avignon she was probably with her boyfriend ... Tristen, correct?"

"That seemed like the only logical explanation at the time. It isn't like Jaq to run off without telling anyone. If anything, she would have told me where she was going. She always told me everything."

"So I take it you two were close?"

"Jaq's my best friend, Officer. She's the sister I never had."

There wasn't a hint of faking in my voice. Jaq really was family to me. The sincerity in my eyes alone spoke volumes. I would have deemed them completely incompetent had they thought I was lying right then. My faith in the NYPD was restored when I saw they believed me. "I've been worried sick these past few weeks," I professed. "Tristen hasn't seen her since school ended and we're both at a loss. It's like she just vanished into thin air."

"I see. Now, is it true that Tristen is presently in the City?"

Fuck.

"Yes, sir. We've kind of been doing our own little investigation to see what might have happened to her. Not that we don't think you're capable, of course," I quickly added. Both of their lips perked up into matching smirks at my admission and I sat there wondering what was so funny.

"So you two makeshift police officers find anything useful?" Officer Romero asked me with a slight chuckle. *Goddamn cops.* I strained to keep my hand from smacking the insolent grin off his face and positioned it firmly on my lap.

"Not as of yet," I admitted with a set of downcast eyes. "We've looked everywhere and no one's seen her. How about you? Do you guys know where she might be?"

"Not yet, but we will. Listen, I want you to leave the police work to us pros. As soon as we got something, we'll let her family know. Until then, sit tight, kid. If you hear of anything at all you think we should know, call," Officer Carroll said placing his card on the coffee table between us.

"I will."

They each gave me a curt nod and left, probably off to consume the nearest donut shop in its entirety. I didn't normally have such animosity toward law enforcement but the way they spoke to me like I was some naïve little girl playing cops and robbers made me want to chuck French crullers at their thick skulls.

I shut the door and let out a long sigh of relief. Now that my unsolicited visitors were gone, I could finally relax and watch some bland, meaningless television. For the first time in far too long I was able to zone out completely. I didn't have to focus on anything at all for the next few hours and, honestly, the idea of rotting my overworked brain felt priceless.

The drive back to Newport took less than three hours thanks to a combination of Andre's expertise behind the wheel and Shadow's supreme turbocharged engine. It was silly of me to make him put on his seatbelt since the man was virtually indestructible in your run-of-the-mill car accident. As soon as the words left my mouth, I realized I was just as overprotective as he was. *Better safe than sorry, babe.* He raised his eyebrows at me perplexedly but thought it best not to argue. We listened to a few of the playlists I had compiled for the trip and it was actually kind of nice being able to look out the window and not have anything to do but admire the scenery for a change.

When I saw the familiar colonials and beautiful waterfront properties come into view, I considered my return to Rhode Island bittersweet. I knew the moment I stepped foot into the little dorm room Jaq and I had once shared would be hard to stomach. The new semester was beginning on Monday and I still needed to go out and buy all of the assigned textbooks and school supplies for my upcoming classes. Now that I had Shadow though, it would be easier for me to get around town and I thanked Andre profusely for making my tragically problematic life just a little bit easier.

I opened the door to my room and as expected, my heart sank. Everything was just as we had left it. The beds were neatly made and untouched. All of Jaq's endearingly risqué clothes still hung on the rack in her tiny wooden closet waiting to be worn. But it was only when I saw the haunting photograph on her nightstand of us in Provence sitting in a field of lavender that I really lost it.

My knees gave out from beneath me as I fell to the floor with my head in my hands. The torrent of warm, salty tears I had so resolutely barricaded inside me for so long were set free and I started weeping uncontrollably. Andre let me have my moment of grief without attempting to console me knowing it would've been to no avail. I was in desperate need of mourning and I hadn't allowed myself to fully let go in weeks.

After a good twenty minutes on the rug, he forced me up and placed me on my bed. He lay down beside me and said nothing for a while. I knew that even if he spoke, his words would be incomprehensible in my current state. We spent the next hour in each others arms as Jaq's passing really hit home for the first time. Seeing the images of her face all around me made me ill. There wasn't a single thing I could do to bring her back and my total lack of control only made the pain worse. I held onto Andre so tightly I thought I'd break him in two and he just lay there feeling as helpless as I was.

"I want you to move in with me," he whispered suddenly into my ear.

I looked up at him speechless. Was he only offering because he saw how distraught I was? If that were the case, living with him would have been for all the wrong reasons.

"Why?" I mumbled suspiciously.

"Because I love you. Because it's what I want. And I don't think this place is good for you right now."

So he had meant it to be a temporary fix. No, I couldn't allow myself to live inside Andre's apartment out of mere sympathy. It wouldn't feel right.

"You don't have to foster me like a stray," I told him. "I'll be fine."

I could hear the sadness in my own voice and prayed he didn't pick up on the fact that this time it had nothing to do with Jaq. Under normal circumstances, I would have loved to move in with him. Living together was taking the next step forward in our relationship and I wanted it badly. But not like this. Not because he pitied me. I couldn't live with myself if I took advantage of his generosity like that. He only felt sorry for me and using him for my own selfish and emotionally fueled gains was totally unacceptable.

"Like a stray?" he asked me stunned. "If you think I'm only asking you out of pity, you couldn't be more wrong. I've wanted to ask you for months now but I didn't want to take you away from Jacqueline so I held off. But seeing you here like this. I can't handle it. I want you with me, Emma. Forever. Please say yes."

Andre had wanted to ask me to move in with him for months? I pressed my blotchy, tear-stained face against his chest unable to look at him directly. He cupped my chin with his long pale fingers and raised my head to face him. There was nowhere left to look but into his incredibly dark, penetrating eyes.

I felt the energy inside the little room fill with devotion and unequivocal loyalty and I knew then that Andre loved me wholeheartedly. He wanted to spend the rest of his existence with me at his side. It didn't fully register how a man so incomparably breathtaking could ever feel that way toward someone like me. I felt unworthy. But if he really meant what he said, I'd be a fool to refuse him.

"Yes."

Without waiting for another word in the hopes that I wouldn't change my mind, he pulled me in closer and kissed me passionately. For that brief moment, every one of my doubts slipped away and in my mind, we were the only two people left in the whole world.

We were practically out the door on the way to Andre's apartment, which was now technically ours, when Oscar, the dormitory security guard, stopped us. He had thinning black hair and the biggest beer belly I'd ever seen.

"Hey, Emma. You got some mail while you were away," the pleasantly plump man said kindly, holding out my bundle of letters and magazines. I thanked Oscar as Andre and I hauled my belongings outside. I immediately recognized that one of the envelopes had been penned in Theron's usual cursive penmanship. Apparently, I was downright incapable of having even one amazing afternoon without at least some bit of drama thrown into the mix.

I decided it best to wait until we got home before I opened the letter. *At least I know it's not a bloody organ this time.* We took a seat on the sofa and I hesitantly unsealed the envelope hoping the note inside held even a fragment of practical information leading to Theron's whereabouts. His customary enigmatic messages were really starting to irk me. Andre handed me a glass of ice-cold water and watched me as I removed the piece of elegant stationary and read the words aloud.

Dearest Emma,

I have faith that the start of the New Year will truly be one to remember for us both. I am sure you must be quite curious as to how I have spent these last several weeks, so I thought it would only be polite to update you on my recent activities. In short, I have brushed up on some current jargon, given how much has changed in the last millennia. I must admit I never was keen on being confined for so long, but the crude way in which this generation speaks is reason enough to go back. I tease, of course. I have recently discovered the term "chivalry is dead" and would certainly add "eloquence" to that idiom as well.

What else? I have already made quite a number of acquaintances, the charming French damsel having been one of them. That Jacqueline was such a saucy little minx. Shame that she couldn't stay for the last act. Which reminds me, did you like your Christmas present? Oh, how I love surprises. I so wish I could have been there to see your face when you unwrapped it.

As for my new face, I must admit it has taken a bit of getting used to. Albeit my original form was much different from this Caden fellow's, it has come to my attention that he is considered very attractive to many of the female conquests I have lately encountered. Needless to say, this vessel has served to make my dinner arrangements advantageously effortless.

I do not intend to take up too much of your precious time, transitory as it is. I only wish to inform you that we will be seeing one another very soon. I apologize that I do not have another gift to bestow upon you as you read this letter. *Though I presume your gallant lover has more than compensated for my frugality. Farewell, sweet girl.*

XOXO,

Theron

I folded the note and placed it neatly back into the envelope, unable to articulate the raging mix of fear and exasperation I felt. *We will be seeing one another very soon.* What the hell did that mean? I was given no location, no time, nothing. It was yet another one of Theron's obscure missives entirely deprived of value. Andre's eyes had become scarlet about halfway through the message and there was a mien of unreserved menace on his face. If I hadn't known him, I probably would have scampered out of the room like a frightened child.

"How dare he?" Andre roared. "Who the fuck does he think he is? Just wait until I get my hands around his throat. I'll twist his fucking head off slowly. I want to savor every agonizing moment."

"Stop," I insisted as evenly as my trembling voice would allow. "We expected this. Nothing's changed, okay? We'll have our retribution. Just, please … calm down."

"I'm sorry."

His eyes quickly reverted back to their usual dark brown and he seemed to have regained some control over his merciless anger. Andre pulled me onto his lap and with those same eyes that were tinged with crimson only moments before gazed profoundly into mine.

"I will never let any harm come to you," he vowed. "Do you understand?"

"I understand."

"Where is the amulet?"

I had it safely tucked away in one of my suitcases and walked across the hall to fetch it for him. He ripped off the silver chain as if it were made of thread and went into his bedroom. When he returned, the pendant was on another, much longer chain, hanging around his neck. Knowing that Caden could now see and hear all that went on between us made me uncomfortable and I decided it was time to come clean. No matter how livid I knew Andre would get, I needed to fess up and disclose the details of our time together.

"I need to tell you something," I began, playing out each prospective scenario in my head and choosing my words carefully.

"About?"

"Caden."

Andre didn't seem to know how to react to my clearly unforeseen response. He shifted in his seat and I could already sense the early stages of both confusion and apprehension settling on his face. I almost changed course in an attempt to spare us from the tantrum he was sure to throw, but I had to tell him. I was left with no other choice. We were now living together and I wasn't about to let us go backwards by concealing the truth from someone who had gone to such great lengths to be honest with me. I decided there would be no secrets between us and somehow, found the courage to say what had been held back for too long.

"The day you left to give Camilla the grimoire," I continued. "Caden stopped me on my way back home from Tristen's house."

Uh-oh.

"Go on."

"He … he bit me."

"What?"

My initial presumption had been dead-on. Andre's eyes instantly mimicked the bright red of Liam's treasured Camaro and I could feel the bitterness clouding the air in my new home. He was seething.

"I woke up in his bed. He wasn't in it, of course," I quickly added. No sense in adding more fuel to the burning fire. "Caden only took me so we'd have a chance to get to know each other. He didn't harm me in any way. I promise. If he had, I would have told you; you know that. But he thought there'd be no way I would come with him willingly so he took matters into his own hands."

"What else?"

"Nothing, really. We had dinner. We talked for a while until I got mad and offended him by accusing him of stealing my phone in case you tried to reach me. Then I went back upstairs and when I woke up the next morning, I was back in my dorm."

"And that's all that happened?"

No, babe. We had a hardcore make out session and I tackled him like the fiery vixen that I am.

I was visibly hurt that he had assumed the worst of me. I would never have cheated on him and he should have known that by now.

"I didn't kiss him nor did I flirt with him nor have I ever given you any reason to doubt my commitment to you and only you."

"I never doubted you, Emma," he admitted stroking my hair. "It's him I don't trust."

"Aside from abducting me for a few hours, he was the perfect gentleman, hard as that is for you to believe."

293

"You sound like you're defending that asshole!" he exclaimed, immediately pulling his hand back and placing it upon his lap indignantly.

"Listen, maybe his tactics were a little unorthodox." *Okay,* very *unorthodox.* "But he didn't hurt me and I'm not sure if you remember, being passed out and all, but Caden saved your life. I don't know what I would have done if I'd lost you."

"What else happened?"

"I met him at The Annex later and he apologized for being so inappropriate. The only other time I saw him was when he found out you were in trouble and he picked me up so we could go save your ungrateful ass."

"I see."

I hated when Andre wore that broodingly pensive expression. It was very unbecoming on him. I took the little amulet hanging around his neck and put it underneath his white t-shirt. Knowing Caden had listened to all that we just said was unsettling. If I didn't see the necklace, it was easier for me to pretend it wasn't there.

"Say something," I begged.

The maddening silence was more than I could stand. I knew in my heart that I did the right thing. Hadn't I? I told Andre the truth and as far as I was concerned, given him no reason to be cross with me. Yet why did I still feel so dirty?

"Thank you for being honest with me, sweetheart. I know it wasn't easy."

He put his hand over his chest where the amulet lay hidden, glaring at the massive black screen of the television just as Tristen had done when we first told him of his girlfriend's death. I couldn't tell what Andre was thinking but felt the haze of resentment in the room gradually lessen when I lightly brushed his cheek with my lips. He turned his head just enough to pull me into a much more fervent kiss than I had anticipated.

It felt like he was proving to himself that what we had was real. I caressed his mouth eagerly, answering some unspoken question. I was his completely and I guessed that he needed the reminder now more than ever. There wasn't a single person, human or vampire, who could've changed how deeply I cherished him, how much I needed him, how intensely I desired him. And for what I thought was the first time since we met, Andre came to believe that as well.

"Let's get that facetious son of a bitch back, shall we?" he grinned. "He and I have quite a score to settle."

Fourteen

"Brilliant!" I heard Blake roar from the other side of the room, rousing me from the monotony of my reading assignment.

In the past two weeks, Andre and I had managed to repaint every lackluster wall and add a bit of feminine flair to the home we currently shared. Now that I spent more time with him, I realized he did indeed have a profession that didn't just involve doing his maker's dirty work. In fact, he was on the phone about as often as my workaholic father, discussing a heap of issues that the manager's of his various blood banks needed his guidance on. While I wrote my long, tedious essays and studied the gruesome history of King Henry VIII, Andre impressively played the role of doting boyfriend slash CEO.

"What is it?" I asked the boys drearily.

I must have read the same passage in my textbook three times and still couldn't remember a damn thing. A powernap was long overdue.

"The Viking has finally figured it out, that's what! I really hope I'm not about to jinx us, but I think he's finally bloody got it!"

I looked over at Andre with a raised eyebrow and the corners of his mouth turned up into the sweet, boyish smile I couldn't seem to get enough of. He startled us all when he let out an uncharacteristically hearty laugh, which reverberated throughout the entire apartment. I had no idea what was so amusing but none of us could help joining him in a fit of unabashed laughter. I walked over to the boys and sat on Andre's lap. I'd gotten my second wind by now and was interested to know what it was exactly that Tristen finally got.

"Tristen has learned to harness his magic," Andre informed me.

"And it took much less time than I'd expected from someone so inexperienced," the chubby mage added proudly. "The kid's got skills!"

I could see Tristen's cheeks beginning to blush self-consciously. "Come on, you guys, stop," he pleaded as if suddenly embarrassed by the amount of praise coming from his new friends. "It took too damn long, if you ask me. I'm just glad I can finally say I'm good at something that doesn't involve a football. Hey, maybe I'll show my dad some tricks. He might be proud of me."

"You can absolutely show your old man, chap. But not until after this Theron mess is sorted," Blake insisted. "We can't afford any potential fuck-ups and *nobody* can know how much I've taught you. If that bloke ever finds out just how valuable you really are he'll kill you in a heartbeat. And we've already seen how bloody impulsive he is. Can't risk it."

"I understand," he sighed.

"So what's the plan exactly?" I asked.

"The plan is really quite simple, lo—Emma," Blake quickly corrected himself. It was evident that any terms of endearment used to address me were only permissible if they came solely from the overly possessive vampire I was seated upon. "We lure Theron back into his favorite tower and Andre's going to—"

"It's nothing you should be concerning your pretty little head with, sweetheart," Andre interrupted. "You've got enough going on with your studies as it is."

"But—"

"But nothing. Now, how about we let these two get some rest? They've been at these spells all night. I'm sure you guys could use a breather, catch up on some sleep?"

I could tell Andre wanted a break as much as they did. They all nodded in agreement as Tristen stood up to grab his coat. I gave him a peck on the cheek and he went out the door back to the massive plantation house he called home. Blake got up as well and bid us all goodnight as he strolled off into the guestroom he'd been occupying for the past couple of weeks.

Having him stay with us wasn't as bad as I initially thought it would be. I liked Blake a lot, but I had to admit that entertaining a houseguest while Andre and I were still settling in as domestic partners was slightly awkward. He offered to get a room at the Newport Inn, the little bed and breakfast he stayed in when he first got to Rhode Island, but Andre insisted that it would be advantageous to have him close by should something go wrong. Blake certainly didn't have the expert hearing of a vampire, but the two-bedroom apartment wasn't huge and the walls were paper thin, consequently making our recent late-night escapades much more subdued than I would have preferred.

Once we were finally alone, Andre picked me up and swiftly carried me off into our newly revamped master bedroom. He hung my old paintings alongside his own and slowly but surely, our place was starting to come together. I still had a bit of reading to do for class tomorrow but turned a blind eye to my boring homework assignment as soon as he removed his shirt and I caught a glimpse of that mind-blowing six-pack that was both familiar and yet remarkably impressive no matter how many times I'd seen and felt it underneath my fingertips.

"I'm excited to see your cottage," I said dreamily as I ran my fingers up and down his happy trail.

"Our cottage," he corrected me. "When I asked you to move in with me, it wasn't just for us to live in Rhode Island together. What's mine is now yours. All of it."

"So you're telling me I have a house in *Spain* too?" I giggled. I couldn't understand how I managed to find a man who was both gorgeous and so incredibly generous. I looked up at him with the biggest grin on my face and stuck out my tongue playfully.

"We do, yes." Andre acknowledged and quickly caught my tongue in his mouth before I had time to retract it. He kissed me sweetly and pulled the warm, heavy blanket over my shoulders. "And I promise you we'll explore the world together in due time. Now get some sleep, beautiful. You have school in the morning."

"Goodnight," I whispered into his chest as visions of majestic basilicas, extravagant Moorish architecture, and sprightly gypsies dancing flamenco cascaded through my mind.

Waking up in Andre's arms every morning made it especially difficult to get to class on time. If it wasn't for Shadow's speed and Andre's insistence to take me there himself, I surely would have been expelled by now for tardiness alone. Newport's attendance policy was far too strict for my liking and I was rather jealous when hearing that some of my friends in other colleges barely went to their lectures at all.

I sauntered into *History of the British Empire* with absolutely no desire to hear stories about life across the pond. I honestly couldn't have cared less about imperial conquests and rebellions. What used to be such enthralling subjects to me became nothing more than wretched tales of bloodshed and destruction. There was enough chaos in my own life and experiencing it all firsthand was more than sufficient. Having to listen to my instructors recount other people's troubles was getting to be excessive for a girl my age. The only place that seemed remotely inviting lately had been my bed and it took quite a bit of willpower for me to open up my notebook and focus.

Professor Knightley was an animated old man with little round spectacles and an assortment of three-piece suits. He dressed as if he belonged in another era and spoke with such joie de vivre that it was hard not to get caught up in his manic enthusiasm. As much as I dreaded the initial process of dragging myself to his course, or any of the one's I had chosen this semester, once I was there, it wasn't so bad. Knightley's slideshows were often accompanied by bustling hand gestures and dramatic monologues. His lively recounts of the bubonic plague made it seem as though the epidemic could return to our doorsteps at any moment.

The hours flew by quickly and before I knew it, the day's lesson was finished. I grabbed my things and headed home, wondering if by chance my bed was still as warm as I had left it. Andre was on the phone with the manager of one of his blood banks in Berlin, ardently discussing the importance of social responsibility as well as some recent changes in supply and demand. He kissed my forehead mid-conversation and continued on about how imperative it was for Plasmacorp to secure more donors.

"Of course they have to be willing, Günther! Have you completely lost it?" Andre yelled at the German man on the other end of the call. "I won't have my entire enterprise defamed over your nonsensical philosophies. Do you understand? Good. Because if I hear a single word about *anyone* compelling humans to up the numbers, your position won't be the only thing I'll take from you. I'm glad. Not only would it go against my very principles, but don't forget the potential PR nightmare on our hands. Not to mention the repercussions we'd have to face from the sovereigns. Brilliant."

Andre curtly hung up without saying goodbye and went straight from unyielding businessman to adoring boyfriend. The former was kind of sexy and I secretly hoped he would retain that assertiveness for a few more moments, at least while I steered him toward our bedroom. Just as I was about to pull him into the other room, I recalled him mentioning sovereigns and started to wonder what he meant by that. Did vampires have a monarchy? I always pictured them as lone wolves. The idea that they might have an organized government was fascinating.

"Sovereigns?" I asked curiously.

"Sovereigns," Andre repeated with a knowing grin. He was fully aware of how much I loved listening to him tell me about vampire culture. His stories were far more entertaining than the one's I heard in class on daily basis.

"Thirteen vampyr elders," he continued. "Led by one, for all intents and purposes, queen. Sekhmet. The other twelve are like a modern-day parliament. They vote on any critical matters and only Sekhmet has the authority to overrule their verdicts."

I vaguely remembered reading about an ancient Egyptian goddess named Sekhmet in one of my textbooks back when I studied at Astor but couldn't pinpoint exactly who she was or what she did. It was hard to believe it could have been the same woman, but then again, there were very few things Andre told me about his kind's supernatural history that weren't totally bizarre and unusual as it were.

"So what do these sovereigns do exactly?"

"I try not involve myself in politics, sweetheart. Climbing the ranks of an authoritarian government never ends well for anyone, at least in my experience. I suppose they keep the peace for us. The elders make sure our kind remains out of sight and out of mind to the humans and they destroy anyone who refuses to comply with their harsh ideals. If any vampire steps out of bounds and reveals our kind to the human race, they deal with them accordingly. The elders also have a rather large stake in most successful vampire-owned establishments, including Plasmacorp."

"What kind of stake?"

"They collect ten percent of Plasmacorp's earnings once per quarter. It's a small price to pay, truth be told.

You can compare it to paying taxes to the federal government. Except if I don't pay, let's just say I won't be thrown in jail."

Andre's smile didn't reach his eyes. I could tell the elders intimidated him and if he of all people feared them, I knew they were not to be messed with. From what he had mentioned, as long as the vampyr elders got what they wanted, they didn't interfere with his business or his life, so I decided to change the subject to something a bit less serious.

He led me into the galley-style kitchen with its cherry wooden cabinets, cream-colored marble countertops and stainless steel appliances. The room's rustic elegance brought a soothingly warm atmosphere to the space. I sat down on one of the four bar stools while Andre pressed a turkey and provolone cheese panini on the George Foreman grill, one of the many housewarming gifts we had received from my family once I informed them that we decided to move in together. It was amusing to consider that a vampire was making me lunch and I did my best not to giggle at the thought. He took out a blood bag from the cooler by the fridge and poured his liquid lunch into the ceramic coffee mug I bought him from The Annex.

"What have you been up to all day?" I asked him while devouring my tasty sandwich.

"Just business as usual. Nothing too exciting. My German division needed a bit of straightening out but that's neither here nor there. How about you? How was class?"

"Same old. I have to study for a test on Thursday, but other than that, nothing new. Why wouldn't you tell me the plan last night? I think I have a right to know what you guys are up to."

"I'm sorry, honey. I just didn't want to burden you with all the tedious details when you already have so much going on. But you're right. You do have a right to know. How was your lunch?" Andre asked grinning.

I looked down and noticed that my panini was virtually nonexistent. I wolfed it down in no time at all and hadn't even realized I was finished with it.

"Delicious, thank you," I answered whilst playfully narrowing my eyes at him.

Satisfied, he continued disclosing the particulars of their plot to bring down the madman. "Instead of waiting for Theron to surprise us," he began. "We're going to track him down ourselves. According to my sources, he's already been in Rhode Island for a few days now. He still has the mentality of a teenager so that should work to our advantage. He's strong, I'll give him that, but his reckless behavior will no doubt be his downfall."

"How do you plan on getting him into the tower?"

"That part is going to be tricky. He already suspects I'm plotting to kill him so he won't come willingly. What he doesn't know is that we have Tristen on our side. In these past few weeks Tristen's learned to harness his magic and with his help, we'll be able to cast the same spell his father used on Caden, but with a few minor tweaks here and there. Instead of transferring Theron's soul into another vessel, we're going to make a switch. Blake's figured out how to do it thanks to Alexander's grimoire."

"So basically, Caden and Theron's souls will switch places? Like one goes into the amulet and the other gets his body back?"

"Right."

"But how do you know that Theron won't find me first?"

"He's already in town so whatever he has planned will happen very soon. Theron isn't the type to take his sweet time and we're going to use that weakness against him. As much as I detest the idea, we'll need to use you as bait, sweetheart. You are the one he's currently after and he'll stop at nothing to get you alone. Because he isn't aware of what Tristen is capable of and knows how much the other Valgard's hate vampires, he won't expect any of them to help us. He also knows that I'd never stoop as low as Camilla by kidnapping or threatening an innocent boy so neither Tristen nor his father would have any reason to get involved."

"So what do you need me to do?"

"When the time is right, you'll take a few of your textbooks and drive over there as though you're working on an assignment for school. You'll sit inside the tower and jot down some notes until he arrives. Tristen, Blake and I won't be far behind and as soon as you get there, you'll call me and speak to me like you're terribly bored and tell me how badly you want to get the paper over with. He doesn't seem like the keenest of vampires and those many years of captivity couldn't have made his wits any sharper.

"One thing that worries me is that he won't be alone. I've gotten word of at least six new vampires he's sired and they'll certainly be with him for protection. His little army could work to our advantage though because he undoubtedly underestimates my strength. I'll finish them off first and in the meantime, Blake will stun Theron with an immobilization spell. He should be out cold for as long as Blake has his hold on him and that should give Tristen enough time to recite the appropriate verses in order to make the switch."

"It all seems so easy," I uttered. Could it all really go as smoothly as Andre made it sound? As much as I had faith in my boyfriend and our magic-wielding friends, I was still skeptical.

"It's not easy, sweetheart. Not by any means. We're relying on my ability to read him from all that Camilla's told me through the years and with that, I've tried to predict his sequential moves accordingly. It's all just one strategic game of chess; a shot in the dark, really."

"How good are you at chess?"

The corners of his mouth perked up into a slight grin. "Good enough."

I sat at the dining room table wearing an extra large red and white Newport t-shirt, clicking my phone on and off repeatedly. I hadn't heard from Liam in six whole days and couldn't shake the troubled feeling that something awful might have happened to him. Andre was off running some errands while I stayed at home to play worrywart. I hadn't told him that my brother might be missing because for one, my fears could've quite probably been invented, and for two, there wasn't much either of us could have done if I were right. But it wasn't like Liam to shut his phone off. He always texted me back within the hour with some clever remark and I had already sent over twenty messages without a single response. I poured myself a tall glass of whiskey and attempted to drown my sorrows in Andre's stash of Johnnie Walker that he kept for social gatherings with us mortals.

By the time I downed all that was left in the half-filled bottle, Andre strolled through the door with a bunch of grocery bags in each hand. He started putting the Greek yogurts and cold cuts into the refrigerator when I joined him in the kitchen. I knew he smelled the alcohol on me before I ever made it to the barstool. Sometimes I really hated those damn vampire senses.

"Are we on holiday, Miss Dresden?" he smiled and brushed his mouth against mine, seductively licking my lower lip. As soon as he noticed the grave look on my face, his expression mirrored my own. "Emma? What's wrong?"

"I haven't heard from my brother. I'm worried that Theron's got him."

"When was the last time you spoke with him?"

"We talked on the phone about a week ago. But Liam always responds whenever I call or text. He's never just vanished into thin air before. I'm really worried, babe."

"Can you think of anything he may have said that could be important? Any new friends he might have met?"

"He mentioned some redhead he met at a bar by his office. He just went on and on about her bubble butt and big boobs. You know, typical Liam. They've supposedly been seeing each other for a couple weeks." I rested my elbows on top of the counter and buried my face in my hands. "Do you think this girl has something to do with his disappearance?"

"I can't be sure but at this point, I don't want to rule anything out. Did he say what her name was?"

"Sarah. I'm pretty sure he said her name was Sarah. Ring any bells?"

"No. But it sounds like she could very well be one of Theron's new progenies. And if that's the case, we may have to move up our date of attack."

"I wasn't aware we'd set a date in the first place."

"Not officially. But Blake and I were considering our options early this morning and decided it may be best to strike in the next few days. And now with Liam gone missing, this just confirms it."

"Just name the time and place. I can't let my brother get hurt because of me. I've already lost more than enough people. If anything were to happen to Liam, that piece of shit might as well kill me too."

"Don't you ever say that again!" Andre shouted so forcefully that I nearly jumped out of my seat. His eyes were searing with rage. "I will *never* let him harm you. Do you understand me?"

"I understand."

"Good. I'll call Blake and Tristen now. We need to figure out just how ready the Viking is. There's absolutely no margin for error in what we're about to do."

Blake answered Andre's call instantaneously and I overheard the two make plans to meet at our place at dusk. My rendezvous with Johnnie Walker only intensified the throbbing fit of nausea I had been suffering since I first got out of bed so I quickly downed a glass of ice-cold water to soothe my aching stomach. I put on my favorite jeans and a grey cable-knit sweater, wondering how cold it would be outside. Once my socks were pulled on and I zipped up my leather steel-toe boots, I joined my pensive boyfriend on the sofa.

The two of us sat there in silence, patiently awaiting the arrival of our brave coconspirators. I convinced myself that there was no time left to worry anymore. I needed to get my game face on. If two mages who were as mortal as I was were willing to risk their lives to save mine, it would have been unforgiveable for me to back out now. I willfully brushed my anxiety under a mental rug and prepared myself for battle. Maybe I wouldn't be fighting Theron and his little minions in the physical sense, but in the next few hours, I understood that I would either exact my retribution or suffer the same fate as those I'd lost so mercilessly. The latter, I reminded myself, was not an option.

Fifteen

I fiddled nervously with the ring Andre had given me over Christmas as I walked into the decrepit tower that had been the scene of so many of my nightmares. I clearly remembered the petrified look on Jaq's face when she stared down at Isabel's corpse sprawled out across the grassy floor. The gruesome memories of that night brought chills down my spine as I sat on the cool surface and took out my notebook and black ballpoint pen. The evening air was bitterly cold and mirrored the stark ambiance that swept throughout the structure. I did as Andre instructed and began to jot down some words regarding the pillars that encircled me. I was bittersweetly reminded of Quinn as I recalled the significance behind their formation.

Removing my cell from the side pocket of my jeans, I switched it on and steadily dialed Andre's number. He answered after two rings, one more than it usually took, and spoke so casually that had I not been in on it, I would have surely believed I really was just there to complete a boring research paper for one of my classes.

"So? How's it coming, honey?" he inquired. "Are you bored yet?"

"Extremely. You know I should have taken you up on your offer to keep me company. This place is so damn dreary."

I heard Andre's hearty laugh on the other end of the line and smiled to myself, silently wishing this wouldn't be the last time I would hear the lovely sound.

"I told you so. Well you just get all the info you need and I'll be waiting for you when you get home. You sure you don't need me to entertain you?"

"And have you distract me from my schoolwork? I don't think so," I giggled. I sounded so convincing that I surprised myself at the acting ability I never knew I had.

"All right, then. I'll see you in an hour."

When I hung up the phone, I felt the bleak energy around me intensify and as I looked up to scrutinize the construction of the tower, I saw Caden standing above me with an insolent smirk on his face. It took a few moments for me to fully grasp that the person looming over me was not the misunderstood man who I'd been indebted to for saving my boyfriend's life, but Theron, a thousand-year-old murderous vampire who had killed my best friend and undoubtedly kidnapped Liam. I remembered the directions

Andre had given me and quickly pressed redial, sliding the phone carefully back into my pocket.

It was such a bizarre feeling to know that as much as he looked exactly like Caden, this callous being was someone else altogether. I couldn't expect any of Caden's usual flippant remarks or charming smiles. This man was pure evil and he wanted me dead. I didn't have to fake the terror in my eyes as I rose to my feet and leaned against one of the pillars for support.

"Do you take me for a fool, darling?" he asked me matter-of-factly. "Did you really think I'd fall for this sorry excuse for a coup?" When I failed to answer, he continued in that same deadpan tone. "And to think, I had so much faith in you. I really have given you much more credit than you deserve. So, where is your knight in shining armor, as it were?"

"Home," I muttered, feeling icy tremors pulsating throughout my entire body.

"I'll give you one more try since you look so much like my beloved Camilla. Where is Andre?" he repeated.

"Waiting for an opportune moment to kill you," I admitted frigidly, clenching my fists.

"Good. Then we're right on schedule. Jack! Scott!"

In a matter of seconds, I noticed two male vampires joined Theron, one at either side. He'd taken his friends along for protection, or perhaps just to keep him company, just as Andre predicted. His brand new progenies couldn't have been older than twenty years old and the vibrant shade of crimson in their eyes was alarming. I was still fighting the notion that I was talking to someone other than Caden. A small part of me wondered if hanging around identical twins would have been as disturbing but the thought swiftly dissipated as soon as the blonde one began to speak.

"Can we kill her now?" he asked his maker eagerly.

"Be patient," Theron scolded him like a stern father would a young child. "I must apologize for Jack's rash behavior, darling. He's still very new to this world. First, I'd like for us to go somewhere a bit less depressing. You and I both suffered a loss here and I want us to have a fresh start. After all, you've managed to take from me the only person I've ever loved, Emma. It's only fair that you offer yourself to me in exchange. Just think of it as a means of restitution for the great sorrow you've brought to my life."

"You'll have to kill me before I offer you anything more than a slow, painful death. That's all you deserve, you heartless piece of shit."

"It seems you and Camilla have more in common than just your looks, darling," he grinned. "We're going to have a lot of fun together, you and I. When I turn you, you will be mine forever."

So Theron never had any intention of killing me, at least not in the supernatural sense. He wasn't seeking to merely drain me and move on to wreak havoc elsewhere. The vengeful brute had planned on making me a vampire instead. He wanted to punish me for Camilla's death, to force me into taking her place at his side for all eternity.

"Over my dead body."

"Precisely. Now how about we leave this dreadful place and I take you to your brother? He's been asking for you, you know."

My heart sank. All of my fears had floated up to the surface and I now knew for certain that my sweet, innocent Liam's life was in jeopardy. Theron took a step toward me and I held my breath unable to move. He grasped a strand of my hair between his pale fingers and inhaled, which was simultaneously creepy and terrifying. I kept reminding myself that he would ultimately lead me to my brother so I gritted my teeth and let him touch me, regardless of how badly I wanted to punch him in the gut for invading my personal space. I shut my eyes until all I saw was darkness and prayed for Andre and our friends to come for me soon. I didn't know how much more of this I could bear.

When I no longer felt the unsettling contact of Theron's hand on my long blonde hair, I decided it was safe to open my eyes. The sight of the two young vampires lying there motionless on the ground made me shiver. Theron was now trapped in between Andre's firm grip, but instead of witnessing any sense of fear or panic on the man's face, the frightening vampire looked eerily amused.

"I was wondering how long it would take for you to join the party," he smirked. "So, after five hundred years of watching you from the confines of my lady's amulet, we finally meet face to face. I do admit it's rather unfortunate that this isn't *really* my face, but I'm nevertheless pleased to be able to formally make your acquaintance, old friend."

Andre tightened his hold on the vampire until he bared a slight grimace of pain. "Camilla was right; you are quite strong for your age. But sadly, not strong enough," Theron scoffed as he effortlessly detached himself from Andre's grip and in half a second, the two had swapped places. Andre was now in a headlock but if he was afraid, he definitely didn't show it.

"Pleasure to meet you, mate," he said in his thick English accent, which I knew from personal experience only emerged when he was either truly enraged or in the heat of passion. "Let me ask you something. How did it feel watching your sweetheart die in this very spot, old friend?" he asked Theron ominously.

The pleased expression on the older vampire's face quickly turned livid as he twisted Andre's arm so far behind his back I could have sworn Theron had managed to dislocate it from its socket.

"I'll remember to ask you that same question right before I kill you."

Without revealing the slightest trace of pain, Andre surprised his opponent with a sudden backflip and the man lost his footing and staggered. They were now standing just two feet apart, silently glaring at each other as if they were Roman gladiators in combat.

The two men were supernatural warriors and the primal looks in their scarlet eyes spoke volumes. They had both spent centuries waiting for this chance to battle it out. One, I had assumed, more so than the other, and this was their long overdue moment of truth. With fangs extended and knees slightly bent, their movements were slow and methodical. They never took their eyes off one another. Like wildcats, they anticipated each other's actions brilliantly and patiently waited for the right moment to pounce.

I felt like a voyeur watching them from across the small makeshift arena and wondered how I could possibly make myself useful. Tristen and Blake were nowhere in sight and I was at a loss. *Think, Emma!* I fumbled in my bag for something, anything I could use to help Andre. I knew I couldn't hurt Theron with a tube of lip-gloss or a compact mirror but even minimal damage would suffice at this point. I just needed to be a momentary distraction and so I threw the contents of my large purse onto the ground and painstakingly began my search.

Because Theron was wearing his tiger's eye talisman, the wooden pencil I could have speared through his Achilles tendon would have done nothing but seriously irritate the shit out of him. I picked up the Swiss Army knife Liam had given me a while back and went through each of the various stainless steel instruments in turn, forcing the gears in my head to keep spinning until I found just one tool that could help us. It was hopeless; nothing I had brought with me served any great purpose and I wanted to smack myself for being so underprepared.

I caught a glimpse of Jaq's little golden Fleur-de-Lis necklace beside me and felt a torrent of rage sweep through me. *Failure is not an option,* I reminded myself and thought about Liam locked away somewhere injured and afraid. I pictured Jaq's bloody heart and recalled the misery in Mrs. Avignon's voice when she called me for the answers I couldn't give her. No, I couldn't fail. I was not about to let this monster get away with my best friend's murder. He needed to suffer for all the carnage he'd left in his wake.

Theron and Andre were still going at it; throwing punches at lightning speed and biting into one other like rabid dogs. Blood trickled down Theron's arms and legs, while Andre had cuts and scrapes all over his hands and neck. I knew their wounds were healing at a staggering rate but seeing my typically dominant boyfriend with all those abrasions was nonetheless frightening.

I was watching a battle that clearly wouldn't reach its end until one of them was either missing a head or a heart. I couldn't afford to add Andre's name to the list of people I'd lost in this past year alone and, suddenly, an idea came to me. I had no clue if it would work or possibly even backfire but there was no time to weigh the potential outcomes. I stood up and screamed at the top of my lungs, startling both men from their hostile sparring.

In the few seconds it took for them to realize I was shrieking for no apparent reason, Andre swung a vigorous roundhouse kick striking Theron's neck as the vampire fell to the floor with a loud thump that resounded through the tower. He was awkwardly pinned between Andre's foot and the grass surface, unable to maneuver his way out of the position without leaving his fragile head behind. In all his rage, I could see Andre about to lose control. He was seconds away from decapitating him right then and there.

"No!" I shouted. "Don't kill him yet. He has Liam."

The crimson glow in Andre's eyes gradually faded and he astounded us both by taking out his cell phone.

"Mate? We're ready," was all he said and abruptly hung up, putting the phone back into the pocket of his dark trousers.

Blake unexpectedly materialized out of nowhere with Tristen following closely behind. After asking me if I was all right, they guardedly walked over to the irate, vicious monster lying stationary on the ground.

"He's got Emma's brother somewhere," Andre informed them. "We can't immobilize this bastard until we know where the boy's holed up."

"If you think I'm going to tell you and your little witches anything, I'm sorry to say you're shit out of luck," Theron grumbled.

"That's too bad," Andre smirked and dug his heel deeper into the flesh of Theron's throbbing neck. I heard the vampire wince in agony and couldn't help but smile. When had I become so merciless? It was most likely on the day I opened Theron's ever so thoughtful Christmas gift. "Blake?" he gestured to the furious vampire at his feet.

The mage bent down closer to Theron, starting to chant some of his usual unintelligible jargon. I felt harsh gusts of wind sweep throughout the tower as I collected my clutter off the ground, putting my belongings back into the large purse my parent's expected I'd use for textbooks.

I strolled over cautiously to stand at Andre's side, savoring the gentle touch of his palm over my cheek. As ferocious as he was in battle, the moment he looked into my green eyes, I knew he was still the tender man I'd fallen in love with. No matter how aggressive even the strongest fighter was in a brawl, it was evident to me that all it took to turn him into a ball of mush was the woman he cared for.

"He's ready," Blake indicated much more casually than the situation warranted.

"What did you do with Emma's brother? I want his exact location." Andre demanded hostilely.

Theron's pupils were dilated and I realized he was now under Blake's influence as if the mage had given him some sort of preternatural truth serum.

"The boy's in some big house off of Bellevue. By Sheep Point Cove," he answered glassily.

Liam was in Camilla's old residence. I remembered the street names on my trip there with Caden. Andre had been there as well and knew precisely where it was.

"How long will he remain this bloody docile?" he asked Blake.

"Not long, mate. I think it's best we perform the enchantment now while the bloke's still tame. We already know where big brother is so the sooner we get Caden back, the better."

"Wait! What if someone hurts him?" I asked wide-eyed. How could we waste any more time if we knew where Liam was? Of course I wanted to return Caden to his proper form but I desperately needed to know my brother was unharmed.

"Liam is likely being guarded by a few of Theron's new progenies," Andre said draping his arm around me protectively. "They wouldn't hurt him until commanded to do so by their master. Best-case scenario is we get Caden back while there's still time and then go deal with the baby vamps. The enchantment must be done here so it doesn't make much sense to go back and forth. We'll save Liam, sweetheart. You have my word."

I nodded meekly and stepped out of the way as Blake effortlessly cast an immobilization spell on Theron, leaving the already dazed vampire completely stock-still. Tristen prepared the small area by lighting eight white candles and placing them between each pillar. He poured what looked like sea salt into one large circle all around the perimeter. I watched as Andre removed Camilla's tiger's eye amulet from around his neck and put it over Theron's head. He took the ring off of the vampire's finger and slid it back onto his own. I could sense he felt somewhat more comforted with it on his hand as the little silver talisman had been his for over five centuries. He walked over to me and held me close against his firm body while we observed the impressive mages in action.

Tristen removed a small page made of vellum from his pants pocket and began to read each incomprehensible verse aloud.

"Sólveret anima. Adducite anima retro," he began and I could tell that he was second-guessing himself as he spoke.

I recalled hearing those same words come from his father the night Isabel met her untimely death and Caden had traded his soul in exchange for Andre's. Blake put his hand on Tristen's shoulder in an attempt to show him he wasn't alone in this and that he was doing fine. He joined him thoughtfully, chanting along knowing his words had no effect to the magic, but it gave Tristen the confidence he needed to harness his magic and perform the reversal enchantment successfully.

When the words finally stopped and a deafening silence filled the space, I noticed the man lying on the floor gradually begin to open his slate grey eyes. I didn't know if the person about to speak was going to be Theron or Caden and I squeezed Andre tighter, mentally preparing myself for either outcome. Tristen regarded Blake pessimistically, wondering if he had failed. Where had his usual confidence gone? I felt like he'd truly lost all faith in himself since Jaq's death. Seeing him so doubtful made me think he really had fallen short and it was only until I saw Caden's familiar grin that I believed the spell really worked.

"Is Emma okay?" he asked feebly.

I released myself from Andre's arms and hastily ran to Caden's side. He peered up at me smiling as my tears fell onto his handsome face. I didn't love him in nearly the same way that I loved Andre, but seeing him alive, by vampire standards at least, filled me with a relief I hadn't felt in far too long. Jaq was gone and I knew there was nothing I could have done to bring her back, but the sight of Caden's beguiling gaze reminded me that all was not yet lost. I cradled him on my lap as Andre watched us rather uncomfortably, and I was unable to stifle the joyous sense of reprieve I felt for all the harm I regularly blamed myself for.

Andre walked over to us shaking his head as the corners of his mouth perked up into a surprisingly friendly and sympathetic smile. He held out his hand, which Caden took warily, and lifted the uncharacteristically frail vampire onto his feet. I was pleased to see them making some sort of effort to reconcile after such a lengthy feud and wrapped my arms around them both. Now that Caden was safe, we had one final task to complete before I could allow myself to feel the peace I'd been coveting for what seemed like forever.

"We need to rescue Liam," I reminded them once I regained my composure and noticed the two mages were eyeing us curiously. Had they gotten the impression that I was some two-bit hussy? I honestly didn't have the energy to justify my reaction to anyone, especially not to two friends who should have known me better than that. Liam's wellbeing far outranked defending my wounded pride.

"Why don't Tristen and I bring the amulet to his old man so he can lock it up with the grimoire while you guys get Emma's brother," Blake offered. "It'll save time and I'd really like to get some rest, mate. I'm sure Tristen does too. You know us mages do require that pesky little thing called sleep, remember?"

"Right, yes, thank you for coming, Blake," Andre said giving his friend a hug farewell. "And I'm sorry again to have involved you in all this. Consider your debt to me paid. If you come to need anything at all, don't hesitate."

He shook Tristen's hand and startled him by pulling him in for a tight squeeze as well. "You were brilliant tonight, Tristen. We all knew you had it in you. Your father will be proud."

We said our goodbyes and headed off to free Liam from the unknown number of Theron's progenies that were guarding him in Camilla's old mansion. I was expecting the worst, unable to shake the feeling that we would be too late. A single salty tear ran down my cheek as I peered out the window and it hit me like a brick just how drained I was. Caden was sitting up front with Andre at the wheel and I decided to sprawl out in the back for the remainder of the drive, struggling to keep my eyes open.

The next thing I knew, my head was resting upon Andre's lap while he lovingly stroked my hair as he often did when we were alone in the comfort of our bed. When I saw Liam safe and asleep in the passenger's seat, I finally allowed myself to fully relax. The usual tension in my face had lifted and for the first time in too long, I felt free.

Had I really been asleep the entire time? I was slightly bothered by the fact that no one woke me up to help, but quickly realized that my assistance wasn't exactly necessary. I was fully aware that I didn't have a vampire's strength or senses and ultimately, I'd have probably been a burden to them both. I let out a drawn-out sigh and looked up at my valiant boyfriend appreciatively.

"How come you let me miss the show?" I smiled.

"And rouse Sleeping Beauty from her slumber? You looked much too peaceful to wake, sweetheart. Caden and I both thought it best to leave you in the car while we got your brother. We couldn't risk putting you in danger when we weren't sure exactly how many vampire's there'd be inside the house."

"I understand. Is Liam hurt?"

"He's lost quite a bit of blood. Fucking newbies," he seethed. "But he's fine now."

"Will he remember anything?"

I envisaged the look on my big brother's face if I were to explain to him the existence of vampires and mages and mystical amulets. A conversation like that was more than I could handle and he'd already been through more than enough as it were.

"No, baby. When Liam wakes up, he'll believe he's been in Newport visiting you for a short while to get away. He'll have no memory of the girl or anything else that went on here. He'll call his firm in the morning to inform them of a sudden family emergency and I'll get him a flight into Boston first thing tomorrow. It'll be as though none of this ever happened."

"Thank you," I whispered drowsily. "How are you feeling, Caden?"

"I've seen better days, love," he grinned as he put the car in park outside our delightfully familiar apartment building. "Nothing a bit of R and R won't cure."

My sentiments exactly, I thought. My warm, comfy bed had never seemed more alluring than it had at that very moment. We were just about to head upstairs when the sound of Andre's phone reverberated throughout the car and startled me from the tranquil stillness of the night.

"You're rambling, Tristen," Andre said chidingly to the other end of the call. "What are you getting at? No. All right. Just stay at home. No, I'll handle it."

He hung up and looked at Caden with the first hints of crimson staining his eyes. He was furious and I couldn't fathom what could possibly have gone wrong. We rescued Liam. Theron had been dealt with. Camilla was dead. We were finally free.

"What is it?"

"Blake. He's run off with the amulet."

THE END